"Yeah, right. Full name, H.

"You want my full name?" Now she was playing for time in part because she noticed the tiny device in his ear. Was he a cop? Security? So what if he was? There was no law against taking a waitress gig for a sick friend.

"That's what I said," came the irritating rejoinder.

Cocky. Obnoxious. And definitely the boss.

"Honey. It's Honey Hill." She braced for the inevitable.

"Honey Hill. You're telling me your name is Honey Hill?" His eyes slid over her body in a way she was ashamed to admit didn't bother her nearly enough. "I don't want your exotic star alias. Give me the one that's on your driver's license."

And there it was. Nope, he didn't disappoint. And she hadn't even given him her full name. Her blood boiled just the same as it had the first time that joke was made. The way it boiled every time.

"In your dreams. Here's what I'll give you."

She let go and sent the tray crashing onto his shoes.

"Oops," she said.

Praise for Charlotte O'Shay

THE MARRIAGE ULTIMATUM was a Finalist in the 2018 I heart Indie contest, Erotic Category, www.LVRWA.org

THE MARRIAGE ULTIMATUM was also listed in Favorite Reads of 2016.

~*~

"Taking the concept of the 'marriage contract' to a whole new level. Lovable characters who seem different on the surface find they have more in common than they thought by having survived difficult pasts. They also have some explosive chemistry."

~romancenovels4thebeach.wordpress.com

~*~

"Charlotte O'Shay uses backstory in a remarkable way to give the reader insight into characters, to create empathy, and to build characters that meet and beat the odds with determination. She has a smooth, very readable writing style."

~longandshortreviews.com

Their No-Strings Affair

by

Charlotte O'Shay

City of Dreams, Book 3

Their No-Strings Affair

Cover Art by *Kristian Norris*

The Wild Rose Press, Inc.
PO Box 708
Adams Basin, NY 14410-0708
Visit us at www.thewildrosepress.com

Publishing History
First Champagne Rose Edition, 2019
Print ISBN 978-1-5092-2562-0
Digital ISBN 978-1-5092-2563-7

City of Dreams, Book 3
Published in the United States of America

Dedication

To NYC.
My home & my inspiration—
every crazy, electric, dirty, busted bit of you.
And to the eight-million dreamers here
searching for their own happily ever afters.
We got this.

Chapter 1
Right Place, Wrong Time

"Stop right there." The deep, take-no-crap voice came from behind her.

She sped up her fast walk down the corridor, her fingers tightening on the silver-plated tray wobbling on her shoulder.

"I said *stop*."

Stopping for a voice like his would be like strolling into the middle of Times Square against the light. She moved faster.

"I know you can hear me."

The irritated, male growl was pitched low; probably so guests who ventured out of the main ballroom wouldn't be disturbed.

Shaking off the sensation of being stalked by an ornery bear, she picked up her fast-clip pace. A highly publicized wedding at the venerated Pierre Hotel was no place for a confrontation—actually, in her case, *another* confrontation—between a service employee and... Who exactly was this guy snarling in that dark voice for her to stop? Nah, she didn't want to know. She moved faster, the swinging doors leading to the kitchen and prep areas straight ahead of her.

A hand closed over her arm, and the tray of empties pitched sideways like the deckchairs on the Titanic. She heaved out a frustrated breath and stopped.

The empties slid to a halt on the tray.

Honey was in no mood, especially not today, to be manhandled by a guy just because he was bigger and she stood only five-two in her sneakers.

"Get...your...hand...off...me. *Right now.* I don't know who you think you are..." She pushed out the words low and slow. She could do this. She could get rid of him and squash her temper. This horrendous day was moments away from exploding into utter disaster.

But no, he wasn't letting go of her arm, and it was either let the whole tray of wine glasses tumble to the floor, or let the bully have his say. Mother Nature had a nasty sense of humor, making Honey the size of a hummingbird and giving her the temper of a hippo.

"Who I am is your worst nightmare. Now plant your feet and give me your name."

"Get lost." Her words came out in a hiss. "Let go of my arm, and I'll forget this happened."

"Oh, really?" A sarcastic black brow lifted. "Give me your name now, and *maybe*"—his sneer said *right, if you believe that, I have some bitcoin to sell you*—"I won't write you up."

Honey stood her ground, lifted her chin, and stared him down in a way her brothers would've recognized as dangerous.

"First, let go of my arm."

The volume of her voice inched up a couple of notches. Loud enough so any passing guests would wonder just what was going on in the midst of this glamorous wedding reception.

He released her arm but stayed so far inside her personal space she caught a hint of the lemon and leather of his aftershave. The heady scent fit the vibe of that TV commercial she loved, the one where the amber Italian sun cast shadows on a gorgeous guy on a motorcycle speeding down some scenic Roman side street at sunset.

Honey suddenly realized if she could breathe him in, he could do the same. Crap! Yep, that's what she smelled like, and nobody wanted to buy a scent called "fifteen hours of waitressing and dumpster diving without a shower." Not that she could do anything about it now.

She poked her chin out in a who-cares-what-you-think jab and straightened to her full non-threatening height. "My name's right there." She arrowed her thumb to the nametag on her shirt with her free hand, the one that wasn't clenched in a death grip over the edge of the silver-plated tray on her shoulder. It was a dry-erase, magnetic tag they gave to the add-on staff, embossed with *Pierre Hotel* in the corner and her name, *H. Hill* hand-printed across the middle in dry erase marker.

"There's no H. Hill on this staff."

Honey took a good hard look at the seriously serious guy who was taunting her temper to full boil. A square was what her artist's eye saw. Square jaw, square shoulders, and square hands with square fingernails. And yeah, no doubt square personality. Glossy too. Glossy teeth, hair, and shoes.

His black tuxedo matched his ruthlessly tamed hair and hugged the defined muscles of his shoulders and thighs in a way that sent a sharp flare of heat to her belly. She crushed the stab of awareness. She could appreciate, as an artist, his exceptional body—he had to be a swimmer with those massive shoulders and lean hips—without feeling. What was she feeling anyway? *C'mon, girl, you* can't *be attracted.* This guy had threat written all over him, and she was not going there. She'd turned out to be the world's worst at judging a guy's intentions or character…

Besides, any random guy would look decent in clothes tailored just for him. And this guy's close-fitting tuxedo had as much in common with the off-the-rack black suits some of the staff was wearing as the caviar towers inside the ballroom did to canned tuna on crackers.

Honey shut down her wayward thoughts. So what if his perfectly molded lips, currently curled into a sneer, bore an uncanny resemblance to those of Michelangelo's *David*? It was no big deal; he could be Mark Consuelos' cranky baby brother.

The question was—who was he? The supervisor? Lizzie should've warned her, but right, Lizzie hadn't worked here before either. She wouldn't know if tall, ripped, and annoying in a tuxedo might be the boss.

Their entire conversation about tonight had taken three minutes, the decision made in thirty seconds. Lizzie was from the same small upstate town as Honey. She'd ventured to the city five years earlier chasing a, so far, unsuccessful acting career. She'd been the first person Honey thought to call when her life took a sharp turn into crazy—was it only this morning?

Lizzie's bad luck had been Honey's one stroke of good luck. Poor Lizzie was down with the flu, and Honey was strapped for cash. Lizzie offered Honey her spot on the Pierre's coveted contract service staff for tonight's wedding reception. Totally not done and Lizzie would get into a boatload of trouble if anyone found out. But hey, who would find out?

"You know how to wait tables, pour drinks?" said Lizzie.

"Of course, yeah," Honey said.

"Okay, fill in for me tonight, a ton of extra staff's been hired, this is a big event, you'll pool tips, and I'll pay you for the night when they cut my check next week. It's a good gig. You won't be run off your feet, and you won't be noticed."

Famous last words because in spite of her size, somehow Honey always got noticed.

Damn, why hadn't she put Lizzie's name on the tag? Now she had no choice but to BS her way out.

"Well that's not possible, is it, since I'm H. Hill," she said in a creamy I-know-you're-the-boss-and-I-couldn't-care-less tone.

She glanced up at him and widened her eyes a fraction as she fluttered her thick, and given her hair color, surprisingly dark lashes once.

Couldn't hurt. Desperate times and all that.

His upper lip curled.

Didn't work.

And why would you ever think it would, Honey? Most guys in Caryville never gave you a second look, and the one you thought you had a future with cheated on you for years. It was weird and it was dangerous, this sudden need to be seen as a woman, as an *appealing* woman by this guy.

"You may be H. Hill, but you were never on the staff list for tonight. I want to know what you're doing here."

His clipped words emerged from between perfect white teeth like he was holding onto his temper by a thread.

You and me both, buddy.

Honey averted her gaze from the laser focus of his.

"I'm working here." She jerked her chin at the tray, which was fast becoming as heavy as a boulder on her shoulder.

"Yeah, right. Full name, H. Hill."

"You want my full name?" Now she was playing for time in part because she noticed the tiny device in his ear. Was he a cop? Security? So what if he was? There was no law against taking a waitress gig for a sick friend.

"That's what I said," came the irritating rejoinder.

Cocky. Obnoxious. And definitely the boss.

"Honey. It's Honey Hill." She braced for the inevitable.

"Honey Hill. You're telling me your name is Honey Hill?" His gaze slid over her body in a way she was ashamed to admit didn't bother her nearly enough. "I don't want your exotic star alias. Give me the one that's on your driver's license."

And there it was. Nope, he didn't disappoint. And she hadn't even given him her full name. Her blood boiled just the same as it had the first time that joke was made. The way it boiled every time.

"In your dreams. Here's what I'll give you."

She let go and sent the tray crashing onto his shoes.

"Oops," she said.

****

Jake had been alerted to an altercation between two wait staff, about to come to blows.

That was *not* happening tonight. Not on his watch. He'd added extra security from his own firm along with the additional service staff he hired from an outside company for this evening to supplement the Pierre's already ample and well-trained staff.

His company had seen to Vlad Grigory's security needs for five years now, and money was no object. The object was to make sure every invited guest, including the politicians and celebrities at the Grigory wedding and most especially the newly married couple, had a smooth, safe, and enjoyable evening.

His mouth twisted. As enjoyable as a wedding could be anyway.

One of the perpetrators in the almost-brawl was cooling his heels in a room off the kitchen. The other, who'd just deliberately toppled a tray full of empty wineglasses on his shoes, was in the adjoining room.

After he quickly buffed his shoes, navy style, back to their previous brilliant level of patent-leather luster, he quizzed the male waiter first, which gave him a few minutes to cool off. He'd *never* been so infuriated so fast as he was five minutes ago. Jake sucked up his annoyance because, damn, he was disciplined if nothing else. Nothing and no one was going to screw up this event—especially not a belligerent employee. That went double for an aggravating, firecracker of a female.

The male server spouted a BS story that the female, H. Hill, had barged into his section of the ballroom and gotten in his face when he pointed out his territory to her. The male had argued back, and she raised her fists. The story rang false, but Jake didn't bother to challenge him—yet. Everybody working tonight would be amply compensated, even before tips. Territorial fights seldom happened when everybody was happy with the end game. But the yelling part, yeah, he definitely believed that. Less than a minute with her and he was ready to spit nails.

Irritated, he lifted a hand to his hair before he fisted both hands in the pockets of his immaculate pants instead. He *would* look as sharp now as he had at eight this morning. His professional image was vital, because he was *it*, the face of his security company.

His security company had grown and was still growing by leaps and bounds, in large part due to his attention to detail. Since he'd left the service five years ago, Jake poured his sweat, knowledge, and heart into his now thriving business. Haven Security was well respected by people like Vlad Grigory. Vlad might be one of his best friends now, but when he'd hired him all those years ago, Jake needed to prove himself to the up and coming tycoon.

And Jake didn't give a damn his mother considered his security business a defiant detour on the road to his ultimate destiny. Let her remain where she wanted to be, across the ocean, gilding her bygone pedigree and chasing status. He'd made a life for himself here in New York and he'd live it. While he could.

Jake ignored the guilt-ridden voice in his head that reminded him the pull of his promise could no longer be put off. In the new year, his time would be up.

Shrugging away those dark thoughts, he checked his watch. It was almost one a.m. The reception was winding down, and it would finish as the most uneventful security event of its kind if he had anything to do with it, and he did. Jake gave himself no more than five minutes to resolve this employee dustup, mete justice, and move on.

His hand hovered over the doorknob as he watched

her through the porthole-style window of the door. Pacing back and forth across the small room, ignoring the folding chair against the wall, with arms crossed under her chest, she was a compact bundle of kinetic energy in spite of the hour. She came to a standstill when he closed the door, and her dark eyes flashed.

For a moment, he zeroed in on the dark chocolate, thickly lashed eyes that seethed with emotion. He read annoyance there, even antagonism, but didn't see a trace of fear. He continued to examine her silently, always his first tactic to keep an adversary or an underling off balance. A pulse throbbed in her throat, and her fists dropped to her sides to clench and unclench like she was gearing up to attack.

Something in her combative stance struck him as vulnerable, but as he watched, she rolled her shoulders much like he might do before a fight. Or when he was exhausted. Damn. He didn't want to notice anything else about her. This was business. So he looked over her head, easy to do since he was at least a foot taller.

"Ms. Hill…or whatever your real name is."

Her jaw clamped shut, and her chin lifted as she struggled to leash her temper.

Join the club, sweetheart.

"Enough of the drama. What happened with the other server? I was alerted to the beginning of a loud argument, told it was about to get physical."

"I handled it." She flicked a small, capable-looking hand with short, unpainted fingernails. "It was all over before you came along."

Jake nodded. Folded his arms across his chest. "Maybe. But what happened? And how did you get in here tonight?"

She shrugged. "There's no way I'm telling you any of that."

He almost admired the way she stonewalled him. It took guts because she had to know she was done working for him.

"All right, moving on. This is a high security event, and you weren't hired for it."

"How do you know?" Her lush, cupid's bow lips pressed together, and a jolt of heat hit him low in the belly. Then she mimicked him, crossing her arms over her chest.

"Because I'm running this gig. I vetted everyone—name, photo, background check." *Why the fuck was he even telling her this?* "And you already know there was no Honey Hill on the list."

He put his hand out, palm up. "I'll take that nametag. You'll be escorted from the premises. And, Ms. Hill, something to remember for your next job—purple hair gets you noticed in a bad way almost as much as dumping a tray of glasses on the chief of security does."

Jake ignored her irritated gasp and the way her hand flew to the spiky hair on the top of her head. He closed his fingers over the nameplate she dropped into his palm and slipped it into his pocket.

For some reason, he didn't want to watch her leave, so he turned his back when his assistant showed up moments later to escort her out. Then Jake went into the adjacent room where the other server lounged in a folding chair at a small table.

"So you were hitting on that server. What happened? She wasn't having it, is that right, dude?"

"She told you?" He raised a combative chin toward

Jake, then shook his head in disbelief. "Snotty little bitch thinks she's too good for me," he muttered.

"She didn't give you up, asshole, but you just did. You should know better. Anybody employed by me keeps it strictly business at work. You're fired." He took the second perpetrator out himself.

All in a day's work.

****

Honey paced around the corner of 61st Street then back again—and again, for long minutes deep in the struggle to cool her temper. Finally, she perched on a fireplug, unfolded and refolded the overlong cuffs of her shirtsleeves as she considered her options. Did she even have any?

Today was a train wreck, and it wasn't over.

Last night, Trey, the guy whose online ad for a roommate she answered, had been upset. Somehow, Trey figured sharing rent in a Brooklyn walkup with her entitled him to a good bit more than just a roommate who paid the other portion of the rent. Yesterday, their second night as apartment sharers, a Saturday, he came back to the apartment well after midnight, full of beer and bluster.

Honey's knee set him straight on the true boundaries of their relationship (thank you, Derek and Donnie). Then she left him to his frustrated yowl in the bedroom, went to the corner of the living room where she'd set up her bed, and lay there, furious at Trey and berating herself for being the quintessential *I'm new to the city* dope. As her temper cooled, her unease at what Trey could do if she fell asleep blocked everything else out, and she lay in her bed, wide eyed and sleepless. She'd never expected his grabby-handed come-on in the first place. What might Trey do when she was asleep and vulnerable?

But packing her whole life into a car and driving six hours into the city was an exercise in exhaustion. At some point near dawn, the need to close her eyes for a second overwhelmed her. Next thing she knew, her cell phone said it was eight in the morning. She crept toward the bathroom, straining to hear sounds of life in his room above the street sounds four floors below their walkup. His door was ajar. Trey was gone.

In the bathroom, propped against the back of the sink under the mirror, a note had been scrawled in block letters on the back of a local craft brewery's postcard:

DON'T COME BACK.

Honey absorbed the threat in those words, swallowed the sour crud in the back of her throat that told her she knew squat about Trey. Wasn't it an unbelievable rookie move to share rent with a dude she knew nothing about?

Moments later, it was obvious. Good ol' Trey had taken all of her stuff—*everything.* The big, old suitcase filled with clothes and shoes, her canvas bags filled with photos and books, and even some of her precious stash of ceramics. Not to mention her purse with her wallet and all of her vital documents, driver's license, bankcard, and old college ID.

Honey bolted out of the apartment to search the trashcans in front of the building and then the rest of them all along the block. She even climbed into every construction dumpster she spotted along the adjacent streets. After a couple of hours of hunting up and down the surrounding blocks, she accomplished nothing besides getting the yoga pants and T-shirt she'd worn for pajamas filthy. Had Trey thrown it all into the water? The Brooklyn apartment was only a few blocks from Jamaica Bay.

Now she was stuck on her second day in the city with no cash, no ID, and no place to sleep. That's when she called Lizzie—Honey had fallen asleep with her phone clutched in her hand, primed to dial 911. But Lizzie dropped more bad news. She and Kurt, her live-in boyfriend, had the flu and scant room in their lower east side studio for a third person.

"You do *not* want to be around us right now. But in a way, it's great luck you called, Honey. I was just about to call out sick, but you should take this job today. You know how to wait tables and pour drinks?"

And so Honey's plans had changed, and here she was.

And right now, it was a major struggle to corral her temper.

Part of her wanted to track down Trey and make him pay for what he'd done to her. The vicious text she'd sent demanding he return her stuff went unanswered. No surprise there. She'd called the landlord but hadn't gotten a call back yet, maybe because it was Sunday.

Would she ever learn? Temper and impulse, her defining vices, and yeah, humiliation and hurt, had driven her to this quick move to the city in the first place. Then powered by the same impulses, she'd decided to share rent with a stranger without being a co-signer to the lease. Without her name on the lease, who knew when or if she'd get her security deposit back, never mind her possessions?

So now what?

Even if she got her stuff back, the small amount of cash in her wallet was no doubt gone forever. And even though she had access to her bank account via her smartphone, there wasn't much there to draw on. Sure, this mess qualified as an emergency, but was it smart to fork over a chunk of her savings to pay Manhattan prices for a place to stay on her second night in the city?

Focus! Things could be worse and had been. Life as a kid with Willow might be termed carefree when it wasn't borderline neglectful. It was all how you looked at it. She'd channel her mother. *WWWD?* What would Willow do? Who knew? But one thing was certain. Willow would *not* allow this setback, a careless error in judgment, to derail her. And neither would Honey. She'd figure out a way to go to her interviews tomorrow and come back with one of the internships she'd moved to the city for.

But come back to where? Yeah, her back-up plan was also not a first. Until Honey found a place she could afford, she'd sleep in her car—at least she had one. Now she was happy she'd forked over several hundred dollars to Joss to buy his ancient Ford, after convincing him that with his curtailed teaching schedule, he could easily carpool to the university.

First thing she could do was go back into the Pierre for her backpack, which now contained everything she owned in the world. Boss Man's sidekick had hustled her out of the hotel so fast she hadn't thought to retrieve it from the staff lockers.

Luckily Trey hadn't got his wandering, vindictive hands on her backpack since she left it in the trunk of the Ford. Even though the car's key along with everything else in her purse was gone, all she had to do was punch in the code for keyless entry and retrieve the spare key from the glove box.

Another rookie move was her decision to drive into Manhattan to work Lizzie's shift. Why hadn't she taken the subway? Instead Honey had white-knuckled it through the unfamiliar streets and unaccustomed traffic and circled for endless minutes before she found on-street parking long blocks from the hotel. Then again, her car would likely be her bed tonight, so there was that. No reason to leave it in Brooklyn.

She pulled the cuffs of her sleeves back down and brushed off the seat of her black pants before she sauntered back into the hotel, nodding cordially to the doorman. Lucky it was shift change time so he was a different guy than the one who'd witnessed her embarrassing march out twenty minutes earlier.

Game face on, she wove her way through the guests meandering across the gleaming, checkered, black-and-white marble floor of the Pierre's elegant lobby. Everybody knew everybody else, judging from the excited buzz in the air in the aftermath of a night celebrating the lavish wedding of the Russian-American shipbuilding tycoon and his gorgeous bride with real-girl curves. The internet was awash in stories of the star-crossed lovers' happy reunion when he'd found out about their toddler love child.

There was no starry-eyed happily ever after for her mom and whoever her dad was. You could call Honey a love child or lust child or a mistake. Willow never concerned herself with labels. Willow had grown up unsupervised by her archeologist parents, and because the three of them were always on the move, she never could decide which of the guys she was dating at the time might be Honey's dad. By the time she realized she was pregnant, she'd chosen to keep the baby and scratched the idea of figuring out the actual father. According to Willow, whose notoriously cynical view of the opposite sex Honey was now grudgingly accepting, none of the teen guys she'd dated were equipped, except biologically, to be a father anyway. And after Willow's affair with Joss resulted in the birth of her twin half-brothers, Derek and Donnie, Honey finally let go of the pipedream of a "Mamma Mia" type reunion with her potential dads.

"Excuse me. I have to run back down to the staff lockers. I left my change of clothes there."

Honey forced her features to relax into a broad smile. The concierge behind the gleaming walnut reception counter had a phone to his ear and nodded distractedly before tilting his head toward the door behind him. Boss Man was nowhere in sight.

Finding her small backpack easily, Honey hooked it over her shoulder, then stopped to assess her surroundings. The locker area was empty. The entire staff was running back and forth, looking after the remaining guests and starting the cleanup required after an event of this magnitude.

Would she dare?

Her interviews were tomorrow—no, today. Before she tried to get a few hours sleep in her car, she was desperate to clean up. When she ran out of the apartment this morning consumed by righteous rage in search of her belongings, Honey had made another mistake in addition to the colossal one she made deciding to be Trey's apartment-mate. Pumped with anger, she'd flown down the stairs and out the door, chasing after her stuff, and hadn't put the latch on the door.

She'd locked herself out without a key. The super lived off the premises, and thirty-six hours into her tenancy, Honey hadn't gotten around to getting his number. Locked out meant no shower, so all she'd managed was a discreet wash up earlier in the staff bathroom when the head of housekeeping loaned her the standard-issue black slacks and white button-down shirt of her position. No way did she want to go to those interviews without a shower.

She scanned the hallway, listening. *When attempting to do anything underhanded, act like you own the place.*

All around her in the back of the house, the hotel's regular staff was hustling to make sure all was in readiness for the VIPs who would stay on site after the wedding. Everyone else was busy with cleanup in the main ballroom.

Right in front of her, the housekeeping manager perused a final checklist. He pointed to the tray on the cart in front of him. "Deliver this to room 1403," he said without looking up.

"Yes, sir," Honey answered, before she hefted the tray and went straight to the service elevator bank.

Chapter 2
A Clean Break

Honey didn't have a key card, but she didn't even have to try to force the lock. When a porter saw her struggling to place the tray on the carpeted floor in front of Room 1403, he obligingly used his passkey card for her.

Home free.

Wasting no time, Honey thanked him, elbowed open the door, and strode inside to the small linen-draped table by the window. She set the tray, laden with a bottle of red wine and a fruit plate, down on it. A quick glance around the pristine room revealed no personal items at all. The room was unoccupied as yet.

She wouldn't get a better opportunity.

All she needed was three minutes for a shower. Decision made, she closed herself into the bathroom, sparing little more than a glance at the understated luxury of fittings she'd never seen outside of magazines. After turning the spray on hot, she kicked off her clothes and stepped under the full-throated nozzle. She efficiently soaped herself with shower gel and lathered her hair, blessing the short, carefree hairstyle.

The violet color Boss Man disparaged would rinse out eventually, but Honey liked it. Her natural hair color was so pale it completely washed out her features.

With her not-there figure and bland hair color, she looked like a tween unless she wore tons of makeup and heels. And when she did that, she looked like a tween who was trying too hard to look like a twenty-five-year-old. The violet color was a statement that made makeup and heels unnecessary.

Besides, her potential superiors at the museums and galleries where she'd interview wouldn't look twice at her hair if her résumé was good enough. The positions were all low-paid internships. So even if she got one of them—no, she corrected herself, *when* she got one of them—she'd still have to work a second job to supplement her income.

But that was all part of the plan. The plan to have no plan other than to double down on her career. She wouldn't allow Trey with the traveling hands to be more than a hiccup in her pursuit of her career and her art. As far as her personal life was concerned, she'd damn well have some fun. On her terms. When she decided the guy and the time was right.

When she rummaged through her pack, somewhere at the bottom would be something clean to wear. Years ago, she'd gotten into the habit of filling the small pack with a change of clothes when her mother started reappearing. One never knew when Willow would show up on Joss Clayton's doorstep for sporadic visits to her children. Usually, she invited Honey, at that time a teenager, on an overnight.

Joss wouldn't let the boys go, he said they were too young, and in truth Honey agreed with him. The upside was that without her half-brothers with them, Honey had uninterrupted time with her mom. Willow usually booked a room at the Crown, a local inn.

They'd stay up all night talking about Willow's latest travels as a journalist and then catch up on Honey's dull high school life and the current events in Derek and Donnie's lives. Willow acted so much more like a girlfriend than a mother that Honey almost felt like she was talking about her own kids when she updated Willow.

Her mom never asked about Joss, nor did he ever inquire about the mother of his sons after Willow's visits. Joss could lose himself in his study of the solar system for weeks. And Willow was never at rest, always on the move chasing down environmental evildoers in the states and all over the world and reporting their misdeeds. In the last several years, she'd garnered more media attention for her work, and Honey was proud to see her mom breaking down complicated concepts on the news and pushing for legislative action and corporate responsibility. Joss, now fifty-eight to Willow's forty-five, was even more of a recluse than ever.

Willow encouraged Honey's interest and ability in art, and even though those random sleepovers tapered off as Honey got older, worked part time, and attended college, Honey was secure in the knowledge that when Willow inevitably picked up again and went on assignment, all of the small ceramic pieces Honey gifted to her would go along with her.

Joss, on the other hand, when he discovered Honey's IQ, told her to shelve the ceramic arts program in favor of an engineering degree at Alfred U. Honey reminded him, as so many people saw fit to remind her over the years, that Joss wasn't her father, stepfather, or even her adoptive parent. She was her own boss. The only person she had to listen to was herself.

What she didn't tell him was she'd decided if she didn't manage to achieve some financial success with her art within two years, or the promise of a future with it, she'd consider going back for the engineering degree—especially if her brothers needed her income.

Nerd, brainiac, weird—Honey had been called every name in the book. Aside from Lizzie, she never made friends at school, and man, it was lonely without her when Lizzie moved to the city five years ago. Lizzie would've warned her about Rick, yanked her head out of the clouds. But without her friend's level-headed advice, Honey was free to weave dreams of happily ever after. Rick could've stopped her with a word, but why would he? Why would he give up the easy A and the easy lay?

Then all the dumb plans Honey built up in her head came crashing down.

Everybody, and that meant every single person in their entire town, assembled for one of the biggest events in decades, a Halloween Harvest Party organized by Cheryl Reese, Caryville's local councilwoman, running for mayor, wife of the COO of their local bank and mother of—drumroll—her boyfriend Rick.

When the time came for one last campaign speech before the crowd, the local police chief, who was the master of ceremonies, introduced Cheryl and her family to the avid audience.

By that time, Honey, wearing the only dress she possessed, stood from the craft table where she was helping young kids carve pumpkins. She'd hurriedly wiped her hands of pumpkin goo and carefully walked toward the stage, carrying a bouquet of autumn flowers for the candidate. It took her a long minute before she figured out what was going on. Rick stood, silent and smirking at his mother's side, as she introduced Darlene Winthrop as his intended fiancée.

Wasn't it a hoot odd little Honey, the girl from the wrong side of the tracks, whip smart though she was, fancied herself good enough for the son of a banker and soon-to-be mayor?

She expected to be introduced as part of Cheryl and Gordon Reese's extended family, as Rick's longtime girlfriend.

Instead, they should've introduced her as the unsuspecting dope, a.k.a. Rick's booty call for six years. The sear of the public humiliation was a raw, open wound. She would never forget how she stopped midway along the path lined with hay bales, sunflowers, and pumpkins as she heard Darlene's name and saw the girl from the next town over, who was still in college, step onto the platform beside Rick as Cheryl made her last campaign pitch before the election.

A Carrie-like rage boiled up as she stood glued to that patch of grass as a kaleidoscope of faces contorted with laughter gawked at the spectacle silly Honey Hill made of herself. How had she, the girl who'd never known her father and whose mother had skipped out on her years ago, fooled herself into believing she was good enough to be a permanent fixture within the Reese family circle?

Temper sealed her decision. Overnight she'd made her plans, and here she was in the city. And yes, November right before Thanksgiving was the wrong time to be looking for the kind of job she was after, and Trey proved to be the very worst choice in a roommate.

Those two decisions might have been avoided if only Honey controlled her impulse to run as fast as she could from the scene of her humiliation.

She'd called Willow to tell her about her move to New York City, if not the impetus for it. She so did *not* want to hear Willow's "I told you so" right now. Willow had escaped small town life, leaving Honey and her brothers to weather the whispers and the judgment. She'd never understood why Honey wasn't eager to do the same.

But Honey's highest ambition hadn't been a swanky career where everybody knew her name. All she ever wanted were stable relationships and a conventional life. Basically, the complete opposite of her life so far. She wanted to get married to the father of her kids. She wanted a solid career that didn't entail travel. She wanted her kids to grow up with their dad, a guy they'd actually met, in a house, not a trailer or a motel room as she'd done in her youngest years.

Wanted. Past tense. She refused to dwell on that day or any of those dreams anymore. Rick's parents had introduced everyone to Rick's girlfriend, Darlene, a preppy brunette, the kind of girl Honey had no hope of being in high school, who had private school written all over her. Cheryl Reese did not want to open her family to a bastard child with purple hair and bohemian clothing, and neither, even more cutting, did her son.

Yep, Willow had it all pegged. Their small town had an abundance of small minds. But Honey, who'd spent her teens with little of a mother's positive influence, craved the friendship and attention Rick seemed to give because she got it nowhere else. Apart from Lizzie who always took Honey at face value, Rick went from being the only guy who never called her brainiac to her boyfriend. That was all it took to win her undying devotion, so yeah, she was so very easy, and she hadn't slept around on him. Once she gave her virginity to Rick, Honey didn't want the labels, which clung to her anyway because of her home situation. Only in recent days had she examined what she was to Rick. A source of easy sex and a classmate who could write his term papers as well as her own and get them both an A.

Willow was right. You couldn't control other people's preconceptions and prejudices. Willow never gave it a second thought. She escaped to what she could control—herself, her career. Honey owed it to herself to pursue her own dreams, to thrive in New York City and make a name for herself in the ceramic art world.

When the anger faded a little, Honey puzzled over how she could've been so wrong. So blind to reality. But she hadn't seen any of it coming, and all that proved was ever-practical, older than her years, genius IQ Honey could be naive.

Now she'd wised up. Rick was the past, and her new life was in front of her.

She'd invite Willow to visit when she got settled again. She grinned as she stepped out of the shower and reached for the thirsty white towel. Her mom was probably the only person she knew who wouldn't balk if she had to sleep in a car when she visited because that was practically old times for them.

****

Jake was satisfied. Almost. The reception was over, and aside from a couple of glitches, it was a major success. He'd made contact with a number of potential clients, and of course the best advertisement for his work was their attendance at a mega-event of this caliber where everything went smooth as silk.

The little dustup with the mouthy server needed further investigation. Somehow, she'd managed to get in and work the event without any clearance.

He reached into his pocket and pulled out her nametag along with the keycard to his room. Honey Hill. Talk about incredible nerve. She hadn't even bothered to come up with a more realistic name. And damned if the name alone didn't bring with it a whole slew of filthy thoughts every time it crossed his mind. Which it had…a lot over the last hour. He wanted to believe it was the stunt she'd pulled that he couldn't forget, but he called his own BS. It was *her*.

Without a second of discomfort or any permission, she'd strolled into his event. When he confronted her, she'd gotten in his face, all five feet nothing of her, stood her ground, then dropped a tray of glasses on him.

His training, his bulk, and his serious workplace demeanor intimidated men much bigger than him. But she hadn't batted an eye at him except when she'd done it as a distraction. And man, in spite of it all, if he hadn't been working and for such a significant client, he would've gone with it in a heartbeat to see where that flirtation led.

He walked into his room—Vlad had insisted on providing him with one even though he had his own place downtown—and saw the tray of fruit and wine was delivered as instructed.

Jake shrugged out of his jacket, yanked off his tie, and unbuttoned his shirt. The tuxedo was only slightly less restrictive than his dress blues, and he couldn't wait to be out of it.

He opened the wine and lifted the cover on the tray. He never had a chance to eat more than an appetizer or two at these events because it was work and he was always moving. Now he'd have a couple of bites of fruit and relax with a glass of wine before he hit the sack.

Jake forked up some sweet cantaloupe and a couple of strawberries, then poured a healthy portion of the wine. He savored the cabernet franc's perfect blend of spice and buttery smoothness.

Getting his mother's vineyard, correction, when *her manager* got his mother's vineyard up to this standard, it would be an accomplishment. His mamma took little interest in anything in the states, including him. It wasn't until after his father's death he discovered her majority stake in the struggling Long Island vineyard seeded by old world vines.

He tossed his shirt on the chair, then froze when he heard the faint sound over the white noise of the hotel's piped-in music. A slight rustle through the thick wood of the bathroom door. He pushed back a step toward the armoire to get into position, then in one fluid motion, grasped and cocked the pistol he slid from the holster strapped to his right ankle.

The door opened as he leveled the gun, chest high at the opening.

Her mouth gaped, and a wild shriek issued in the short seconds it took him to uncock the pistol, push it into his waist, take one long stride to reach her, and shove his hand over her open mouth.

"What the hell?" Her muffled words tickled the palm of his hand, and heat flooded his chest as electricity ran in a hotwire from his hand to the tease of her soft lips against his skin.

Jake, pull your shit together!

"Damn right, what the hell! What the hell are you doing here?"

She was slippery as an eel as she jerked back and forth to get out from under the arm pressed across her chest from shoulder to shoulder and the hand covering her mouth. She wasn't at all concerned he had a gun or with his superior strength, he could do serious damage to her without breaking a sweat.

Or maybe she was well aware what froze him in a cold sweat was the shock of seeing a fantasy come to life. There was nothing imaginary about the round little ass pressed against his body and the precarious state of the towel that was about to slide off her. She squirmed, and a torrent of curses flew out of her mouth against his hand. Yeah, she was in a temper all right, but so was he. Because this person, this *woman,* who had trouble written all over her, was back again. Somehow, angry and aroused as he was, somewhere deep in his gut, he knew. The rest of his life would be divided into the time before he met her and the time since.

"Stop. Right now. I have a weapon." He put his lips a breath away from the delicate shell of her ear. Kept his voice low but didn't disguise the snarl in it. "If I take my hand off your mouth, you shut up. I ask the questions and you answer. Got it?"

The spiky roadrunner head bobbed up and down.

"Okay." He lifted his hand slowly.

She stepped away from him, and right away her hands jumped up to tighten the towel around her body. She jerked her chin up, keeping silent as instructed, but her lips pressed into a determined line, and her dark chocolate eyes sparked outrage.

By now he didn't even find it weird the emotion showing strongest in her eyes was indignation. Nor did he wonder his strongest desire was *not* to find out how or why she'd gotten in here. Nope. His hands itched to remove that towel. His jaw tightened, and the rest of his body hardened into painful readiness. He forced out a harsh breath, unclenched his fists. Searched for logic.

"Ms. ah…Hill. Somehow, we meet again. I guess it wasn't enough for you to get fired. Do you want to be charged with breaking and entering and theft of services as well?"

Her annoyed eyes widened further before she said, "That's your question? You almost gave me a heart attack pointing that gun at me. The answer is no."

He raked a hand through the pristine smoothness of his hair. *Smart-ass.*

"What are you doing in my room?"

As she opened her mouth to speak, he raised his right hand up chest high. "Hand to God, if you say you were taking a shower, I'm gonna lose it."

He watched her pale pink lips press together again and one eyebrow rise, and he knew she was suppressing a smirk.

"Okay," she said. "I won't say it, but that's the reason. And it's pure bad luck this is your room. That's just the kind of luck I've been having lately."

She started to shrug, but the movement caused the knot of her towel to unravel. She grabbed the edges of it again, but not before he caught a gut-clenching glimpse of the creamy skin at the top her breasts.

No apology, not a hint of embarrassment. The

woman was certifiable. If he could think about anything other than what was under that towel, he'd tell her so.

He went for sarcasm. "Of course, you could've avoided this altogether by taking a shower at your own place. You know, where you live."

"Yeah, that would've been smart. But I don't have my key. I locked myself out of my apartment, and anyway, it's a long story, and I'm sure you've got better things to do than hear it. I'll just get my things and get out of your way here."

The little speech poured out of her mouth fast as she executed a quick sidestep away from him.

"Where do you think you're going?"

"To get dressed. Then I'll get out of your hair."

Jake ran an aggravated hand through that hair. "Yeah, okay."

He angled his jaw toward the bathroom door and watched it close behind her, frustration clawing at him. He had to get to the bottom of this: how she'd worked tonight without proper authorization and her astonishing reappearance in his room just now, but hell, the woman was practically naked. The sight of all that pale skin, damp and rosy from the shower, unnerved him.

Because her mere presence pushed every sane thought out of his head. Because now that she was no longer in his employ, he could act on the attraction sizzling between them. Or was it just on his side? No, he never got that kind of signal mixed. But it wasn't like him to leave the mystery of her being here unsolved in favor of getting her into his bed. This chick was seriously messing with his head.

He poured another generous portion of the cabernet

into his glass and tossed it back in a gulp. He'd find the whiskey in the minibar in a moment because wine wasn't gonna cut it tonight. But first he'd wrap up this mini-interrogation and send her on her way. Then tomorrow, no later today, he'd dig deeper. When she was gone and he could think straight.

Then she was out of the bathroom in skinny cargo pants and a long-sleeved white tee. Even though every inch of her skin was now covered, his pulse amped up even more. With every muscle tense and on edge, he was a rocket about to go off. The well-worn, too-snug clothes clung to every curve of her tight little form. For the first time in his life, he appreciated the term second skin.

She hitched her small knapsack onto her shoulder.

"Okay," he said looking over the top of her spiky hair, looking anywhere but at her unadorned face or her body. "Let's see your ID, and then you can go."

She opened her mouth, then closed it, stuck her hands into her back pockets.

"I lost my ID when I lost my house key." She lifted her chin.

He rolled his eyes at the ornate ceiling. "*Basta!* Are you kidding me? Isn't it too late for this kind of nonsense? It's two in the morning. I'm not going to prosecute you. I'm just going to note your name and information." *And flag it so you're never allowed anywhere near anything I'm in charge of again.*

She chewed her bottom lip, shook her head back and forth. "Listen, I want to be gone as much as you want me to leave. I don't have my ID, though."

A thought occurred to him, which should have hit him much sooner.

"If you have no house key, where are you going now?"

"Not that it's any of your business, but I'm going to stay with a friend."

"Where?" The question shot out fast enough to fluster her.

"I, um, the address is in my phone." She looked down and fumbled with the screen, but not before he saw the rush of deep pink that washed over her skin from throat to hairline. "It's about ten blocks from here." She pocketed the phone, still not meeting his gaze.

"You're a terrible liar. Fake name. Lost ID. You're insulting my intelligence, H. Hill."

"I don't care whether you believe me or not. My name *is* Honey Hill, and I *did* lose my ID. Unless you're going to call the cops, I'm leaving now." She turned smartly and walked to the door.

Puzzle pieces fell into place as he studied her—her straight-backed, proud posture, her neck tilting slightly to the side. She reminded him of a slim-stemmed flower with delicate, silvery petals. A summer flower that somehow made it into late fall with no protection from the elements. It was two a.m. Though it was unseasonably warm for this time of year, it was still late November in New York. The temperature outside had dropped to forty degrees. She had no jacket, just a death grip on that miniscule backpack.

The words came out before he knew what he was saying. "If you need a place to sleep tonight, you can stay here."

Chapter 3
Sleep Is Highly Overrated

His deep voice was casual, almost matter of fact.

Honey kept her hand on the doorknob and made an effort to compose her face before she turned back to respond.

It was a struggle not to react when part of her wanted to do a sky-high fist pump and the other part wanted to slump over in exhaustion. Absolutely the last thing she wanted to do was go back out into the chilly November night, walk ten blocks to her Ford Escort, which she'd christened Fred and who was the friend she'd be staying with tonight.

Right now, the warmth of a bed and the thought of a bathroom, the glory of *a bathroom,* the blessing of not sleeping in her clothes, especially with her interviews tomorrow, was beyond tempting.

She turned around then, and yeah, there was one more, very alluring thing. She was looking at—no, practically drooling over—hands down, the most gorgeous guy she'd ever set eyes on, a tanned, shirtless, six-packed god with a pistol stuck in the back waist of his pants.

No, she couldn't do this.
How would she ever sleep?
She had to say no.
"Okay," she said.

Her face flushed hot as she said it, and she willed him to turn away because she couldn't make herself stop staring at the T of black hair hazing across his chest before it arrowed straight down to the unbuttoned waist of his pants.

She swallowed the surge of lust in her throat, croaked out a thanks. "I really appreciate it. I have a big day tomorrow, and uh, not having to go all the way to my, um, friend this late…it will help."

After everything else that had happened between them tonight, his offer was the last thing she ever expected to hear. Two days into her move to the city and she'd let herself down in a big way. But she couldn't drum up the energy to care right now because she was exhausted. All she needed was a couple of hours sleep to regroup.

She forced her gaze away from his chiseled torso to the welcoming, plump chaise in the corner of the room. Yep, she could be comfortable there. Being short had some benefits.

"If it's okay, I'll borrow one of the bathrobes to sleep in. I don't have any pajamas with me."

Now it was his turn to look uncomfortable, and Honey marveled at the stripes of color that scored the olive skin of his cheekbones.

"Sure," he said. "I'm going to take a quick shower before lights out. Feel free to undress…ah, put on that bathrobe." He nodded at the bathrobe on the hanger hooked to the top knob of the armoire.

He disappeared into the bathroom, and as soon as Honey heard the water go on, she quickly shed her clothes, folded them, and slipped into the thick, cotton unisex robe that covered her from neck to ankle.

The bathroom door opened. He reappeared inside a cloud of steam with the same size towel that had previously covered her entire body hooked at his hip to cover his thighs. He rubbed another smaller towel over hair the water turned into gleaming black ringlets.

Then he walked toward her, swaggered was more like it, before he stopped, feet planted wide. He raised a wicked, black brow in question.

She froze in place as heat bloomed in every secret place of her body even under the heavy weight of the cotton robe. God, he was hot. More ripped than the models in her artists' anatomy class. More alive. The room receded, leaving only him and every luscious defined muscle he had in her vision. She couldn't look away, and she couldn't seem to catch her breath. A tight pulse began to throb between her thighs, begging for relief. What if she reached out a hand to him and…?

Finally, she understood.

Duh. He has to get into the armoire behind your back. They did an awkward little dance then, where she sucked in a breath and sidestepped his big body so he could reach the handle, open it, and grab a leather gym bag inside.

She inhaled the same intoxicating scent she couldn't help noticing earlier this evening. *And oh, man, why hadn't he shaved? Just to torture her?*

"I didn't bother to shave." He rubbed a hand along his jaw. "I wanted to be quick. It's almost two-thirty," he said.

Honey nodded, and her usually smart mouth went from dry to drooling. She was *so* out of her league here. She raced into the bathroom, mumbling, "Teeth."

She located the hotel-provided, cello-wrapped

toothbrush and toothpaste and took her time brushing so he'd have enough time to dress. Tucking the toothbrush into her backpack pocket to save, she thought, *do guys like him even wear anything to bed?*

But when she stepped back into the bedroom, he still hadn't dressed. At least, not enough to stop her from salivating some more. His basketball shorts hung low on his lean hips. His leather carryall was open on the bed, and he rifled through it, pulling out a dark blue T-shirt. He shrugged into it, biceps flexing all the way. She had to consciously snap her jaw shut as she tracked the flex of his shoulders and pecs as he pulled it down and finally concealed his defined torso from her avid gaze.

This was such a bad idea.

"I wasn't sure what I had in the way of—" He cleared his throat as he glanced at her with a half-smile. "—sleepwear."

Honey nodded, her question answered—yep, he usually slept nude—totally forgetting how to say words in the face of his smile. It was the devil's own smile—pure sin. And there'd been no smiles between them today. A tiny part of her wondered how good it would feel to be on the receiving end of that smile on a regular basis.

Stop it right now, Honey.

She busied herself setting up the chaise with a pillow and a blanket, set her alarm, and plugged in her phone.

"I set my alarm for seven. Just so you know." The last thing she wanted to do was surprise a guy with a pistol hidden somewhere.

"Not a problem. Better get some shut eye, then."

He switched off the classical music wafting from the small night table system, hit the off switch on the lamp. The heavy drapes and blackout layer of curtains on the windows plunged the room into complete darkness.

Honey slid into her makeshift bed on the chaise. The rustle of crisp sheets and the breaths he hummed out meant he was making himself comfortable in the bed. It was a strangely personal sound. She'd never shared a room with a man. Which was unbelievable to everyone on the outside of her little town looking in, but there it was. She'd lived in a dormered third-floor room at the top of their shabby Victorian house, her brothers sharing the large second-floor room. Joss occupied the converted bedroom on the main level.

Yes, she and Rick had been intimate. But there was nothing of beds or sheets about it. It was always a hurried few minutes somewhere like his truck, an awkward, fumbling kind of encounter. In retrospect, it was obvious he never wanted anything but the easy sexual release he got from her. She was convenient with the added advantage of a home-cooked meal on occasion and homework help.

She'd been too caught up in her *one man, one home* fantasy to see it. What had made her think Rick didn't mind her background and upbringing? How had she missed his snobbery? The answer was obvious now. She'd wanted a happily ever after so badly she lived in a fantasy and called it reality. If only she could mold real people like she did with cement and clay.

Even worse, even though it had only been a month since they broke up, Rick her fantasy and Rick the nasty reality were both hazy memories in the face of the gorgeously ripped, incredibly irritating, and yes, because he saw through her fake *I'm staying with a friend* ruse, kind-hearted guy in this room with her. Rick was rapidly moving into the category of lesson learned.

I finally get it, Mom. Family ties were mere biology. Relationships ended. Career and work were what lasted. It was past time to pursue her art with everything she had. Time to put away childish aspirations of happily ever after. Maybe she was cut out for temporary relationships anyway. *Stick with what you know, Honey.*

Permanence was something she'd never actually seen and something she obviously wasn't good at. She wouldn't hanker after things like certainty and stability. Those things only looked better on the outside. They must be mind-numbingly boring in reality.

She shifted on the chaise and turned her face toward the wall. She needed sleep, but her restless mind and needy body wouldn't give her peace. How in hell could she sleep when he was only three feet away from her in bed, and all she could think of was the way he'd looked wearing nothing but a towel after his shower?

The surprisingly boyish curl in his damp black hair, the small drops of water that lingered and clung to his broad shoulders for a moment before they slowly made their way down his anything but boyish chest. The way every visible inch of his skin was deeply tanned to a lustrous almost unreal bronze.

There was something protective about him. Something reassuring in his raspy voice. His large capable hands, that, yeah, even when one covered her mouth, felt disarmingly good. She could hardly recall her anger earlier today—*hello, the guy fired you, Honey!*—because for some reason underneath the annoyed, boss-man exterior was a sense of something deeper. She wanted to discover what that was almost as much as she wanted to explore his seriously amazing body.

"So what's tomorrow? Your big day?" His voice was dark, warm, and rich as melted chocolate, and she added the sound of it to her growing catalog of his good points.

"I have three interviews."

"Oh. In the service industry?"

"Um, no."

"That's good."

She caught the amusement in his rough voice and smiled into the darkness.

"They're for entry level positions at galleries and a museum." Somehow, it was easier to speak when he couldn't see her expression.

"So you were filling in for somebody tonight?"

"Yeah, for a friend, it was a mutual favor. I don't want to cause my friend any trouble."

"Understood. One more thing. Where would you have gone if you hadn't stayed here tonight?"

She pushed out a breath. It was marginally easier to say in the dark.

"My car." No, she wouldn't lie, but there was no way she'd elaborate on that shameful admission either. At least the room was pitch black and he couldn't see the scorch of embarrassment marking her face.

There was silence for a moment before her eyes snapped wide and heat raced through her all over again.

"I have a question too." *Late to the game,*

considering we're sharing a hotel room. What would Rick's judgey mom say if she could see her now? No doubt something crass and offensive that would flash around town before dawn.

He grunted something like "go ahead."

"What's your name?" she whispered, part embarrassed part defiant.

"Jake. I'm Jake Ricco." His rich voice carried the hint of a smile.

"Okay. Goodnight, Jake."

"Goodnight, Honey."

The smile lingered in his rough voice, and she let her eyelids close.

****

No wonder her husky voice was tentative. She didn't want to talk about her situation. Well, yeah. Whatever events led to her current state, he heard the dread in her voice at the prospect of discussing it. Equally, he appreciated her sense that it was only fair to provide him with some information since he'd offered her a place to sleep.

Not that he was likely to get any...sleep, that was. His buddies would laugh. This was not a scenario the Jake any of them knew would ever be involved in.

He was known for being deliberative, never impulsive. His career both in the military and as a civilian was all about creating and adhering to lists. In addition to his mastery of anything to do with the water and swimming, he was at his best organizing and carrying out his exact plans to completion. Lists of procedures and protocols for the training that kept his teammates and those they protected safe. Then recently, business rules which succeeded in pushing his second career to the forefront of the security industry.

Deliberation was what kept him sane. Rules existed to be followed. If a rule didn't work, it was replaced by a better rule that did.

He'd borne the consequences of breaking rules. He was still bearing them.

So why had he broken multiple personal and professional rules tonight and offered her a place to stay?

Everything about her was wrong.

From a job standpoint, she'd snuck into the gig here and had a set-to with another server, the only blemish on an otherwise smooth event. She was combative as hell and had somehow snuck into his room. So no, *not* employee of the year.

What was it about H. Hill? Why was he lying in bed with a massive hard-on brought on by just the thought of a kooky woman who called herself Honey and whose even breathing told him she was already asleep? He flipped onto his stomach and buried his head deep in the pillow. He'd block her out—her unexpectedly appealing looks, her bossy voice, her salted caramel scent, her everything. And he'd get some sleep.

A couple of hours later, he was roused awake in the sweaty aftermath of an erotic dream featuring that same face. The face he saw every time he closed his eyes. Big, dark eyes, short, sleek hair, compact, supple body. In his filthy imagination, she was straddling him in this enormous bed, the white robe covering her otherwise naked body sliding from her shoulders. She rode him hard, her eyes glittering and focused totally on him, her teeth planted in her pouty bottom lip. He pushed his hands into that silky, silvery hair, before he pulled her head down and covered her mouth with his.

Damn. His body was on fire. He couldn't go for another shower or even take matters into his own hand because they were sharing a room and he had no interest in having her wake up to find out exactly how she'd affected him.

What the hell, Jake. He flipped the sheets off his body and lay there as his skin cooled, willing his muscles to relax. Then after long, painful minutes of backward times tables in Italian, he managed to settle back into sleep.

At six he jolted awake again from another fitful half-sleep. This time he was breathing hard in the aftermath of a vivid nightmare. No, it was more than a nightmare; it was the total recollection of that long-ago day swimming with his brother Francesco. The nightmare that had dogged him almost every night for twenty years and his pounding head assured him further sleep wasn't happening.

He was already wearing the shorts and T-shirt that were his workout gear. He slipped out of bed, grabbed his sneakers from his bag. He'd head to the hotel's gym. After he sweated for an hour, he'd get them both some coffee.

She was out cold when he looked over, barely a bump under the blanket on the chaise with only the violet spikes of her hair visible. Maybe that color was a good thing. At least he could keep track of her. He was grinning as he let himself out the door.

After his work out, he hit the coffee shop down the street. But when he got back to his room at seven fifteen, she was gone. On the chaise, on top of the neatly folded blanket, she'd placed a sheet of paper ripped from the hotel's notepad.

Jake, I'll never forget your kindness. Thank you. Honey.

Jake didn't realize he was squeezing the disposable coffee cup until the hot liquid spurted all over his hand. He strode into the bathroom and dumped the whole thing down the sink.

Chapter 4
A Small Town Called New York City

Five Days Later

He'd wasted three precious days telling himself he couldn't care less.

Then after the third straight night of erotic dreams featuring white sheets, white towels, and feathery silver hair, he called in a favor at the precinct and ran her name through the DMV.

Turned out Honeysuckle Hill—hell, yeah, that was her actual name, and yeah, the name alone made him sweat—had accumulated two parking tickets on her Ford Escort on the lower west side in the last week. With that information, in between meetings with clients to discuss or set up security at their homes, offices, or event spaces, Jake had spent the last couple of days walking concentric circles around the site of those tickets, hoping to spot the blue, ten-year-old vehicle.

So far—nothing, and he was starting to question his sanity. He'd spent a restless, platonic night with a sneaky, tray-dropping, violet-haired crazy woman, and he wanted more? What the fuck was wrong with him?

It could only be she intrigued him, and he needed to close the loop. Somehow she'd slipped out that morning, leaving a note that messed with his equilibrium. She'd left with no apartment key, no jacket. Did she get a job? Where was she living? The city was big. And the city could be unforgiving.

He had to satisfy himself she was okay.

Really Jake?

He called his own bullshit. She'd shown she could take care of herself by handling the creep who harassed her at the hotel that night. With no one the wiser, she'd snuck into his room right past the tight security he put in place for the Grigory wedding and reception. The woman was more than capable.

For all he knew, she could be in a terrycloth robe right now spouting bull to another dude who figured her small stature and big eyes meant she was helpless. *Good luck with that, buddy.*

His fists clenched at the idea of her with someone else, but he had to face it. The woman had hustled a job and a bed for a night. He didn't want to think she was used to hustling anything else, but that could be her reality.

And he had to admit it didn't matter because he didn't care what she'd done. He only wanted to find her.

Without knowing how he got there, he was inside Duffy's. It wasn't game time yet, but hell, he could use a drink. Monday night habits died hard, although on this particular night he'd be watching football alone. Connor was out of town, and Vlad was still on his honeymoon.

He was heading to their usual seats in the corner of the bar when something caught his eye from the back of the room. A flash of motion near the stockroom, silver hair topped with a violet fringe.

He froze, then started a swift, silent walk back

there, never letting his gaze waver from the spot where he'd seen the top of her head. Because it *was* her. And he wasn't going to let her slip through his fingers again.

****

Honey squirmed at the uncomfortable bead of sweat trickling down her spine as she bent and heaved another plastic case of twenty-four pilsners. Outside, the weather was ridiculously warm for the last days of November. Inside the thick plaster and brick-walled pub, it was a cool kind of muggy with sweating walls and sticky floor no matter what it was washed with. Cleaning and tending bar for the better part of two hours drenched her *Duffy's* black tee, and sweat coated her back. The skinny jeans she'd scored at H & M stuck to her skin like a rubber sauna suit.

She'd already worn the handful of tees Jim Duffy gave her last week when he hired her. Opting to take every shift offered left her scant time for anything else, including filing a police complaint against Trey. Anyway, a complaint would be nothing but a symbolic warning for any future impulsive apartment renters from the sticks. With no hope of ever getting her stuff back, Honey put all of her focus on finding another place to live.

But she'd gotten one of the art internships she interviewed for, and she had this bartending job to fill the pay gap. And for a couple of more days, she could stay at Lizzie's while Lizzie and Kurt visited his parents for the Thanksgiving holidays.

She was almost too busy to feel lonely on Thanksgiving…almost. Last year, as usual, she'd cooked Thanksgiving dinner with all the trimmings for her brothers and Joss. Rick had showed up after dinner to hang out for a while, and Willow called them. That had been their custom for years.

A few days ago, Derek had called her on Thanksgiving morning. A fist clenched around her heart at the sound of her younger brother's changing voice, confirming he had one foot still lingering in childhood and the other scratching the surface of adulthood. She kept the conversation brief because God forbid Derek figured out his big bad sister nearly burst into tears at the sound of his voice.

"Honey, glad I caught you."

"Yeah, you are lucky. I was almost out the door. Taylor Swift invited me over for turkey."

"Ha, soooo, you're having a blast in New York City?"

"Of course. I love it. It'll be perfect when you and your sidekick can visit when school gets out for winter break."

"I can't wait, Honey."

"Me either, Derek. Say hi to Donnie and Joss. And don't burn the turkey."

"Won't happen, we're going to the Crown."

"I knew you beanstalks would miss my cooking if nothing else."

"We do miss you, Honey, and not just your cooking. But I'm glad you're doing this. For you. And it's cool to tell my friends my sister is an artist down in the city."

"Not yet, but I'm working on it. Right now, I'm a bartender. My internship doesn't start till January."

"Yeah, a bartender's even cooler."

So her brothers were doing just fine. It was time for her to stop inflating her mother-hen importance in their lives and find a place to live.

Thank God for Lizzie. After a grungy two days sleeping in her car, she'd welcomed Lizzie's text saying they were recovered from the flu and heading up to Vermont for a few days—*and I have a second set of sheets.* Honey grabbed the chance to take regular showers and sleep indoors. Lizzie had offered up her on-trend wardrobe to Honey till she could replenish her own, and she took a few tops. But at five-nine to her five-two, even Lizzie's blouses swam on Honey.

After the Trey disaster, Honey was hesitant to room with a complete stranger, but she'd be smarter this time. Her name would go on the lease. Between shifts, she culled through options on online rentals sites. Rentals in the city went faster than Hamilton tickets, so she had to take a look at anything suitable right away before someone else got there first.

She twisted round with the heavy case of clean pilsners and rammed straight into an immovable wall of hard-muscled man. Her grip loosened in shock, and his hands come out to cover hers on the side handles of the plastic case.

"Whoa! Way to creep up on someone!" Her heart rocketed into her throat as she absorbed the reality. *Jake—here.* Too close for comfort and yet with the case of pilsners between them, not close enough. Awareness crackled between them, and the familiar leather and lemon scent of him washed over her.

"Well if it isn't Ms. Honeysuckle Hill herself." His black eyes glittered as he drawled her ridiculous, actual name.

The same rich, taunting voice of her vivid imagination. Jake had starred in her dreams every night and figured into her daytime fantasies as well. A fresh wave of warmth flashed over her already overheated cheeks as she recalled the words they spoke in her fantasies, the delicious details of everything they'd do to each other, how she teased and egged him on every step of the way. *Shake it off, Honey.*

She shook the damp hair off her forehead and stepped back till her shoulder blades pressed the clammy wall. He was crowding her space, and he wasn't about to move out of it—if the gleam in his eyes was anything to go by.

Half the reason she'd run out of his hotel room last week was instinctive self-preservation. On top of the genuine fear exhaustion would set in and she'd sleep through her alarm and miss her interviews was the knowledge she'd never had such a visceral, confusing reaction to a man before.

He'd tossed her out of a paying gig, and even though it riled the hell out of her, she didn't belong there, and they both knew it. Then when she snuck into, of all rooms, his, to shower, the cosmic joke was on her because she couldn't explain to him why she was there, and she couldn't explain to herself why she didn't want to leave.

The smartest thing she could do was run in the opposite direction...so she did. But that didn't mean she wanted to. No, she left because she wanted to stay so damn badly. After Rick, after Trey, after all of the clear indicators of her ineptitude with men, she wanted to stay so badly. And that scared the living daylights out of her. All week she alternately kicked herself for missing out on the hookup of a lifetime and patted herself on the back for dodging an ego deflating one-night stand bullet.

It shocked her to admit so soon after Rick's defection and Trey's forceful come-on, she'd even consider anything personal, never mind sexual, with a guy. Like were they all jerks? Or just the ones she came into contact with?

So when the door clicked closed as he left that morning, Honey roused from her half sleep and moved fast. His tuxedo was hanging in the closet, so she knew he meant to return. She'd washed and dressed quick, written a note, and ran.

She'd never thought she'd see him again.

But here he was, and he was solid, dangerous, smelling like…some combination of heaven and him, and wearing that challenging, sinful grin.

"What are you doing here?"

"I could ask the same. Still in the service industry I see." His mouth was a sexy straight line, but his eyes danced with mirth.

Honey ground her teeth. "What are the freaking chances…" she muttered.

He laughed, and those gorgeous lips opened to flash gleaming white teeth. She couldn't look away. The reality of Jake was even bigger and better than her fantasies.

"The staff shouldn't talk to themselves. Bad for business."

He was so close his breath ruffled the hair at her temple with every word. She wanted to laugh as much as she wanted to scream. There didn't seem to be anything in between about her reaction to Jake.

He was her dream, her fantasy, and her nightmare all rolled into one, and he was right in front of her, blocking everything in her sightline with his bulk. She yanked the case of glasses away and shoved past him to walk behind the bar. Her hands were shaking when she set the container on the back counter.

His gaze stayed on her as she walked away—she could tell from the feathers of awareness that tickled every inch of her skin from her neck to her ankles. She took her time putting the glasses away and finally sucked in a big breath when he settled onto a barstool in the corner farthest from the door.

To hide her nerves, she tugged a bar towel along the gleaming oak she'd polished to a shine ten minutes earlier and stopped when she was near enough to mutter, "Why don't you find another place to play?"

"It's also bad for business to send customers away. What would Jim Duffy think if I told him you were trying to get his clientele to leave?"

"You know the owner here?" *Man, could this get any worse?*

"Yep. I've been coming in here for years."

"Holy sh…"

"You know, Honey, I don't believe you have the knack for customer service."

His devil's grin inflamed her ready temper, but she bit her lip on the retort that sprang to her lips. Joss, never effusive with compliments, always told her she could sell snow to Eskimos when she worked their farm stand every summer.

She forced herself to look straight into his wickedly amused eyes and let a phony smile curve her lips.

"That depends on who you ask. I haven't had any complaints. What can I get for you?"

She pressed her lips together and waited—all fake polite while he scanned the offerings. She'd served several people over the last couple of hours, but right now the place was practically empty. Jim told her there would be a good crowd later for Monday night football. She glanced at the clock whose plastic face proclaimed *Beauty is in the eye of the Beerholder*. Eight o'clock game time couldn't come soon enough.

"I like that Belgian ale on tap."

Of course you do. The taps, set into a throne-like platform at the center of the bar, were a challenge to someone her height. She stepped onto the ledge behind them and stretched up to pull the handle, fully aware of the way the hem on her tee moved up to expose a large swathe of skin around her middle. A fresh coat of heated perspiration washed over her as his gaze drifted frequently to the tiny purple crystal piercing her belly button.

Jake's narrowed gaze tracked her every move. He shrugged out of his leather bomber and relaxed back on the barstool. "Getting warm in here," he said. Crossing his arms over his chest, he stared, not even pretending to watch the kickoff.

Honey clamped her lips over a curse. She was so right to get out of that hotel room the other night because Jake looked at her like he was a starved jungle cat on the prowl and she was his chosen appetizer. But, oh, man, she hated to admit it—it turned her on.

If she'd stayed the other night, if they acted on the heat sizzling between them, where would she be now? Feeling awkward and regretful? Or would she view him as a very sexy experience and make a lighthearted joke about the encounter? Did women walk away from Jake totally satisfied and never look back, or did they wallow in regret there couldn't be more?

Then the surge of football fans Jim Duffy predicted started to stream through the door, and it was a little easier to ignore her over-the-top musings because any relationship with Jake, brief or otherwise, with someone like her was a product of her wild imagination. Her appeal was as basic as being half-naked in a towel. *Let's be real.* Jake was a Roman god packing heat, and Honey was the girl her classmates used to call Pippi Longstocking.

She moved back and forth, taking orders and pouring. Crazy busy or not and even though the Giants were having one hell of a great game, Honey's skin stayed hot as Jake's gaze brooded on her. When he raised his glass for a refill, self-preservation had her tilting her head, forcing him to slide the glass toward her so she wouldn't have to go to him.

Gary, the young bar-back, assisted her by running for extra glasses or lemons and limes as requested. She'd been a waitress as a teen but never tended bar, so last week Jim showed her how to pull beer and fix a couple of the mixed drinks some of his customers liked. But this was not a complicated cocktail clientele. This was a beer, shots, sometimes wine, or soda crowd.

Honey had it covered because tending bar, like waitressing, had a lot in common with everything she always did at home cleaning up after Joss and her brothers. She found her rhythm moving back and forth serving and almost—almost—forgot he was there.

When the game was over, the bar started to clear out, and Honey began to restore order. As Gary helped her clear and wipe up tables, Jake remained planted on the same barstool, nursing a beer. Now the bar was emptying out, he didn't bother to pretend his hooded, fallen-saint's eyes hadn't been on her the whole night. His searing black gaze was more open now as it stripped the black tee and jeans right off her. She froze, her skin prickling with moisture, and she shivered, opening her mouth for air as her heart forced its way into her throat. No. This was her space, and this had to stop.

She looked him full in the face, took his stare, and raised him a glare. Then she strolled toward him like he was anybody, not the guy who'd starred in her torrid dreams for almost a week. Still, she stopped a safe distance away.

"You still here?" She tucked her thumbs into her belt loops and jerked her chin toward the post-game show running silently across the screen. "The game's over, and your team blew a big lead."

His lips quirked, and she forced her gaze away from the amused curve of his lower lip.

"Like I said, customer service doesn't appear to be your strong suit." He grinned then, and his white smile dizzied her as surely as if she'd been downing beer instead of serving it all night.

She looked back over her shoulder as more customers left, many of them calling out a goodnight to her. Then she raised an eyebrow, thinking of the tips she'd earned. "I don't know about that."

"Jim Duffy is a canny, old man." His voice emerged on a growl.

She shook her head. "He's kind."

Jim had given her a chance at this job, barely blinking an eye when she couldn't show him any ID.

He'd also been okay with the fact she'd be leaving when her internship started. "I'm always good with less paperwork," Jim'd said with a shrug. Gary was his grandson, and Jim hired him while Gary figured out whether he wanted to go to college, into the service, go out for a union trade, or *wouldja believe* as Jim put it, try his hand at becoming a writer. Jim was good people.

"When do you get off?"

"I…um…" Every fantasy of getting off with him rolled across her mind's eye like a dirty video. Her voice stuttered to a halt. She couldn't stop looking at him, and he appeared to be having the same problem. As she watched, faint flags of color darkened his cheekbones.

He cleared his throat. "What I meant was…" He closed his heavy-lidded eyes for a moment and shook his head before lifting his gaze back to hers.

"I know." She lifted her shoulder and looked down at her sneakers so he wouldn't see her secret grin. Weird. She enjoyed his discomfort almost as much as she hated to see him embarrassed. It had to be because she might've been looking into her own expression. Her cheeks were burning, and her eyes must be glittering like his because the same painful lust hit her square in the chest every time he looked at her.

"I leave at two or sometimes earlier like tonight. The bar closes at four on weekends." *Stop babbling, Honey.* He was a regular here so he knew this.

"Anyway, thanks again for your, er, help, the other night." *Brilliant, Honey.* Now both of them were picturing the other wrapped in towels and nothing else at the Pierre. And she knew how that little scene ended. Or some of the ways at least. She'd fallen asleep fantasizing all the scenarios her avid imagination could conjure every night this week.

He shrugged off the thanks, then pierced her with a laser stare. "Where are you staying?" His question shot out fast.

He was nosy and obnoxious, but he'd seen through her BS the other night at The Pierre, and she wouldn't forget. At least she didn't have to lie this time.

"At my friend's place. They're away visiting for Thanksgiving."

He raised a brow but said nothing, settled back on the barstool. She refocused to cash out. Gary hoisted chairs on top of the tables and mopped up the floor some more. After he carried the mop and bucket to the closet, she locked the safe. Everything on her mental list was checked. The old place was as orderly as it was going to get...time to lock up.

"Time to go." She cast a raised brow to the clock on the wall. Gary, maybe five feet seven in his Sunday shoes, stood stiffly at her side.

"Agreed." Jake nodded over to Gary. "Good night, son. I'll see Ms. Hill home safe."

Gary looked over at Honey, his Adam's apple bobbing with indecision.

"Gary and I are going to share a cab, Jake."

A cab halved the cost of both of their rides home, and she didn't have to find a gas station—who knew there were virtually none in Manhattan?—or look for parking at either end of her workday. It dawned on Honey fast that her car was more of a burden than an advantage in New York City. But even though she stood to make some cash on the resale, having a car was probably a necessity again once she started her internship on Long Island. It all depended on where she ended up living. Not to mention, Fred, her Ford, had been her bed for a few nights already. No, she was keeping the trusty old vehicle for the time being.

"I'll do that tonight."

Her body clenched in rejection of Jake's authoritative statement. He wasn't even asking—he was telling, and Honey wasn't having it.

"Hey, Gary, hang out a second, 'kay?"

She took several steps beyond Gary's earshot, turned, and put herself squarely in Jake's space. Tilting her chin, she shot him the look. "Take your overbearing macho and go home."

He lifted a derisive brow, not giving her an inch. "You leave work at one a.m. with a skinny teenager as your escort? Really?"

"Yes, I do. Jim usually comes in tonight, but it's his and Jeannie's anniversary, and they went to a play. It was the only night he could get tickets. I told him Gary and I would be okay. And we are."

Honey crossed her arms over her chest, as always on the defensive regarding her lack of height, her supposed feminine weakness, and all the other bogus nonsense uttered about women, especially women her size. Hadn't she just served a crowd, cleaned up, and counted money practically on her own?

"Besides what's it to you? Who died and made you king?"

His face tightened—not with annoyance but something approaching pain. In a moment, his expression morphed into statue-like hardness. She shook off the hand he put to her elbow.

"Where are you staying?"

She gave him the address.

"Off Avenue C? This gets better and better."

She rolled her eyes. "It's a studio and it's fine. I'm beyond happy I can stay there."

He punched the address into his cell, and a car service pulled up in moments. Gary and Honey got in. Before the driver could roll away, he put a business card in her hand.

Gary piped up. "Thanks Mr. Ricco. We appreciate the ride."

"Yes, *Mr*. Ricco," Honey chimed in with a syrupy we're-just-kids voice.

"Can you"—the next word came out through gritted teeth—"please text me when you're inside the apartment?"

Honey raised an eyebrow, shrugged. "Okay. Sure. How do I get along without you?"

Chapter 5
Truth or Dare

"I don't want to think about that," he muttered, watching the vehicle drive off.

In five minutes, he was back to his townhouse. That was only one of the many beauties of Duffy's, one of the first places he'd found when he left the service to come back to New York and his dad. It was an old school, unpretentious bar where he could unwind after a long day building up his security business and working on the renovation of the townhouse his father bought, his dad's last project. Duffy's was rough comfort, easing the exhaustion of witnessing his dad's painful decline, a place where he tried to forget the cancer claiming his dad by inches. Sometime during those months, he introduced his buddies Vlad and Connor to the place.

During the renovation, he worked alongside his dad, doing everything imaginable from demolition to sheet rocking to laying oak floors, installing marble countertop, and finally putting down sod and planting a fig tree in their prized backyard space. It turned out to be the last project his dad started, and Dante had almost seen it to completion. Near enough that they'd spent those last weeks together in the house with the hospice nurse in the background.

His decision not to volunteer for his last tour was

well worth it in retrospect. Even if he'd exhausted himself seven days a week to ease the hole in his life of missing his teammates and the raw grief of watching his father fade before his eyes. The townhouse was a showpiece now, and he took immense pride in every brick, cornice, and fitting. At four floors and with a basement, backyard, and a roof deck, it was a six-thousand-square-foot island of perfect solitude.

When the solitude started to get to him, he couldn't recall, but it didn't matter. With his inevitable move to Italy, he'd sell it or lease it soon enough. It was a cavernous space, when all he needed was an office and a bedroom. His assistant was a family woman who often worked remotely. He wouldn't need this New York space in the future, for the life he'd promised his mother. For that, he'd find an apartment in Rome.

He checked his watch again. Honey still hadn't texted, but crosstown traffic was brutal at any hour in Manhattan. Besides, post-Thanksgiving qualified as the holiday season, and good luck getting anywhere fast.

Jake leaned into the fridge, grabbed a beer, then shoved it back in again. He paced over to the floor-to-ceiling windows, stared unseeing out into his backyard oasis.

When her text came through—*home safe* with a smiley face—he closed his eyes on a long exhale. His life was all about security, and there were multiple things wrong with her situation. He ticked off the list in his head. She was a petite person working alone tonight in a New York City bar with only a gangly teen for assistance. It didn't help that Gary lacked any kind of protective skills and gazed at Honey like a lowly vassal ready to do the bidding of his princess. The rest of the patrons at Duffy's stayed belly up to the bar, like him, their eyes more on Honey and her belly jewelry than on the game. Could be Jim figured he'd found himself a goldmine with someone like Honey tending bar at his place…and Jim would be right.

When it came to doing his job or protecting people he cared about, Jake went over the top. He worried. He planned. That tendency had always been part of his orderly personality, but it was one hundred percent ingrained after that day long ago swimming with Francesco. Now fear gripped him hard whenever he took on a new responsibility. The fear was never conquered, but he could neutralize the fear with a Plan A and B. But Honey wasn't part of a job, she wasn't his responsibility, and he had no claim on her. No wonder she pushed back…and damn, when was the last time he'd pressured a woman about anything? He'd never had to.

What was it about her? She didn't want to be looked after, which bothered him. She didn't overshare. There was no blow by blow of her issues, her day, her troubles. She was always trying to get away from him in fact. Which only made him wonder.

Did she get the job she interviewed for? Maybe not, if she was working at Duffy's.

Where she was living was a whole other story. Her current neighborhood was trouble to the unwary, especially millennials trying to save a buck. That went double for females new to the city. Did her friend's place even have a secure lock on the door?

He forced himself to face facts, not to blind himself to reality, whether the reality was safety precautions in the city or the certainty he'd soon give up the life he'd built here, for a promise extracted so long ago it seemed he'd always existed under the weight of it. His pride might want to reject the truth, but he'd promised. Soon his mother would pimp him out, and he'd marry the woman she'd handpicked as his bride. He'd join his generations' deep but meaningless, to him anyway, royal pedigree to a stranger who would parlay it into financial stability and high-society stature for his mother.

Long after Francesco, and even now with his father gone, his mamma wouldn't let go of her goal, and he was bound by his promise. And he allowed it because—guilt.

So much time had passed, and yet nothing had changed. Their relationship consisted of nothing more than his guilt and her blame unrelieved by any tender feelings. She was unashamedly forthright about her ambitions and intentions for him. The last time they'd spoken, she didn't bother to sugarcoat her plans, nor did she care enough to pretend.

All he was to her now, maybe all he ever had been to her, was a means to an end, a stand-in for a person and a life, both long gone, she was determined to recapture.

"You promised me, Giancarlo. There *is* only you now. Francesco, my beautiful golden one, is gone." The tears were never far from her voice when she spoke of his brother. Long ago, the pain of those tears had cut him. In the past, her tears had been answered by his own guilty tears. Now he was more likely to reach for a drink to squash the heavy weight of the loss he alone was responsible for.

"And the less said about Dante the better. What a

mistake that alliance was. Go sew some of those oats, get it all out of your system in America. But remember, you owe me. *You promised.* There are several suitable candidates whose parents will consider a match. And you are handsome; I'll give you that. Just like your father."

If that didn't make him feel like a piece of meat, nothing would.

The way his dad told it to him, in the beginning, Mamma had been an integral part of the success and expansion of Riccobono Construction, running the books and putting her CPA to good use.

But Dante's charm faded rapidly when business reversals left the handsome Italian-American with only a tenuous foothold in the *nouveau riche* society his Italian born wife coveted.

After Francesco, there was no going back. No expectation on anyone's part they would ever be a family here again. Well maybe he harbored some hope, the way only a twelve-year-old could. In those early days, he used to close his eyes and wish. Wish himself back to the day before it all happened. If he could do it all over, he'd be strong, strong enough to save Cesco. Or maybe convincing enough to change his older brother's mind about the idea of swimming out so far in the first place.

But even when he tried to capture a memory from before Cesco was gone—there was nothing of softness or any special affection for him from his mother. No exclamations of *figlio mio* or *il mio dorato*, my golden one, from her. Those words were never for him, and those words died with Francesco.

After Cesco was gone, Franca completely

withdrew from her husband and Jake. She ignored her husband and her remaining son, returning to Rome full time to focus her prodigious energy into social climbing. Over time, on the other side of the ocean, his father clawed his way back up from the economic downturn. But Mamma had moved on. She did her best to rejoin the old-money, used-to-be-royals class of her youth without her New-York-bred spouse. They spent increasing amounts of time separated by the width of the Atlantic as his dad put his all into the construction business, and she spent her time as well as the remaining funds of her meager inheritance in Rome.

After the first wave of their collective grief subsided, his parents were divorced in all but name. Jake begged to move into his father's place in New York, but Franca would have none of it. She hadn't kept him with her either. The autumn after Francesco died, she sent twelve-year-old Jake to boarding school in Connecticut. His father scraped together the tuition, and Jake spent every break with his father. But on Christmas Day, like clockwork, he went back to Rome and his mother.

He hated Christmas.

He'd spent years channeling his grief first into the navy to become a SEAL and now his security business. Why was he rehashing this now? These kinds of thoughts only churned up emotions he'd buried along with his brother and completely cemented out of his psyche when his father passed.

It was Honey. She ignited something in him, something beyond the basic carnal spark he recognized in her eyes that was reflected in his own. But his first impression of her was on the money. She was trouble;

she would mess with his promise if he let her. He avoided any female who couldn't be slotted into a category called sexual release. He had no room for anything else in his life.

But still he couldn't stay away. It didn't help Jim Duffy told him the days Honey worked. Once he had that intel, he couldn't *unknow* it. So there he was in his usual spot at the bar on Wednesday.

Honey was down at the front of the house, charming the mix of white- and blue-collar, after-work crowd that found their way into the Greenwich Village bar. Her relaxed way, her habit of tilting her head to the side as she listened, made them all feel like the most important person in the room to her. Except for him. When she saw he'd slipped into his usual stool at the end of the bar, she stiffened. Then her lips curved up in a phony smile, her eyes sparking annoyance as she concentrated on the crowd closer to the front while Jim handled everyone clustered down toward Jake.

"So you've taken a personal interest in the new bartender." It wasn't even a question. Always blunt and to the point was Jim. No wonder Honey liked him.

"I…" Jake's gaze flew from where it was pinned on Honey over to Jim, and he lifted his shoulders in a "what-are-you-talking-about" way. Jim knew him better than most. He knew he lived nearby in the townhouse his father was renovating at his death. The property his dad gave to him in his will as a final insult to his mother. That if he was in town, he found his way into Duffy's like clockwork on game days, especially during football season, usually with Connor and Vlad.

But Jim didn't know Jake used to have a brother.

Or that his brother Francesco was dead because

Jake let him die.

Whatever Honey had or hadn't told Jim about her circumstances, it wasn't his place to speak for her. Besides he didn't know much either. That's why he was here. To make sure she was okay. Something about her brought out his need to protect.

"Nah, nothing like that." He ran a palm over his heated face like a teenager denying his first crush. He searched his beer for inspiration, but the foam was as opaque as his thinking. "She's…" A vise squeezed his heart when he looked over to where Honey was laughing and pouring drinks like she'd been doing it for years instead of days.

"I know. Cute as a button in spite of that crazy purple stuff in her hair. So don't get any ideas, Romeo." Jim wagged a thick, work-roughened forefinger in Jake's face. "She's what the missus calls a keeper."

Whoa now. Jake extended both hands, grinned through an exaggerated shrug. "What me? You know me better than that, Jim." One thing Jim did know was Jake's staying power with a woman could be counted in days or occasionally weeks but never anything approaching keeper status.

Jake's ready smile gave nothing away. "Really, no worries." He was *not* looking for a keeper.

"Hummh." Jim grunted as he moved to wait on someone else. It was busy for a Wednesday night, and young Gary was down with the flu.

That little exchange unnerved him enough to make him throw a few bills on the bar and head home.

In his office on the first floor of the brownstone, he organized next week's appointments on his virtual calendar. Then he printed contracts and specs sent over by his assistant and placed them in folders. It was bogus non-work—nothing that couldn't be handled tomorrow. He was marking time till Duffy's closed.

****

She looped her recent sidewalk find, a silver-tone, cross-body purse, across her chest as she tugged the old door shut behind her. Jake stood at the curb across from the door, his serious demeanor erased by a smile as his gaze met hers.

She went on the offense. "What are you doing here? I thought I saw you leave at ten."

Would she ever have a moment with this guy when she wasn't sweaty and looking her absolute worst? And why did she have to admit first thing she'd noticed he left?

"Aw, you missed me." His teasing grin flashed bright under the glow of the lamppost.

She sucked in a determined breath and relaxed her shoulders. "Bored without me, were you?" She pursed her lips on the tease.

Jake paced toward her, two deliberate strides until he was a foot away and she could see the heat igniting his eyes to blast furnace coal. She swallowed hard, returning his look without speaking. Because words weren't needed. A message was passing between them, and they were both on the same page.

Did he read the interest on her face? No, interest was for job interviews and bank statements. What was surging through her was sexual awareness, and it was the polar opposite of polite. Her face burned, but somehow her hands were ice. Someone had a boombox blaring Christmas carols, and the usual late-night street people were crisscrossing around them. Ubers and taxis fought their way along the narrow downtown streets in a beeping, honking road race, but nothing took her focus off him.

Oh, yeah. This guy.

This guy looked like he just stepped off a pedestal labeled *Roman god*. Anyone would wonder how it would feel to take him home for a night. *Anyone.* Close fitting, worn jeans and a leather jacket looked just as good as a damn tuxedo on him. But not quite as good as when a white towel barely covered the essentials.

Stop it! Stop staring up at him like a fan girl, like those women in Duffy's do. Honey had actually seen one do a double take the other night when the woman spotted Jake in his usual corner seat at the bar.

Like she was watching a NatGeo show called *Cougar on the Prowl*, Honey followed the action out of the corner of her eye as the woman, a bountiful brunette with legs for days, had reapplied her lip-gloss, shook her hair back, and gone for it.

They spoke for a few minutes, the brunette's voice low and teasing as she edged, bit by bouncy-boobs bit, closer to Jake's seat. She tried and failed to sidle between his man-sprawled legs, but he still handed over his cell, and Honey would bet her paycheck Jake now had the brunette's number. When Honey glanced over, all casual, after she finished serving her waiting customers, the brunette was gone. Had they met up later? Honey had despised the sour taste of jealousy in the back of her throat.

And now she wondered, would she be featured in tonight's episode? The one called *Big Black Bear Toys with Dumb Bunny*?

She squeezed her eyes shut for a second because it

was the only way she could jumpstart her brain. When she opened them, he was still there, still running his gaze over her from head to toe, and it would be a lie to pretend it bothered her because she liked it way too much. Enough to wish she was dressed in something other than a T-shirt and sneakers.

"Why did you come back? Did you leave something behind?" She folded her arms across her chest.

He nodded. "I did. You."

That broke the spell. She narrowed her eyes and cocked an eyebrow. "*No*. I'm not a something, and I'm not your concern."

But she wasn't as annoyed by his caveman words as she should've been. She'd been irritated to see him leave Duffy's. The moment the heavy door swung shut behind him, a little of the sparkle had left her and her night. Now she had to get away from him before she did something crazy like tell him how she didn't want to get away from him.

She craned her neck to look down Washington Street for the navy-blue sedan on its way, but it was nowhere in sight.

"You still living over on Avenue C?"

Refusing to look at him, she issued a quick nod and peered down the street again. Lizzie would be back on Sunday. Time was ticking, and she still hadn't found another place to stay. But she'd used every off day going around to possible rentals. She loved Lizzie. Which meant she'd never lose her friend, her only friend, overstaying her welcome in Lizzie and Kurt's tiny studio.

She pursed her lips and raised her brows. She

pulled her loose jean jacket, an old one of Derek's or maybe Donnie's she'd found in the trunk of the Ford, tighter around her, saying pointedly, "Goodnight, Jake."

He held her gaze, folded his arms across his chest. "I'll wait till the car gets here."

"Whatever." She waved a hand and ignored the way his brow darkened at her offhand dismissal and peered up the street again. Then looked down and refreshed her screen. "It says the car'll be here in two minutes." *Would he just leave already?* "I've got this. Goodnight, Jake."

"How do I know you're not going off to sleep in your car?"

"Because I told you so." Why was he so persistent? Didn't he know he was like chocolate to her? The most decadent Italian dark chocolate—sweet, salty, and super intense. The kind she could gorge on given the chance.

"Why do you want to get rid of me?" He leaned in as he said it, and she wanted to go there so badly. She couldn't stop eying his lips and licking her own, thinking of him and chocolate. But she wouldn't. How could she forget what a jerk, what a humiliated fool she'd been about Rick only one month ago? Rick, the guy she'd known *or thought she'd known* for years? She was clueless about guys, what made them tick, or how to turn them on or off. And Jake was one sophisticated piece of machinery. She'd need both an owner's manual and an advanced degree if she ever wanted to figure him out. But she didn't.

"Why *shouldn't* I want to get rid of you? C'mon, now. Go home and feed that line to your girlfriend." She flicked her hand in a shooing motion.

"There's no girlfriend at home, Honey, but thanks

for asking." His wicked smile dipped into serious for a moment. "I don't play like that."

"Is that so? Well, I'm not a game. I don't wanna be played at all. I'm not good at it. I'm straightforward. I don't know how to be any other way. So don't confuse the point, don't confuse me."

His words were gravel rough. "You want me to come out and say it? So there's no…confusion?" He moved fast till they were toe to toe.

"Yeah, go ahead. Say it." She braced her hands on her hips as she tipped her head back to maintain eye contact.

"I don't know why or what this is, but you're driving me crazy. I want you."

His gaze sizzled straight into hers as he said it, daring her to deny the current that pulsed between them anytime they were together. His boldness took her breath, and as the words settled in her mind, she let the possibility of what could be overtake her before she said what she had to. Before she shook him off.

She tilted her head to the side, regret tingeing her voice. "You know what the Stones say—you can't always get what you want."

With perfect timing, her ride pulled up to the curb, and she opened the passenger door, but as she slid in, Jake's hand came over the top of the doorframe, and damn, she had to look up at him again. He bent his head to her ear, and the low rumble of his voice was like a jolt of electricity to her core. "If it's what we both want, where's the problem?"

Her rock-n-roll logic had no answer for that one.

****

She walked her feet off the next day viewing

potential rentals till they all melted together in her mind, under a heading called hella expensive closets. Queens County was her ideal for proximity to her internship on Long Island, but she'd need her car, or she'd need to garage it and take the railroad. All of which would cost her. The places she found near transportation were too expensive. She was wavering on a cheapish one, a share with three roommates several blocks from the E train.

When she'd exhausted every possibility on the day's list, she took the subway to the precinct in Brooklyn to file a complaint against Trey. The duty officer eyed her with cynical pity as she told the tale of Trey and her stolen belongings. Once more it was crystal clear where her temper and impulse always landed her. She told the officer neither the super nor the leasing agent would confirm whether Trey still lived in the apartment she'd occupied for less than two days. With skepticism about the likelihood of success running through every syllable, he wrote it all down and said they would see what they could do. Then he handed her a slip of paper with the address of landlord tenant court scrawled on it. Welcome to New York.

Jake's words and the heat in his eyes came back to taunt her at random moments of her long apartment slog. But she wouldn't kick herself for turning him down. *That's the one smart thing you've done since you arrived in the city, Honey.*

There was nothing good to be gained hooking up with the hottest guy she'd ever set eyes on.

Was there?

Willow would tell her to go for it. In fact, her mom's casual attitude about everything except work and career was one of the reasons Honey always took her goals of a home and husband so seriously. The roll-with-it attitude about relationships so intrinsic to Willow completely skipped over Honey. Besides her name, the only thing Willow bequeathed Honey was her hair color and her love of classic rock. In all other ways, they might as well be strangers. No. She'd made the right decision. The last thing she needed now was more complications of the male variety.

Friday came, and she still hadn't found a place of her own. Honey offered Lizzie money toward staying on a while longer at her studio, which she and Kurt accepted. She made every effort not to be there when they were. But now they were back from their family visit, she slept cramped on a futon behind a screen.

"It's okay, Honey. It's a bitch finding a place in the city," Lizzie said, ever the stalwart friend.

Kurt's half-smile was stiff. "You should ask around at your job," he said.

****

"You look like you didn't get your full cuppa caffeine today, Honey."

Honey's grin was forced. "No time. I'm still on the hunt for an apartment. I spent the weekend and most of today at it."

Jim nodded over to the carafe on the burner in the corner of the bar. "Help yourself."

Honey only gulped down half the coffee in the chipped black mug before the regulars started streaming in for the game.

"And, Honey." Jim came to her side to speak quietly. "I meant what I said the other day. You can come stay with us in Sunnyside. The place is big

72

enough; you'll have your own bed."

"Thanks, Jim. I appreciate it. But it's only a matter of time. I'm sure I'll find something soon."

No way would she take Jim up on his generosity and upset his household. He and his wife Jeannie had kids and grandkids coming and going at all times even though they were ostensibly empty nesters. If she could swing it, she'd live on her own.

She sensed rather than saw when Jake came in. Her back was to him as she grabbed for a bottle in the lower fridge when that ripple of awareness hit. Her ears were hyper alert to his low-timbered voice.

"Buddies ditched you again, Jake?" She pictured the teasing grin on Jim's full face.

"Yep. Vlad cancelled, and Connor's suddenly spending all his time out east."

The rest of what they were saying was lost in the steady rise of voices after kickoff.

It was a rout for the Giants. Money changed hands. Celebratory beers were downed. Jim started to clear the bar area, and Honey stayed well away from it wiping up the tables.

"Honey, you're out on your feet. Gary and I can finish up here if you want to get out a little early. And remember what I said, okay? The more the merrier."

"Thanks. Thanks for both. I will head out now. See you Wednesday."

Honey grabbed her backpack from the hook under the bar and headed to the door. Jake had his cell to his ear and his back to her as she slipped out. Another night seeing, breathing, and feeling Jake was in the books. She had this. Temptation presented. Temptation denied.

It was a little after midnight. She'd save a couple of

dollars if she walked part of the way. There was no direct subway route from Duffy's in the village to Lizzie and Kurt's place on the lower east side, but if she walked up to the Fourteenth Street L train, she'd save the cab fare.

She stepped outside, winding her fuzzy scarf, another corner peddler find, around her throat as she strode to the corner. She was searching her purse for her transit card when a hand gripped her elbow from behind and yanked her to a stop.

"There's my girl looking pretty as a picture."

Honey swung round to see her ex smiling for all the world as if they hadn't broken up in an epic way over Halloween weekend.

"*Your* girl? What the hell? What are you doing here, Rick?" She shook off his hand.

"Did I scare you?" His gaze slid over her, and Honey cast her own cursory look his way, noticing how much closer he was to her diminutive height than say, Jake was.

"I'm not scared. Surprised is all. Really, what're you doing here? And how did you find out where I work?" Honey stepped back, cocked a fist on one hip, and narrowed suspicious eyes.

"So many questions. I was in the city, so I thought I'd look you up. Your brothers told me where you work."

It was a mistake not to tell Derek and Donnie she and Rick had broken up. But she'd been in no hurry to lose her cred as their all-knowing big sister, and man, miraculously it seemed they hadn't heard the gossip. Or maybe they'd just pretended not to. Now she wondered if they knew but chose to spare her the pain of recounting the events of that humiliating day. Or maybe they figured telling Rick where she worked would help, in a misguided attempt to foster a reconciliation. They knew in the way siblings did, though she'd never said it plain, she'd planned a future with Rick.

She'd call tomorrow and tell them because there was no way she wanted them to keep Rick informed of her day-to-day life in the city. Funny, there'd been absolutely no doubt in Honey's mind she'd never see Rick again. He hated the city. So what was he doing here?

Rick grimaced at the peeling green paint on the brick face behind him. "Don't know why you had to run all the way to the city just to be a barmaid."

Honey pressed her lips together hard at the dig. She would *not* be drawn in to losing her temper. "You always said you hated the city. What're you really doing here? Is Cheryl out of town?"

His careless shrug was all the answer she needed, but he yammered on. "Yeah, Mom left on a cruise this past Saturday. Election celebration. And I don't hate the city." He looked around, smirked. "Not if you're here."

Regret washed over her at her stupidity, at the recollection of all those wasted moments—who was she kidding, years—when she might have been anywhere else, with anyone else but had chosen to be with him. Well, starting right now, never again.

"Listen, once I was dumb enough to think we were friends—and more. But now I know you were using me."

Honey took a breath because damn, it still hurt. But the reason it hurt had changed. It hurt knowing she'd been that unaware, so dumb. She firmed her chin.

"How do you have the nerve to show up here? I don't have to tell you a thing. Go on back to your *intended fiancée*. We're over." She couldn't help sneering. "I noticed Darlene didn't have a ring? Daddy didn't pick it out yet? Or are you screwing around on her too?"

"Honey, I…" He gripped her elbow again, and just as quickly Honey shook him off.

"*Let go*. My life is here now. Did you think you'd pick up with me like nothing happened after announcing your intended engagement to someone else in front of everyone in Caryville? Forget it, Rick. I've already forgotten you." Her lips twisted, and she couldn't resist saying it. "Tell your mom I'm having a blast as a barmaid in the city. I'll be sure to get Darlene's number and let her know you couldn't wait to chase me down here." She turned back toward the corner. She'd take the first cab she could now.

"No, c'mon, wait!" He grabbed her arm again and gave it another yank.

"Get lost Rick, no kidding, *leave* me alone!"

"What's going on here, Honey? This guy bothering you?"

Jake's menacing growl came from just outside Duffy's scarred wooden door. Then he was right there, breathing heavy, his furious gaze fixed on Rick's hand. The younger man loosened his grip on her upper arm and dropped his hand.

"I'm her boyfriend, Rick." Rick thrust his chin out at an aggressive angle even as he took a small step back.

Honey exploded. "Are you for real? Ex-boyfriend. Cheating ex-boyfriend."

"All I want is to talk to her." His voice was accusing as he looked back at Honey. "You've blocked my calls…"

"If she wanted to talk to you, she would. So she must've said everything she wants to say. That's why you're an ex, Dick." A glimmer of a smile fell over Jake's hardened features.

"We had a misunderstanding. I'm here to talk to her."

Honey rolled her eyes at Rick's words. Had his voice always been this whiny?

"By showing up at this hour and scaring her when she just got out of work? That's bordering on stalker behavior, buddy. Don't put yourself into a situation. I want you to get lost now, Dick."

"It's Rick."

Honey felt her lips curve into a slight smile. *Oh, Jake.*

Jake folded his arms across his chest. "Right. You need to leave now."

"Listen, both of you." Her voice was steel, and her hands came out, palms forward to ward them both off. "Do *not* talk around me like I'm not here."

"But, Honey," Rick broke in. "This is all a mistake."

"But, Honey, nothing. You have a nerve. Seems everyone understood what was going on except me. *You* cheated on *me,* Rick. You humiliated me in front of our whole town. There's nothing mistaken about you and your intended fiancée, is there?" She jerked her chin toward the street. "Go away. I've moved on. And I never want—"

"So that's it? What, now you work in a bar? A

weird-ass, certified genius with a full scholarship to college and now this?" He looked down his nose at the street they were on, the uneven curb, grubby sidewalk, and dim doorways that were almost second nature to Honey already.

"You've moved on?" His peevish voice stung her with its contempt. "With *this* guy?" He looked from one to the other of them and slowly nodded his head. "I knew it. Mother was right. She told me you'd never be satisfied with one guy. How could you be anything else with a family like yours? And who is this old dude? Your father? Oh, yeah." He snickered. "I forgot. You don't have a clue who your father is, do you?"

Jake snarled and seized Rick by the scruff of his neck. Rick struggled to pull away from Jake while Honey pushed her way into Rick's face.

"Cheryl was right about one thing, Rick. I'll never be satisfied by one guy, if the guy's you. Get lost before I call Darlene and tell her *everything* about how lame you are."

Honey tugged at Jake's other hand, the one that wasn't attached to Rick's neck. It was amazing to realize she didn't give a horny ho what Rick did as long as he went away.

"Let go of me," Rick yelped, "before I call the cops."

"Go ahead, Dick," Jake drawled. "I know every single cop in this precinct."

Honey yanked again at Jake's other hand. "Let's go, Jake."

Jake did a shove release of his hold on Rick's collar, and he stumbled noisily back against a garbage can.

Then he looked over at her and lifted one black brow. "Where to, pixie?"

Honey lifted her chin. "Let's go home."

Chapter 6
Never Say Never

When they were around the corner, Honey dropped Jake's hand. The in-Rick's-face possessive grip that gave him the final "get the hell out of here" message wasn't necessary anymore. But when Jake reached down and threaded his fingers through hers again, she had to set the record straight.

She stopped in the middle of Jane Street, put both hands in the crooks of his elbows, and faced him. "Thanks for…" She shook her head, embarrassed at all he'd heard, all the no doubt accurate surmises he made about Rick and the current melodrama in her life. "Just thanks."

Jake's lips twisted. "No need to thank me. Sooner or later even Dick was gonna figure out just how much of a dick he really is and come chasing after you."

"It's Rick." She grinned, suddenly relaxed, and a laugh sputtered out with him where a minute ago she was ready to spit nails.

"A dick by any other name." His heated gaze stroked her face like a warm, velvet glove, and the slow, easy curve of his lips was intoxicating. His smile was so perfect he could win Olympic Gold with it. Her heart shoved its way into her throat, snatching her oxygen, and she was lightheaded.

She finally found a tiny bit of sanity and cleared

her throat. "I'll head home now."

"Where's home? Did you find a new place yet?"

She shook her head. As usual, impulse overruled common sense, and she spilled her guts.

"I'm staying at Lizzie and Kurt's. They're okay with me being there a little while longer." She crossed the fingers behind her back, recalling the caustic look in Kurt's eyes as Lizzie told her it was okay to stay on.

"Kurt?" Jake spat out the name, and his perfect smile vanished like the sun behind a storm cloud.

"Lizzie's boyfriend. That's why the studio's so crowded because it's the three of us."

"The three of you," Jake repeated, nodding to himself. "I have a proposition for you."

"Oh, yeah?" She raised her brow at the turn of phrase, but Jake's only reaction was to level serious eyes on her.

"Yeah," he said, daring her not to give him her full attention. "My place is a block from here. A townhouse. It's four floors, and when I'm there, I only use two of them."

She started shaking her head because immediate rejection was the only sane response, but he kept talking.

"Both the third and the fourth floors are self-contained apartments. With their own hallways and their own keys, their own everything. I could rent one of them to you."

"No," she said, her voice firm, separating still more from him by stepping back another few inches. "First thing, I could never afford…"

"I'd charge you something fair for one month. By then you'd find your own place, but in the meantime, you'd have somewhere safe to live, your own space, and in walking distance to Duffy's."

"Second thing," Honey continued as if he hadn't spoken. "I wouldn't live with you."

"Are you hearing me? It's not living with me. They're each separate apartments. The work on the place, the renovation, is done. So I would've been looking for tenants right about now. I put a call in to my realtor the other day."

"I probably couldn't even afford one month anyway." *Was she really considering this?*

"You could. Then you'd have the time to find another place, and I'd have the chance to get a tenant on a lease."

"Oh, I would definitely want to sign a lease." She *was* considering it.

"Of course." They walked on for a few paces.

"I need to think some more about it."

"Why don't I show you the apartment now and maybe answer some of your questions?"

"Now?"

"It's right here." He nodded over to an elegant corner building, with repointed brick and a gleaming, black, wrought iron fence surrounding a front garden embraced by a lilac hedge.

Honey took the picture-perfect exterior in, waiting for the annoying, internal voice that always told her the right thing to do—even if she usually wanted to ignore it. Silence. Huh. She wasn't doing this, was she? It couldn't hurt to look? *Yes, it could.* Oh, yeah, there it was. The voice…telling her this place would spoil her forever, that nothing she'd ever find would match the beauty of this property, and that was just the bricks and mortar. Jake was an entirely different kind of perfection.

He unlocked the heavy outer door, and then they were crunched together inside a small vestibule with a new-looking but old-school feel, black-and-white tile floor while he dealt with the lock on the inner entry door. Jake settled his bomber jacket on a hook just inside the inner door and led the way down a long hall over gleaming oak floors past a staircase on the left. The hallway was lit by nineteenth century style lamps, which cast a golden glow over the plaster warming the walls into the color of thick, creamy, homemade butter.

Jake pushed open the final door leading into a kitchen taking up the entire back of the townhouse. It was a chef's fantasy tricked out with modern appliances set in and on lush, old-fashioned Carrara marble counters. Floor-to-ceiling, six-over-six windows were clear and pristine on either side of an enormous oil painting depicting a table adorned with a large ceramic bowl overflowing with lemons, figs, nuts, and berries.

Honey clasped her hands together and turned in a circle to take it all in—from the wrought iron chandelier hanging from the coffered ceiling to the delicately hued ceramic tile that graced the backsplash behind the stove. Riveted, she walked to the stove and put a forefinger to the ceramic.

"Handmade?" she asked, leaning in to examine it closer.

Jake nodded. "Yeah, it's Tuscan."

She continued to rub the tile with her forefinger. "This is just… Wow, look at that color; man, it's just as gorgeous as I imagined."

"Talk tile to me, baby." His black eyes sparked

with laughter.

Honey rolled her eyes, suppressing a smirk.

"Not just tile, it's artisan crafted and painted ceramic tile. You really are a walking, talking ad for basic male…"

"Oh, yeah? Seriously, you should hear your own voice."

"Really? What does it sound like?" She stared him down till the back of his neck flushed pink.

"Let's just say, there's not much any guy wouldn't do to be on the receiving end of that voice. And you use it on an inanimate piece of clay."

"Any guy?" She raised a brow, never letting her gaze stray from his.

Jake returned her intense look. "Right now, I couldn't stand it if any guy heard you talk about ceramic or anything else in that low, excited voice. If you're gonna be talking like that, I'm the guy who wants to hear it. Me. Just me."

He leaned in, and Honey froze. *Whoa.*

Was she ready for this? Jake was a man…unlike Rick who was only a few months older than her own twenty-five and proved he was as immature and selfish as they came. She was an adult—hell, she'd been an adult at fourteen. When Willow left, when she was fourteen, Honey reckoned she'd gotten a first-class ticket to the wacked-out world of grown-ups the very same day. But was she ready for the invitation she read in Jake's eyes? She wanted to be. Right now, she couldn't think of anything she wanted more.

"So basic," she heard herself say, and she kicked herself for sinking back into cowardly safety. "But yeah, I'm a ceramic artist, so I don't hear myself when I geek out. At least that's my degree and that's my excuse, so I'm going with it." She felt her lips soften. "Right now, the only person who appreciates my work is my mom. Talk about cliché, right?"

He shrugged, and his mouth and his voice flattened. "It's cliché because it's what everyone wants, right? A mother's admiration, her approval."

Oh, man—she'd said something very wrong. His teasing voice went tight, his eyes blanked, and his whole attitude went south.

"Hey." All instinct, her hand covered his arm, and she squeezed, her hand pale against the black hair covering his bronzed forearm. The sinew of his muscle twitched in reaction. "I, uh, didn't mean to…did you lose your mom recently?"

He shook his head. "I lost her a long time ago." He didn't exactly shrug off her hand, but he turned away, and it was the same thing. He rejected her sympathy. He didn't want to share anything about himself. *Fine.* She tucked her hand behind her back.

"Anyway—" He cleared his throat. "—glad you like the tile. When I say this is my place, I mean I chose or designed or installed everything here." Pride colored his deep voice.

Okay. Message received. He didn't want to talk about himself, just his home. If Honey wanted to know anything about Jake, she'd have to piece it together from her observation of his home. She did another slow three-sixty in the kitchen, the artist in her fascinated by the way every element, bold and subtle, flowed into the next to make up the warm whole. So different from the narrow, old Victorian she'd left, with its rotting wood and un-insulated windows. The house she'd lived in since she was nine. Nothing wrong with it really. *It wasn't the house, Honey. It was how you felt inside it.*

She'd been too young to have more than snapshot memories of any of the other places she lived, the many precarious stops along the way with a very young Willow that preceded Joss's home on the outskirts of Caryville. In the ever-changing landscape of her youth, Willow was the one constant…until she wasn't.

Sadder still to know she'd never felt welcome in Joss's home. Yes, he took care of them—if caring was paying the heating bill. And yeah, that *was* something. But personal warmth was never there—how could it be when she reminded him daily by her very existence of Willow? He wasn't fatherly or friendly or protective or at all interested in getting to know her as a person. He was in his world, and she created her own, eventually peopling it with Rick and imbuing Rick with the kinds of feelings and traits she wanted him to possess.

Already independent, she figured out how to care for herself and her brothers. She was the one to show interest in Derek and Donnie, to see the differences in them, and there were many in spite of their identical looks. Now at fifteen, Derek was the introverted one who favored the bass guitar while in-your-face Donnie was all about drums.

But to Joss, she was and would always be Willow's daughter and Willow's mistake. Donnie and Derek didn't fare much better, and they were his blood. So five years after they moved in, Joss and Willow parted ways. Except when Willow left, Honey stayed behind. She was in ninth grade then, the boys only five and in need of a mother or the next best thing—a sister. Joss, never warm and fuzzy even when Willow lived with them, withdrew, became more completely wrapped up in his academia.

Their relationship fell apart because Joss was jealous of Willow's life before him, her work friends, and her contacts in journalism. The introvert in him couldn't see Willow was only half a person without her career. Willow finally made it clear in the only way he could understand. After increasingly long forays into projects during those years that took her all over the state, along the east coast, and then the entire country and beyond, after one trip, Willow simply failed to come home.

These days she called every so often, so they knew she was okay. She showed up at odd times to visit for a couple of days when her schedule allowed. With nowhere else to go, Honey made herself useful caring for the boys as best she could after school. One of Honey's main tasks, as far as Joss was concerned, was to field Willow's calls to the house so Joss didn't have to speak to her. Honey saw the pain in his eyes when the phone rang, the hope and fear, the expectation, the dread. It highlighted the message, in the kind of in-your-face neon she saw driving through Times Square for the first time a few days ago. *Falling in love doesn't mean happily ever after.*

Willow and Joss never married, so there was no formal, legal parting of the ways. But it was no less painful than a drawn-out court proceeding. They were all sad, in a kind of mourning for the family they might have been. For Honey there was a realignment of priorities. She stepped up to the task of big sister and surrogate mom, loving her brothers, willing them all to thrive, and she held tight to her dream of becoming an artist.

Overriding everything, she cherished the goal to have with Rick the kind of family life she'd never had before. The kind where both parents lived in the same home, the kind where she'd have a career while also raising a family.

That was crazy talk. An inane pipedream. Had she really expected she'd fix every crack in her home life as easily as she mastered her studies? How could she have been dumb enough to let that childish plan inspire her throughout the remaining years of high school and all the way through college?

Even after college, the dream was still fixed in her head, and her head was in the sand or the clouds or wherever dumbass girls like her dreamed stupid dreams. She'd doubled down and dreamed some more, imagined she and Rick working side by side with their growing family and with the blessing of her brothers, Joss, and Rick's parents. But the death of her dream? That happened right in front of the assembled citizens of Caryville. Every single one of them had been witness to it.

She'd been so easy. Rick hadn't promised a thing. Honey supplied all of the ridiculous layers of their future life. When it all blew apart, her ever-ready temper took over, and for once she'd been thankful for it. Raw with anger was better than sobbing with humiliation.

"It's beautiful. I mean I don't know what it looked like before, but I…" She stopped, totally blank, no clue what she'd been about to say. Her complete attention riveted on Jake, his face, the faint shadow of whiskers on his jaw, the unconscious way his hand rasped over that same stubble.

"Look." He pulled his cell from his pocket. "You wouldn't believe what a mess it was. But you know what they say, good bones." He pulled up a photo on his phone. "Here, check this out."

Honey stepped closer, leaned in to look at the device cradled in the palm of his broad hand. He started swiping past the photos, and she hitched herself up onto the counter stool to get a better view.

"Look, this is where we found the old oak floors underneath the vinyl." His long finger traced a short path over the screen. "And here's where we uncovered the boarded-up fireplace." He flipped through some more photos, and Honey's hand came up to stop it.

"We? Who's that? Right there." She slid off her stool and tapped her finger over the figure of a tall, slightly stooped-back man with a thinning head of white hair.

"Oh, yeah. That's my dad. We did the project together; I mean, he was the brains behind it all. I was the brawn." His smile faded, and he swiped the screen closed. "He's dead."

"Oh, Jake, I'm so sorry. I didn't mean to…" She was a regular barrel of laughs tonight. The more she discovered about him, the more she wanted to know.

"Nah, it's okay. It's impossible to talk about this place without talking about him. We hashed out every detail. He let me make the final decisions, but yeah, that's why this place is…"

"So special to you. Yeah, I can see that, feel it. It's a really beautiful home." Honey lifted her gaze to his, and his black eyes warmed her. His hand tightened over hers, and a languorous shiver slid down her spine.

"Are you cold? Is that your only jacket?" He ran a disparaging eye over the worn denim.

The last thing Honey wanted to talk about was her lack of wardrobe and the impulse that led to losing all of her stuff.

She lifted her chin. "I'm not cold."

He settled his big hands gently on her shoulders and slowly pulled her toward him till she was between his legs as he sat on the counter stool. His hands edged down to move from shoulders to wrists and then back up again. Oh, man, he had the best hands. Even through the denim, she savored the warm strength of them. If he ever quit his day job, he'd make a fortune with those hands.

She swayed against him, boneless but anything but relaxed. Her lids were heavy, her breath stuttering, oxygen lost to the weight of her heart crowding her throat. The confident movements of his big hands soothed then incited, over and over. His long fingers and palms tantalized. Her skin burned hotter with each stroke, and her belly tightened with each shaky breath she pulled in and released.

When his hand cupped the back of her neck and warm fingers found the hammering pulse behind her ear, she jolted and swayed, then grasped his thighs to steady herself. Every thought coalesced into one.

Kiss me. Don't make me wait. Don't make me ask. Kiss me.

But he didn't. He only tucked her head under his chin, and now the scent of lemon and leather and him was right there as she sucked in another strangled breath.

Enough waiting.

She flicked out her tongue to taste the warm skin at the base of his neck for the barest second.

Chapter 7
Same Dance, Different Song

He jerked back in reaction, almost fell off the stool. Was that her tongue? Damn right it *was*, and the wet slide of its heat packed a punch that went straight to his gut. And if she had that effect on his neck, he didn't want to think about that hot tongue on any other part of his anatomy. Not unless they were going to do something about it. *Pull yourself together, Ricco.* He took a breath. Found his cool.

"So you're not asleep," he murmured into her hair. "Thought I'd bored you with all the details of this build."

She tipped back her head, and a slumberous smile lit her eyes. "It wasn't the build I was thinking about." Her voice was breathy and prim at the same time, her small hands planted like brands on his thighs.

"Oh, no?" He chuckled as he tugged her more firmly into the vee between his legs. His fingers continued the slow stroke of the skin at the back of her neck. She was all soft skin with tender bones, like one of the pair of pale gray turtledoves that came into the backyard every morning. He consciously gentled his hands.

Go easy. Till you know what she likes.

"So beautiful," he murmured, bending his head.

Her eyes widened as she saw his intent. Was that

anticipation? Did she want this as much as he did? She did. When had he ever been wrong about that kind of signal? Never. She'd just nuzzled his throat, and the tease of that soft tongue went straight to his groin.

But still, he prided himself on having some finesse. He wouldn't move on her like an out-of-control teenager even if every ounce of blood in his body was pulsing and pounding through him, urging him to do just that. He put his lips to the corner of her mouth, breathed in her scent, some combination of salty skin and caramel as he rubbed his cheek along hers.

Slow down. Slow the fuck down.

Breathing deep, going for restraint, he pressed his lips to the other corner of her mouth. But when she opened her mouth on a moan, he covered the sweet softness of her lips, hands cupped on either side of her jaw, keeping her mouth just where he wanted it. A shudder rolled through her, and he lifted his head, satisfied to see the rosy flush suffusing her skin. He gathered her closer to the heat of his chest.

"Still cold?" He ran a forefinger down her cheek to her chin. Like the skin of a peach—velvet. And fever hot. He couldn't stop touching. He trailed his hand slowly over the exposed skin of her neck then down her chest over the fabric of her T-shirt. Her heart was pounding just like his—straight out of his chest. He rested his palms against each breast in turn, carefully cupping them, feeling her nipples as they tightened and pressed hard against the soft cotton. Yes. She wanted this as much as he did. He lowered his head to take another taste.

But now she was pulling away, shaking her head.

"No, no, too much," she said, pushing him away.

His hands fell to his side. What? What was happening? What was going on?

She took a step and then another backward as she released herself from his arms. When she was a couple of feet away, when he couldn't reach out and hold her, she looked up at him. Her eyes still held the glitter of want, and damned if she didn't run her tongue over her lush, pink lips.

She kept shaking her head as seconds ticked, then finally she spoke.

"There's a reason I don't have a winter jacket, and it's the same reason I can't take you up on your offer of a place to stay." Her voice was so low he had to lean in to hear. "When I got to the city a couple of weeks ago, I rented an apartment. The plan was I would split rent with a roommate I found online. A guy I'd never met before." Her gaze shifted away; she looked over his shoulder.

His jaw clamped shut on a curse, his spine tensed, and the hair on the back of his neck stood at painful attention. Man, he didn't like where this was going.

"The same weekend I moved in, like I was there less than two days, my roommate came back to the apartment late—he was drunk. And he came on to me, you know—really strong. He wasn't taking no for an answer."

"Honey, tell me now what he did, because so help me I'll find him, and I will take him apart." He pushed to his feet, and his hands clenched into fists on his thighs.

"No, it's…I'm fine." She waved her hand in an it-all-came-out-okay way. "I mean it wasn't fine then, but he was drunk enough I could surprise him with a knee and an elbow—ya'know? He was butt hurt, but he got the message." She folded her arms across her chest and nodded, her pointed chin firming.

This was the Honey he knew.

"So he backed off. I went to the outer room, to where I had my bed set up. Because he paid a few more dollars rent, he got the actual bedroom."

Oh, yeah, what a guy...a real prince.

"Even though I told myself to stay awake, I must've fallen asleep for a time, because when I woke up the next morning, he was gone."

Jake pushed out a harsh breath and waited.

"Yep, he left, but then I realized he took all of my stuff with him while I slept. *Everything.* All I had left were the clothes I was wearing and a backpack of extra things I always keep in my car. That was the night I took the shift at the Pierre."

"You agreed to share rent with this asshole?" He raked his fingers through his hair, looking around the kitchen at the same time, trying to find something he could crush his fist into to relieve the need to crush the asshole's head instead.

"Yeah, that's what he is, and I did." She pushed the silver wisps of hair back behind her ears in the way he'd seen before, the way she did when she was thoughtful or distracted, her aggravation obvious. "So the question I ask myself is, what's the message in that scenario for me? And the answer is, what would be dumber than to be roommates with a guy I barely know again?"

Now he appreciated where she was going, and his vision went red. Literally for several seconds, he couldn't see anything but big bloody blotches bursting like bombs across his eyes.

"Are you actually comparing me to some drunk jerk who tried to attack you, then stole your stuff? Are you really going there?" He fisted his hands again, trying to get a grip on his temper. He tamped his voice down to an irritated growl before he continued.

"Remember that night at the Pierre? *You* snuck into my room, and when I got there, *you* were in a goddamn towel. I could barely keep my hands off you—but I did." Had he just told her that? It didn't matter. She knew. He'd never forget her eyes that night, a mixture of defiance, want, and need.

"And, pixie, you wanted me just as much. Just like a minute ago. Don't even try to deny it."

Defensive, she crossed her arms over her chest but threw her chin in the air anyway. "So what?"

"So as for my offer, we wouldn't be roommates. I'm the landlord, and you'd have your own key to your own separate apartment." He bit off the words, his fury a heaving beast inside of him. She was actually comparing him to that loser…

She stood silent, still considering, and dammit, that did him in.

"Are you kidding me right now, Honey? How smart *are* you? You can have a month's fair rent in a brand-new apartment in a building owned by a security expert. Or you can stay with a couple on a sketchy street in a cramped studio on a futon. If you can't see the difference between me and that dirtbag Dick and that asshole…?"

"Trey," she supplied.

"Then maybe you aren't as smart as you think you are. I swear you've got me so mad right now you're gonna have to beg me if you want me to lay another finger on you."

"Don't hold your breath, buddy. You're not the only one with a temper."

"So?"

"So what?"

They sounded like second graders on the playground. He spoke very slowly. "So are you taking the apartment?" Anger clawed a hole in his chest when she didn't respond, and he grabbed the keys off the hook near the door. "Here." He threw them down onto the center island. "You can show yourself up to the top floor. Or not."

Fury pounding hot blood in his ears, he strode to the fridge and yanked the door open. He grabbed a cold one, twisted off the cap, and chugged the whole thing in one long gulp, leaning into the blast of cold from the open fridge, because he couldn't look at her without wanting to protect her from those two miserable idiots Tweedle Dick and Tweedle Trey and rail at her for not knowing he was nothing like them. For not knowing who he was.

Beer finished, he pushed a couple of slow breaths in and out before he turned back around. She was gone. Good. And so were the keys. Better.

Still amped up, still angry, still, if he admitted it, the smallest bit *hurt,* he took the stairs two at a time to his second-floor suite. Changed into swim gear and headed back down to the gym he'd set up next to his office. He and his dad spared no expense on this part of the house either. He dove into the pool and powered into his laps.

****

They said people with genius IQs often lagged behind knowing how to function in real life, in the world. But that wasn't exactly true for Honey. If everyday life was the ordinary stuff she had to remember to take care of the house and look out for her brothers, she was covered. Her lack was very specific. It was the relationship stuff she sucked at. Particularly male relationships.

Jake flipped when she compared renting an apartment from him to the disaster with Trey. But only the broad outlines were the same. Jake was self-made, the head of his own security company, and as Jim Duffy told her, an ex-Navy SEAL.

Trey had no visible means of support. Hadn't he told her something about his parents fronting his portion of the rent? And—hello, he'd jumped her.

No genius at work here. She'd been hell bent on leaving Caryville, and she ignored every possible warning signal but the reasonable amount of money Trey was asking for rent.

So yeah, she stunk at figuring guys out, and she let temper and impulse rule her. After Rick, she should've known better with Trey, and damned if she could figure Jake out either.

But that was for the best. She was putting all the stuff she couldn't figure out about guys in a mental box labeled *Not Now*. Honey was officially in the *Me* zone. It was past time to concentrate on her career and banish men, or at least a permanent guy, from her life. All she needed was a reasonable rental in the city, and now she had it. Even if her landlord was the surliest, sexiest guy she'd ever met.

Taking the last few steps before opening the door

to what would be her home for the month, she texted Lizzie to give her the good news not to expect her back except maybe as a normal guest not the awkward, endless sleepover kind. The *woohoo, so happy for ya!* she got in response made her impulsive decision to accept Jake's offer worth it on that level alone. She'd mooched off Lizzie long enough.

And wow. Living here even for a month would be a slice of heaven. The space was well worth the dent it would put in her savings. She'd be living like a rockstar because the fourth-floor apartment, like everything else she'd seen of Jake's place so far, was an HGTV wet dream.

Resting against the bathroom doorjamb, she brushed her teeth. Yep, her luck had finally turned. This place, her very own space, the entire fourth floor of the brownstone, was amazing. The bathroom was stuffed with more luxury products than the Pierre and twice as cozy. There were tons of towels, and a combination of lighting—ambient for relaxing baths and overhead modern fixtures you could perform surgery under.

She ran a reverent hand over the coverlet on the king bed, the velvet and linen combination so simple it was decadent. Smoothing her fingers over the heavy iron base of the bedside lamp, she acknowledged this place had every feel the tactile artist in her craved.

It was everything a backroads bumpkin like her never thought she'd experience. Everything she never thought she wanted. What was it Joss always said? That she was lucky enough to have the things she needed? Yes, she counted herself lucky on that level—in Joss's house she was safe and physically secure. But she wanted and needed more, and it wasn't the house. The dilapidated Victorian they lived in had a ramshackle charm, but she'd never been welcome there. As Willow's daughter, she'd always be a reminder to Joss of their broken relationship, and her half-brothers were a permanent, ever-growing, always-hungry reminder of their parents' ill-fated affair.

What Honey wanted was a home—a place of welcome where she could welcome others. A place where she didn't feel like her mom's forgotten baggage.

And though she didn't *need* this place, she could appreciate it. Jake hit it out of the park with his townhouse, creating a modern living space while enhancing every old-world detail already in place— from the wood-burning fireplace and the nineteenth century plasterwork to the moldings surrounding the ten-foot ceilings.

For the first time since she arrived in the city, the creative pull overwhelmed her, and she sat to sketch, her mind overflowing with new designs for her stock in trade, ceramic Christmas ornaments. These would be a take on Dickensian but more modern in flavor. Later she'd create a prototype design and measure out the actual dimensions of the molds, but for now she heeded the inspiration seizing her, and she lost herself in the flow.

After she got the bare bones of her ideas down in black and white, she couldn't resist the lure of the decadent shower. When she stepped from the marble enclosure onto the thick cotton of the rug, she slipped on the new terry robe hanging from the hook in the bathroom. No way did she want to wear the sweaty clothes she'd worn all day. It was past time to buy something new to replace the clothing that wasn't so great to begin with and was surely gone forever. Wearing Duffy's tees twenty-four seven was getting old.

She belted the robe, and as she plugged in her phone, she formed a plan because she was wired that way. Her impulsive side flipped into organized chaos. Tomorrow she wasn't on the roster at Duffy's. Checking apartment listings and trekking around the city was over for the time being thanks to Jake. So first she'd get her backpack of stuff at Lizzie's, then check out the new ceramic tile exhibit at the Museum of the City of New York.

No. *No.* First, she'd find the nearest *Miranda's Moments* and replace the heinous undies she'd bought on the fly. That pack of plain panties she'd picked up in a hurry at the drugstore was a cross between granny panties and a toddler's drawers, and even though all she wore over them were jeans and tees, they *had* to go. Then she'd hit an H & M or maybe a Goodwill and score some recent vintage as her mom used to call it, maybe a skirt or a jacket, something that'd help her look like a practicing adult for her new internship role.

Her hand was on the bedside lamp switch when the hard knock sounded at the door.

Jake.

She walked to the door, her stomach muscles contracting tighter with each step, nervous anticipation jacking her heart rate. Just like she was on the last *tick, tick, tick* on the climb of a rollercoaster at the country fair, she forced herself to keep her eyes open even as she cursed her impulse to prove she could master her fear of the nauseous unpredictability of it. She tightened the belt on the robe, opened the door.

He narrowed his laser gaze on her, his black eyes glittering as they roved from the top of her towel-ruffled, damp hair to her bare feet.

She gripped the door, half thoughts forming, then sinking back into the pudding that replaced her brain.

Get rid of him, Honey, self-preservation ordered. *Push him out. Lock the door.*

Puh leeze, weakness argued. *That's the last thing you want to do. Just yank him in and finish what you'd barely begun downstairs.*

Jake's gym shorts hung low on muscular, hair-roughened thighs, and the faded navy tee stretched taut over his shoulders and chest. Right now she'd trade everything on her non-existent Christmas list for alone time with him.

That would be crazy, wouldn't it? No, crazy was expecting to get through weeks with Jake and come out unscathed. Could she live here for a month in close proximity to this guy without giving in to the *I know you want me, come and get it* vibe he was so good at putting out? Bigger question: did she *want* to?

His gaze honed in on her face, and his lower lip curved in a half smile that said he'd read her struggle, and his features were stamped with confident knowledge of the loss of equilibrium his presence caused.

Of course he knew his effect on her. Didn't Jim say, bushy gray eyebrows drawn fierce in fatherly concern under a furrowed brow, that Jake was over thirty years old and he rarely saw him with the same woman twice? Hadn't she smirked back and assured Jim she could take care of herself even though she'd seen Jake in action too, saw the way women drooled over him like he was the featured pastrami behind the deli counter and they all wanted a taste? Honey had her pride. No way did she want to take a number in their supermarket lineup.

That was before she agreed to this rental idea.

Because the put-together Jake-the-boss in a custom tux with the perfect hair had turned her on even as he was firing her. How would she survive for a month sharing his living space? She already knew his hair turned into shiny, ebony ringlets as soon as it was wet. And yeah, the bronzed skin covering his sculpted physique made him look like he spent all his time in the Mediterranean, lounging on a yacht, wearing only suntan oil and a smile.

She was only human.

She swallowed and lowered her gaze, focused instead on his hand, his square, tanned hand, currently holding an envelope. Why had she thought his big, capable hand boring? The strength in his work-roughened hand made it a work of art. Hadn't the disaster with Rick proved she knew *nothing* about men? Especially a man whose image would pop onscreen if you Googled *sexy as sin*.

"This is the lease. As we…discussed, a month-to-month tenancy."

She took the envelope, careful not to let their fingers touch because he might be talking business, but her body was teetering on a hair trigger with the anticipation, the expectation of his hand anywhere on her body.

"Not month to month." She quick-stepped farther back into the apartment. "One month. My internship starts late January."

He folded his corded arms across his chest, invading her space without crossing the threshold.

"You got the internship? Congratulations." The warmth of his smile enveloped her, and she craved it all the more knowing its rarity. But then stern Jake was back. "I wanted you to have the lease immediately—so there's no misunderstanding our *business* relationship."

He was harping on Trey, underlining the differences between Trey and himself, as if they weren't obvious. Jake was a responsible, accomplished man. Trey was an entitled boy.

She managed a shrug, coupled with a careless don't-bother-me-with-trivia smirk. *Say goodnight, Honey. Shut the door in his face. Do. It.*

Business relationship. *Hang onto that concept, Honey.* She smoothed out the envelope she was crushing in her hand, cleared her throat.

"I'll venmo you the rent, okay?" *Get...him...out. Now.*

He nodded, his hooded eyes inscrutable. "Sure. Sweet dreams, Honey."

Honey closed the door on his taunting smile, her palms sweaty as she sagged against it. He knew exactly what he was doing coming up to give her the lease, reminding her of her comparison of him to Trey and his promise not to lay a finger on her unless she asked for it. If the last few minutes weren't a recipe for a sleepless night, she didn't know what was.

****

Honey pried open gritty eyelids. It had to be dawn because the sun screamed through the luxurious drapes she'd so admired last night. Sex with Jake kept her tossing and turned on all night. In her dreams, that is.

Congratulations, Honey. One more impulsive decision and now she'd set herself up for a month of torment sharing space and keeping it all business with a walking, talking sex god.

But what if?

What if...she went for it? What was wrong with full-on stress relief? What if they gave in to the pull between them and just hooked up? Like Jake said, what was the problem if they both wanted the same thing? Simple and uncomplicated, a hookup with a time limit.

Why shouldn't I? she asked herself as she splashed cold water on her face. If Jake was half as good as his cocky attitude, Jim's warnings, and her erotic fantasies led her to believe, this could be the beginning of a few unforgettable weeks and the first steps toward her own sexual independence. Now that she'd acknowledged happily ever after wasn't going to happen for her, what was to stop her from a fling with an end date of her moving on to her new job in January?

The whole concept was scary exciting in a way that hollowed her legs and carved a pit in her belly. Or maybe it was that she hadn't eaten since yesterday afternoon and needed a dose of caffeine to knock some sense into her.

Certain he had something resembling breakfast or a power bar in his gourmet kitchen, she carefully closed the apartment door and started a stealthy tiptoe down the stairs. The house had a solid silence that soothed. Like the place had been there forever and would last through eternity. She pushed out a nervous breath and checked her phone. Six o'clock. Was Jake still asleep? Working out? Already out the door?

It didn't matter. All she had to do was grab a quick

something from the fridge to tide her over, before she got on with her day.

Ahhhh. She closed her eyes on a blissed-out sigh as she crept into the empty kitchen. Coffee was coming down, brewing on an automatic setting. She pulled in a long inhale, then examined the cupboards with purpose. The one over the coffee machine would have mugs for sure. She opened it ever so gently and...score. Getting on her tiptoes, she grabbed a mug and poured. Found sugar in a ceramic bowl, dropped in two cubes, and took one, long, sweet gulp. A door *thunked* closed on the floor above her, and she felt the quick, heavy tread of feet coming downstairs.

Jake.

It was too late to do anything but own it.

So she took down another mug and poured him a cup.

"Good morning." She ignored the startled look on his face and held the mug out to him with her best barista smile. "Cream and sugar?"

Chapter 8
Pint-Sized Perfection

He ran his palm over his face, scraping over the stubble he'd shave after his workout. Then he blinked his eyes open and shut, but yeah, she was still there. He was conscious that he was staring; his mouth might even be hanging open.

The terry robe swam on her, but somehow it worked for him—big time. She was Tinkerbell after a shower, or Tinkerbell right after she woke up or had sex. Oh, man, was he really equating Honey to a Disney character? The answer was yes, and he'd gone batshit crazy.

The clock on the wall said six oh five, and his morning wood was raging. And now there was no way to erase the triple X dreams he'd just awakened from, fantasies complete with details of every surface he could take her on in every room of this house, not when his fantasy was smiling like an angel and holding out a mug of coffee.

Oh, man. This was a mistake. *You're freakin' brilliant, Jake.* A tenant was one thing. He was ready to find one. It was the natural next item on his list, for the easy cash flow one would bring while he figured out when to put the townhouse on the market.

But a living, breathing temptation who slept upstairs, someone he'd come home to every day of the week? Someone who pissed him off so much he'd sworn he wouldn't touch her unless she made the first move?

Was she even twenty-one? Damn, he'd never seen her ID. When his buddy at the precinct ran her plate, why hadn't he gotten her personal info too? But how to ask that? *Hey, so there's this girl I have the hots for. Bro, is she legal?*

His gaze skidded over her pure profile, then he forced himself to look away. To look at anything but her unpainted lips and youthful cap of hair. *What the fuck, Jake?* He swallowed, racked his brain for what she'd said—and hadn't said—in their conversations going back to that first night's confrontation at Vlad's wedding. What was it? Yeah, right. She was filling in for a friend for the night. And she had an interview. Then last night she'd said she was an artist. *Keep your eyes off her and remember, Jake.*

"Black is good," he said, taking the mug she held out.

"I helped myself to the coffee." She shrugged, smiling, and he'd swear her silver hair took on a halo-like sheen around her head, and the effect of all of her angelic perfection hit him with a satanic jolt of lust.

Moving fast, he stepped back round the other side of the center island before she saw the hard evidence of her effect on him in his gym shorts.

"No problem. But, Honey?"

She raised her brows till they reached the bottom of the feathery fringe of pale hair on her brow.

He cleared his throat and took a sip of the coffee. It was scalding, but he gulped some more anyway.

She moved to the counter, slid up to perch on one

108

of the stools at the center island, and once she was situated, sitting there like a sweet apparition on the head of a pin, she pulled the sides of the robe up and over her lap.

Eyes to yourself, Jake. He refocused and found his voice.

"How old are you?" He barked out the question in his head-of-security voice. The one she'd scoffed at all those nights ago at the Pierre. "And bear in mind I can verify everything you say."

She laughed, and the low, sultry sound of it made him wish he was a stand-up comic or Santa Claus or her favorite sit-com because how good would it feel not to be rule-bound, list-making Jake but the guy who made Honey laugh on the reg? How good would it feel to shed his business persona, the ass-kicking, ballbuster he showed the world and just be his own damn self?

"I'm twenty-five."

He eased out a breath. Felt relief that he wasn't lusting after a teenager. But still raised a skeptical brow because she was so…little.

"Yeah, yeah, I know, I'm short, and I've no makeup on now, but"—she waved a dismissive hand—"I graduated college and stayed up around my hometown to work before I decided to come to the city." She spoke with the ease of someone long used to explaining why she looked like a teenager, and his gut told him it was all true.

"What made you decide to come to the city now? Your ex, the dick, wasn't happy about it, that's for sure."

"Yeah, well"—her lips firmed under a smile—"he's the ex, right? I stayed to help out with my two younger brothers. They're fifteen now though, but that kept me there too, and…" She looked away from him.

"Too?"

"What?"

"You said that kept you there *too*?"

"What is this, an interrogation?"

She was agitated, and that wasn't what he wanted. He just wanted to get to know her a little.

"I thought it was a conversation."

Her face flushed, and she raised her chin before answering.

"I…it's probably the first time I'm talking about… You're the first person who's…asked me about myself. And I've decided I don't want to. Talk about it, everything yet, right now."

He raised both brows. The first person to ever ask her about herself? He had questions, a lot of them, and a burning need to know every single thing about her. Damned if he knew why. He'd never wanted any background detail on the women he hooked up with. There was no point. Things between him and the women he was with never got beyond basic stats. The kind of conversation that started with what kind of drink she preferred and ended with what sexual position she favored. He always aimed to please for the short time he was with someone. But when the woman in question overshared her stuff, he had a hard time keeping up his interest, a tough time pretending that it meant anything more to him than quick and easy.

He promised his mamma his future, but he'd been determined to have a damn good time in the present. But time was running out. He was thirty-two, and that was almost twenty years more than Cesco got. Soon he'd do his duty and move forward without regrets.

In the intervening years, he'd created charming Jake, laughing Jake, Jake the prince of superficial relationships. Why was Honey different? She had layers, and the more she kept her stuff private the more he needed to know it all. He'd have major regrets if he didn't take the chance to get to know her. It wouldn't hurt anything or anybody if they got to know each other a little during the month she'd be here.

He took an easy breath, loosed his trademark, lazy smile on her, and gentled his voice, honing in on the first thing she'd said. "You were responsible for your two brothers? Alone?"

However old she was now, that was a hell of a responsibility for the young kid she'd been.

"No, no, it's not like that...my um, their father lives with them, but he's a professor, and we sort of shared responsibilities around the house."

"And their mom?"

She took her time answering, and in a moment, he memorized her face with its pointed chin, the strong arch of dark brows, the cupid's bow lips that were a pink as pale as the inside of a rose petal...

"My mom, and Derek and Donnie's mom, doesn't live with us. She's...Willow Jansen."

Jake's gaze stroked over her face again, more comprehensively this time, and he nodded. He knew the name, and once he put the name to the face, he saw the resemblance. Although her mother was taller, Honey and the globetrotting environmental journalist shared the same coloring, the same delicate bone structure and arresting look he recalled from her television pieces.

"And that trash Dick was spewing last night, about

111

you?"

"Yeah, it's all true." She shrugged in a practiced way. "I'm illegitimate; it's no big deal." She looked past him toward the window, and he could see the shaft of dawn light that illuminated the determined unconcern in her dark eyes. "I don't know who my dad is." She lifted her shoulder. "My mom doesn't either. She was"—she met his gaze—"young when she had me."

He nodded back, mirroring her look of unconcern. On his part, it was genuine—he didn't give a flying fuck who her people were. That's the kind of bull his mamma obsessed over. He wasn't so sure Honey didn't care though. He'd bet his navy pension she cared, and the usually delicious coffee turned sour in his gut. He put the empty mug back on the table and gripped the edge of the marble. There was hurt in her solemn profile, and right now all he cared about was putting a smile back on her face.

"You don't have to talk about your personal stuff…but"—he grinned his patented, big, Jake smile, spreading his arms wide—"when a man finds a woman in his kitchen at six in the morning in a terry robe, well, he has questions."

She guffawed, picking up his vibe immediately. "Oh, yeah? And the question is, where's my breakfast, am I right?"

Her smile was back, and so was his hard on. He'd go for broke and then take an ice-cold shower after his workout.

"No, the question is more like, I'm betting you have nothing on under that?"

Her eyes glittered like chocolate topaz. "We have a

winner here." She raised her hands to start a slow clap, and the robe gaped wide open. She crushed the lapels between her fingers, but not before he saw the deep pink perfection of her nipples and the flush beginning to darken her champagne-colored breasts and torso.

"Well, then." He cleared his throat for the millionth time that morning. "I need to set some ground rules. I mean…"

Rules? Really, Jake? What would they be? *Rule one: you can't go parading around naked under a robe? Or wait, no—you must always parade around…*

"Jake," she interrupted, cheesing broadly now. "Let me ease your…mind." Her eyes flashed down to the tent in his shorts and then back to his face. Heat powered through him along with barely contained lust. Damned if she didn't make him feel like a frustrated teenager.

"I borrowed the robe because my clothes are dirty and I didn't want to sleep in them last night. But I'm going to put them back on now and go get the rest of my stuff at Lizzie's place and pick up some groceries too. But I smelled the coffee brewing and"—she slanted another smile—"it was too good to pass up."

"That does little to ease my…mind, pixie. But guess what? Your apartment has its own washer dryer."

He chuckled at her involuntary gasp.

"It's a stackable behind the door to your left as you walk into the hall. Right before you get to the kitchen."

"No way!"

"Way."

"Then I'm going straight up there to do a wash."

She looked like he'd handed her a pot of gold, and he was pleased. Way happier than he should've been.

His cell, sitting between them in the middle of the countertop, vibrated and sounded a cymbals blare. That ring tone was Regina Romero, his PA, and she never called him unless she had to. Her hyper-professional method of communication was email, then maybe text and never before eight a.m.

"Sorry, I have to take this." He jerked his chin toward her to finish her coffee and picked up the call.

Chapter 9
Game Changer

"Regina? What's up?"

Honey glanced at the clock then at Jake as concern formed grooves on each side of his wide mouth, a stab of something like jealousy slicing through her stomach. It wasn't even six thirty. Regina and Jake had to be close if he picked up her call so early.

"Of course. No, I… Of course, it's okay. A girl? Wow. That's… Right, sure. Yes. Don't worry. Go. I'll figure it out. Yeah, and congratulations to all of you."

With one hand, he ended the call while the other raked deep into his short hair.

"Fuck me."

Honey raised her brows at him. "I take it that, er, isn't part of your ground rules?"

His scowl morphed into a laugh.

"Wiseass. I'll remind you of that when I figure a way out of this mess. Regina's my PA, and her daughter just had her first baby. In Florida. A month early. I was *almost* prepared to have her leave for a few weeks in late January, but…" He scraped a hand over his face. "Every day's a full day; I've got a jammed calendar leading up to Christmas. I'm screwed."

"So what is it? Tell me. Maybe I can help."

"Help?" He stuck a hand into his hair again, and now it was pointing in six directions.

"Yes, help. I'm not on at Duffy's today. Up in my hometown, I worked as the personal assistant to the COO at our local bank."

And yeah, Rick's dad was the Chief Operating Officer at the bank and Rick's mom was just elected mayor and Honey was so damn gullible. She would *not* go there right now. She was a natural at organization and certain she could figure out his calendar and get him where he had to be at least for today.

Jake's big body was hunched over his cell as he strode toward what she presumed was his office. He pushed open a thick oak door into a windowed room with built-in shelves, a leather sofa sitting on a velvety rug, a huge desk with two chairs facing it. He went behind the desk, set down the cell, and booted up the desktop.

"Here's my schedule." He tapped the screen with a forefinger. "And the calendar for the month is in there too. I spend a lot of my time going to specific sites to scope out security issues for current clients and meet new ones. Lately, a lot of my time is also spent interviewing. My business is expanding. I hire a lot of retired cops and ex-military. There's a bunch of contact info, emails, résumés. Regina was culling through it all, then giving it to…"

"To you so you could make the final decision on whether to interview someone. Okay, I've got it. First thing's first. Let's get you through today, and while you're out doing your thing, I can pick up where Regina left off and set you up for tomorrow."

"No!" He slashed his hand through the air. Then finished more quietly. "Sorry but the absolute first thing has to be you put some clothes on." He cleared his throat. "Be hard to work with you otherwise."

"I can see that." She eyed him and pressed her lips together, trying not to smirk.

He scowled. "Honey, I swear if you don't stop…"

"I know. You said I'd have to ask. Well, what if I did?" She waited as he filtered that statement and saw the incredulous lift of his black brows when her meaning sank in.

He narrowed his eyes on her, spoke carefully. "What's that now? What if you did what?"

"What if I said I changed my mind? What if I said I wanted to be a tenant with benefits?"

He swallowed then, and out of nowhere Honey fought a strong urge to reach up and taste the golden skin of his throat. Just like she had last night. When he didn't respond but simply searched her face, she didn't attempt to blank her expression. She wouldn't take the coward's way out and look away. *I want to jump your body* was no doubt written all over her face. As the seconds slipped by, he took a couple of controlled breaths, and she watched as they expanded the broad wall of his chest.

"I'd say"—and the next words came out dark and gritty—"hell, yeah."

"Well, then. To be continued." She looked him in the eye and then allowed her gaze to travel the length of his beautiful body. The body she might soon see in its entirety. But because he was still standing there looking like Michelangelo's *David*, if David wore gym clothes and sported a hard-on, she changed the subject.

"Do you think I could get some more coffee?" She tilted her head and watched as he came out of his trance. He shook his head from side to side before staring at his phone like it held the secrets of the universe. Then nodded as he spoke matter-of-factly.

"It's six thirty now. Sure, yeah, get yourself some coffee. And there's plenty of breakfast stuff in the fridge and pantry. I'm going to work out, and we can meet back here by eight. Is that enough time for you to, you know, wash your stuff?" He backed toward the door as he spoke.

Seeing this big, gorgeous guy, this straight-up sex god, so uncomfortable gave Honey an unaccustomed feeling of power. Man, was she tempted to use it. To tell him no—she'd keep the robe on all day, thank you, because it turned both of them on. And wow, just the thought of saying that and damp heat saturated every pore.

No, she wouldn't. Mainly because she didn't quite have the nerve to put it out there—yet. To ask for exactly what she wanted, yeah, it felt good, but it was too much at this moment to dwell on the follow through.

"Absolutely. See you back here at eight. Fully dressed." She resisted lifting her hand in salute and settled for giving his hard body another raised-brow once-over.

****

She was already there when Jake returned to his office as buttoned up as his jacket. He grunted a goodbye and left for his scheduled meetings. Honey set to work following up on the resumés Regina and he'd chosen from the printed stack on the desk and set up appointments for interviews later in the week.

She quickly adjusted to Regina's methods, the operating system, and the bare bones of his business.

She sifted through Jake's pile of resumés, filing, and phone calls in no time.

By noon, things were under control, and Honey forwarded Jake an email detailing a tentative schedule of appointments for the remainder of the week.

This was so much like the job she'd had back in Caryville Fidelity & Loan. The memories of that job shoved their way in faster than she could push them away. She'd started as a summer helper between sophomore and junior year in high school. The role had expanded into a permanent part-time then full-time position after college that she held until this past fall. Halloween weekend to be exact.

She squeezed her eyes shut and massaged her temples, willing the embarrassing slideshow away. But yeah, it was happening. She was in for a full-on walk down an ego-deflating memory lane. She flopped back in Jake's desk chair and let the film roll.

In high school, she and Rick had shared a few of the same teachers and then started to share lunch. When the job opened up at the bank after sophomore year, it was natural for Rick to mention it because by that point he knew she was light on cash and helping at home. She'd done it all at the bank; filing, phones, calendar, events, and then two years ago became personal assistant to Mr. Reese, Rick's dad and COO.

By the end of senior year in high school, the furtive kisses she and Rick shared behind the taco shop turned into a sexual experimentation then consummation.

In hindsight she finally got it. Honey looked at Rick and saw stability. He looked at her and saw an easy lay.

With Honey at Alfred U and Rick at a private

college two hours away, there wasn't a ton of time for them to spend together, but Honey didn't need Rick's words. Oh, no. She formed plans of permanency all on her own. Every break from school, Rick found her ready and willing to hookup. Then he'd be gone again, and no doubt she'd find out if she cared to check that Darlene had followed him to Clarkston University.

The funny thing was now she didn't care to check. She wondered if she'd actually missed him as a person when he was away at school or if she simply wanted the reassurance that they were a couple.

And what did that say about her?

Rick had represented something approaching the stability she lacked in her home life. When Rick was away, she hadn't missed the sex either. If this was love as in commitment and if she didn't get all hot and bothered for Rick the way other girls did with their boyfriends, she figured what she and Rick had was different, as in better, as in more than sexual. Rick as a first lover was neither here nor there. Honey had nothing to compare him to, and she figured this was what married long-term relationships meant. Regular sex, but not exciting I-can't-wait-for-you-to-get-home-so-I-can-rip-your-clothes-off sex. If she were honest, she never felt that way about him. She'd been curious about sex, and then she figured okay, so that was what it was.

Not one moment in all the years with Rick compared to the anticipation she experienced when Jake so much as stroked the skin behind her ear or looked deep into her eyes. Like she mattered. Jake called her beautiful. Even if it was a lie, he'd said it.

No, no, no. Honey stopped the train of thought—

dead. This was so not the way it was going to go. A sexual relationship was just that. If she hooked up with Jake, it would be on her terms and her decision to go for a no-strings affair. No more weaving dreams and building fantasies.

She closed the door on his office, got her purse, and left the apartment. Nobody strolled in New York City, but she relished the warmth of the sun on her face in the chill December air as she rode the wave of pedestrians surging along the sidewalks in Soho. She peered into the depths of the old warehouses turned chic retailers, mentally noting their trendy New York take on the holidays. There would be a market for some of her stuff in these shops, either the seasonal items she still loved to create or her more recent abstract designs of functional tableware. If only she had more inventory.

Now without a full-time, fully boring bank job, she'd have plenty of time to create, and she'd already compiled a list of likely ceramic workspaces in Brooklyn to check out. Fingers crossed there was one at a reasonable rental price she could grab for a month.

It was a struggle to hang on to the thought of the idea that she needed to set aside money to rent workspace when she found herself in the biggest *Miranda's Moments* she'd ever seen on Broadway. Her small collection of underwear was gone with the rest of her clothing. No way would she keep wearing drugstore baggy panties that were already starting to fray.

So yeah, goodbye granny panties, hello a week's worth of lacey thongs in every color from nude to black.

She used similar reasoning when she scored vintage, leather, Gucci, knee-high boots in a consignment shop. Not an impulse purchase because the weather was turning colder, right? She needed something to wear besides black sneakers, and oh, man, they were so pretty. When the saleswoman admitted the only reason they hadn't sold as soon as they came in was multiple women failed to fit into the small size, Honey Cinderella'd her way into them, and the woman let them go for half the stated price.

Final stop was a green grocer where she stocked up on enough food to make walking back with it all a challenge. Her stomach growled. She'd grabbed a power bar from Jake's pantry for breakfast, and now it was almost four thirty. Early dinner for sure.

When she was almost back, her cell pinged. She let the shopping bags drop down onto the sidewalk, stretched her back, and pulled the phone from her pocket.

—*To thank you for helping out today, I want to take you to dinner. Eight o'clock work for you?*—

She wanted to say yes.

She would say yes.

But she literally had jeans, T-shirts, and a couple of random tops from Lizzie to wear. *And new underwear…*

—*Sure but nowhere too dressy, okay? Limited clothing options*—

She told herself she was standing there on the grungy sidewalk because she wanted to give herself a rest from carrying all those groceries, but damn, she couldn't breathe. This wasn't a date. It was more of a courtesy, a thank you—but still.

Or maybe it was a date, and yeah, Rick had never taken her on an official date where it was only the two of them, whether fancy or not. Ever. It was always a hang out with classmates in a fast food place or chill time with her brothers while she did all the cooking. *How blind could you be, Honey?*

—Of course. I'll figure it out. See you at eight—

Honey raced back to the townhouse, the weight of the bags in her hands forgotten as she mentally catalogued her meager wardrobe. A hot guy like Jake wanted to take her to dinner. All at once, every insecurity she'd experienced growing up, without a steady female influence and with limited money to spend even if she had an ounce of dress sense, came back to her. She was a sloppy tomboy who wore overalls to school till she was twelve because they fit and later because they were her fast-growing brothers' hand-me-downs. Waiting for her figure to become more feminine like Lizzie's turned out to be futile. She remained as she still was, flat chested and petite. In high school, she graduated into combat fatigues and cargo pants, inexpensive options which suited her boyish figure.

In college, still stinging from comments made by the pretty preppy girls in high school, she affected a bohemian, gothic, mish-mash style with thrift store finds and an assortment of cheap carnival jewelry she wore when she wasn't working with clay. For her job at the bank, she rotated a black skirt, black trousers, and a gray dress with pastel oxford shirts, all cheap, all boring. She hated everything about the bank's dress code, but she'd dragged the skirt and dress to the city just in case she needed them at her eventual internship. Now they were gone with everything else of hers Trey had ditched.

In fact, the only other dress she'd ever owned was the violet one she wore to the ill-fated Halloween fundraiser for Cheryl Reese. It was one of Lizzie's cast offs, and she'd thrown it out in a fit of anger after that day. Besides, the stretchy material failed to cling to her much less well-endowed body, and the mini-skirt length on Lizzie was an awkward knee length on Honey. Once more the vivid nightmarish video played in the back of her mind as she saw herself smiling as she strode purposefully up the center aisle toward the podium to take her place in the midst of the Reese family at Rick's side, the bouquet chosen for Cheryl clutched in her shaking hands. Then Cheryl's horrified face and Darlene's puzzled frown when she was mere feet away from the platform. As Rick and his dad stood stone faced, she backed away from them, surrounded on all sides by the snickering of Cheryl's assembled supporters. Then she'd thrown the bouquet to the ground and run.

I want to take you dinner, he'd said.

Tonight, she would look put-together, adult, appealing, and yes, sexy if she could possibly manage it. Her pride demanded it.

Honey held the blouses Lizzie gifted her up to her neck. One was tunic length, pearl gray, and flowing. On her, a dress. She stepped into it with the boots and sent a photo to Lizzie.

—*Could I wear this out to dinner?*—

—*Absolutely, yeah, it's a Ted Baker, and it's got a sweet vibe happening on you. LOL that it's a top on me and it goes almost to your knees*—

—*You don't think it makes me look idk? The gray suits you with your hair, but do I look like a sick bird?—*

—You just have to put some makeup on, Honey—

—It's gone...everything I had which wasn't much anyway—

—So go to Sephora and get some more. You live in the city now, sweetie, no excuses—

—Ok, right—

—So spill it. Who's the lucky guy?—

—It's more like a business dinner—

—Hmmm. Call me tomorrow with the deets. You look fantastic. Go for it. And put makeup on!—

Chapter 10
Nothing's Sweeter Than Honey

"P.O. Navarro, Sixth Precinct."

"Tommy, it's Jake. I need the rest of the pedigree info on that individual I called you about the other day. One Honey…"

"Oh, yeah, sure, sweet porn name, right? I wonder…?"

"Never mind, rocks for brains."

"Jake, don't be a—"

"I said never mind, pal."

He ended the call. He wouldn't look her up. Honey said she was twenty-five, and he believed it.

Bad boys go to hell.

Jake had been halfway there for a long time, and now he was taking the final step. The step that would assure his entrance into its fiery depths.

Because when Honey came strolling down the stairs, her eyes big and shimmering like topaz, in a floaty almost-dress with fine Italian leather boots hugging her slim legs, all thoughts of the polite conversation he wanted to have with her, the getting to know her stuff, went straight out of his head.

Watching her skip downstairs like a freakin' faerie, not knowing she was entering the devil's lair, he was helpless to do anything but put out a hand to grasp hers. He forced a smile when all he wanted to do was pick her up and carry her back into his bedroom, strip the filmy dress off her, and do everything his body was begging him to do right now.

"You look like an angel."

Oh, for the love of all that's holy, Jake.

Her cheeks tinted a golden pink, then she tilted her head sideways and sucked in her bottom lip, giving his go-to leather jacket and jeans a blatantly needy once-over.

"You clean up pretty well yourself."

He relaxed a little then. They were both on the same page, wanted the same thing. This urge was mutual.

The host showed them to the corner banquette he'd pre-selected in the trendy Japanese dining spot walking distance from his place.

"Do you think I could sit here?" She pointed to the spot next to him. "Then we can both, you know, see out, see what's going on here." She shrugged. "I've never been to a Japanese restaurant before, and this one looks pretty spectacular."

"Yeah, of course." Had he made a mistake? Had he ever been so nervous about a dinner with a woman? He wanted to show her he was hip, and this place was a hot destination for the millennial crowd.

She flushed. "It's gorgeous here, kind of exotic, and I just want to see what's going on, you know, and from here…"

"All you can see is this and *me*." Ego rapidly deflating, he jerked a thumb toward the polished bamboo paneling behind him and his face. The face she was in no hurry to examine apparently. "I get it. Come on over here." He went for a no-hard-feelings grin and patted the seat beside him.

She sidled across the leather till her right thigh and his left one brushed together for an all-too-fleeting moment. But she stayed close, and he could swear the heat of her naked thigh against the denim scorched him.

He cleared his throat. "Is this okay?"

She swiveled toward him, her entire body moving too, and suddenly her—damn, were they braless?—breasts pressed against his arm through the cotton of his shirt. He was a goner. Side by side dining was officially his thing. Now and forever.

When she turned again to look at him from under her lashes, he inhaled that hint of caramel that always seemed to cling to her skin. He'd stumbled into heaven, and he refused to dwell on the hell to come.

"It's just that"—her wide-eyed gaze swept the room—"I need to take it all in. If the food tastes as good as this place looks…oh, man, yeah."

She surveyed the open kitchen, the floor-to-ceiling granite pillar surrounded by a circle of stones in the center of the room complete with a xeriscaped garden dotted with succulents. The other diners were equally fascinating to her; Japanese couples, business types finalizing deals, hipsters and millennials toasting each other with exotic cocktails.

"The food *is* good. The menu gives the English translations, but this is an authentic place. Best miso cod in the city." At least that's what the foodie reviews said.

"Tough to decide…" She sucked in her bottom lip again as she studied the menu.

"We can get a few small plates and share, cod, angus beef, eggplant?" He raised an eyebrow.

"Great idea." And then she actually licked her lips, and his body tightened in pain, blood pooling in his groin turning him to steel.

When the server brought their food, Honey examined the plates and bowls in front of them. "See, this is what I mean. I knew a place like this would have handmade ceramics." Her eyes were dark stars.

"The food on top of them is pretty good too," he teased, lifting his chopsticks, ready to dig in.

"I know. It all looks amazing, and I haven't eaten more than a clementine since breakfast." She took her own chopsticks, then stopped, tilting her chin toward their hands. "See this?"

"No. Yeah. Ah, you have nail polish on. It's pretty." His face heated. Had she expected him to comment on the translucent pink-gold color on her short nails?

She giggled. "No, I meant look at our hands. I'm a lefty, so there's no awkward bumping into each other when we're eating."

"You know what that means?" He caught on fast, bringing his left arm out to circle her waist. She quivered at his touch, then settled into it.

"What?" She turned her face to his, and their noses were inches apart, her eyes sparking with humor.

"I can steal your food," he murmured in his best big-bad-wolf voice as he snagged a morsel of beef from her plate.

"Oh, you better not try that with me." She popped a square of cod into her mouth. "I like my food. And I always had to get mine fast before my brothers decided they wanted my helping too." A little of the sparkle left her eyes.

"You miss them."

"Yeah. A little… This is my first time away from them since they were babies. But I know they're okay. And it was past time for me to go."

Jeez, Jake, way to bring down the mood.

"Thanks for your help today."

She lifted her shoulder in dismissal, raised her wine glass, and took a long swallow. "Happy to help. You're in a bit of a bind."

Whatever lipstick she'd worn was long gone what with eating, drinking, and the way she worried her lower lip. For the life of him, he couldn't keep his gaze off the pale lush bow of them.

"I'm still in a bind. So I've got a proposition for you."

"Always with the propositions, Jake," she teased, and that was it, folks, the tables officially turned. Honey was in charge.

He gulped his beer. "Do you really want to go there?"

"Go where?" She blinked her eyes wide, all fake innocence.

He blew out a breath, disgusted at himself for his hesitation, his nerves.

"Let me get this out. How about I hire you, pay you to run my office a couple of hours a day? On the days you're not at Duffy's or every day if it suits you? Obviously, you can handle it all with one hand tied behind your back. I'd be grateful, and you moving on to your new job will likely coincide with Regina returning to work." He turned in his seat and switched on his full "charming Jake" smile.

"And here I thought you were going to say

something else entirely." Her gaze darted to his, in a look that was half-flirty and half-nervous, and two things hit him. She was a petite person who'd already consumed quite a bit of wine. Also, her eyes were not truly brown. Right now instead of the chocolate he was used to, he saw the deep gray of a stormy sky.

"And what might that something else be?"

"I…" She chewed her bottom lip in a way that tempted him to reach out and soothe it with his finger, with his tongue…with his…damn.

"Honey, I'm gonna be upfront with you. I've never had a female live anywhere near me. And to have you, someone I want to…that I…" He shook his head. *Spit it out, Jake.* "I'm attracted to…"

She withdrew—her body shrank into itself, and a sudden breath of air cooled the heat between them.

He looked down at his hands clenched in a death grip on the table, seeking the right words. "I'm not a long-term guy. I can't be. You said it, I'm basic, the go-to guy for a good time." He lifted a questioning brow. "If…knowing that, knowing there's this thing between us, if we let it happen, there'd be a definite end date—then let's get it out of our system."

"Whoa, okay." She ran a finger back and forth along the smooth surface of her chopsticks before folding her hands in her lap and looking him in the eye.

"I guess I owe you the same honesty. I'm here in the city to pursue my career. Things got way sidetracked when I met up with Trey…"

A growl rose out of his throat, but she stopped his protest with a look.

"Hang on. My one purpose here in New York is to work on my art and keep a roof over my head. I don't have room for a relationship right now, and honestly I suck at picking out worthwhile guys."

He let out a low rumble of protest, but she interrupted.

"If you and I were to hookup—that's what it would be. Temporary. Fun with an end date. Just"—she looked him square in the eye—"sex."

"So…"

"So sure, I can help you out in your office a couple of hours a day to keep your head above water. And…" She paused for an endless second, looking away from him, and then refocused her gaze on his face, her lips curved in a small smile. "And, yeah"—she took a breath—"if we want to hookup, great. I've come to the conclusion I know squat about what I want in a relationship. Or if I even want one. Don't even know if I'm capable of having one. So yeah, short term works for me."

Her hand came up from her lap, and she held it out to him.

"Are we actually shaking on this?" He covered her hand with his, unable to keep the bemusement out of his voice. She was so serious.

"Yeah, we are." She raised her eyebrows in challenge.

And so they shook on it, and it was without a doubt the weirdest conversation he'd ever had with a woman about sex. But it felt good to get it all out into the open. Honey deserved that. He'd never felt the necessity to explain anything of himself to another woman. Not that he'd given her the full truth of him. They wouldn't be together long enough for it to matter. But a weight lifted. They wanted the same thing.

He glanced over to see she was studying him surreptitiously, the forthright bravado of a few seconds ago gone, a cloud of uncertainty in her eyes. He didn't want her uncertain when she was with him. Everything about their time together should be relaxed and happy. And it would be.

He folded cash into the restaurant's billfold and stood up.

"Let's go for something sweet. Cupcakes or ice cream?"

"Do I have to decide on one or the other?" Her impish grin was back.

"No, you don't. I know just the place." He grinned back at her, and it wasn't his "Jake the Fake" patented show of teeth; it was a smile as real as the unfamiliar stab of warmth in his gut.

Once they were out of the restaurant, he slung his arm loose along her shoulders as they strolled along Hudson Street. He resisted the urge to plaster her into his side but allowed himself to stare down every guy who dared to look too long at her booted legs and barely-there dress.

The West Village Cake Bar was only a few blocks away. Once they were inside, Honey went straight to the counter and stood rapt, looking down into the offerings.

"It's going to be hard to decide." Honey shook her head from side to side, glancing back and forth among the confetti cookies, the truffles, and the soft serve.

"Everything's good here. Why don't you choose something, and I'll get a couple…?"

"And you can taste mine, and I'll taste yours…" Honey raised a brow suggestively.

"I swear," he lowered his mouth to her ear and grumbled, "if you keep teasing me in a public place…"

She smirked and pointed at the tin of cookies. "That one has an assortment in it…"

"Perfect." If he didn't get her out of here and back to his place, he might push her into the counter in front of all the waiting customers and kiss her teasing pout of a smile till she begged for mercy.

"How about the variety tin of cookies and a small box of chocolate cake truffles, Angie?"

"Sure thing, Jake."

"So you're a regular here?"

"Yep. I go here whenever I want something sweet." His gaze didn't leave her lips, and she met the look head-on even as a flush slid up her throat to cover her cheeks.

She shivered.

He shrugged out of his jacket and settled the leather on her shoulders where it swallowed the denim she was wearing. "Put it on," he said as he paid for their desserts. "Let's get out of here."

Yep, he was going to hell. But maybe it was okay to get a sweet taste of heaven first.

Chapter 11
Pixie Princess

Jake strode down the long hallway, flicking on a couple of lights as he went. Honey followed him at a slower pace, relishing the enveloping warmth of the kitchen, trying to put her finger on how it could be so sleek but so welcoming at the same time.

"Espresso? Wine?" He lifted a brow as he walked to the counter.

She clasped her shaking hands together in front of her, suddenly all nerves. Caffeine would make it worse.

"Wine would be great, thanks."

"I've got all the colors"—his grin flashed—"red, white, pink… Do you want to stick with white since you had chardonnay with dinner?" He opened the wine fridge set under the counter.

"Sure." She licked her dry lips as he uncorked the wine. Looked around and spotted the dessert.

"I'll open these." She spied small plates in the open cabinet under the center island and pulled two out. "I like how you've done this. Put some plates and stuff into the center island…makes life easier."

"Exactly." He handed her a wine glass. "Ideal for early-morning quick breakfast…"

"Or late-night snacking. Especially for short people." She needed a stool every time she wanted to cook even the simplest dish in Joss's tall Victorian in

Caryville.

"Or kids. The realtor says it'll be a good selling point."

"You're really going to sell this place? After all the work you did to get it the way you wanted it?" She looked around the room from her perch on the counter stool. She'd have a hard time saying goodbye to a place that was the perfect combination of modern and homey.

"That's the plan." His lips firmed as he lifted his own glass of wine. "*Salute.* To your health."

"And yours." Honey raised the glass in turn, then took a long pull. "Wow, this is delicious."

"My mother would be happy to hear it."

"Oh?"

"It's from her vineyard. Her family's estate vineyard anyway. Long gone over there, but there's a small outpost here on the north fork of Long Island. Her cousins brought some vines over a few generations ago."

"Wow." She examined the label. "*La Principessa Perduta,*" she pronounced slowly. Science and math were her thing, and she was hopeless at languages except for the random curse words she picked up in school.

"What does it mean, the name?"

"The lost princess."

"So cool. I've never known someone who owned a vineyard."

"I don't. She does." His words were clipped.

"I thought your mom had passed…?"

"Oh, she's very much alive." His lips twisted. "But she's not hands-on involved with the vineyard, nor did she want to involve me." He took another gulp of his wine and set it aside. Picked up a cookie.

Honey hid her reaction, lowering her gaze to the dessert plate, certain Jake had no clue of the pain evident in his words.

This is none of your business, Honey. This is none *of your business.*

"Try these yet?" Jake was changing the subject, and his sexy grin was back.

"I want to sample this first." She lifted a truffle donut, took a bite, and let out an involuntary moan.

"Oh. My. Good-ness." She pushed the whole thing into her mouth and reached for another.

Jake laughed. "I know, right?"

"Is there anything better than this? Stop me before I eat them all right now." She flicked her tongue over her lips in search of stray crumbs.

Jake moved toward her. "Stop me, she says," he murmured.

When he stood next to her perch on the counter stool, their faces were almost level, and he put his forefinger under her chin, tilting it up slightly so her lips were right there in front of his.

His intent was clear, and her breath clogged her throat. Without her conscious say so, her eyelids fell shut, anticipation ratcheting up her heart rate so fast and hard it hummed like a thousand bees in her ears.

When his tongue stroked along her bottom lip, her lips parted on a moan, and his tongue, tart and sweet with wine and chocolate, invaded her mouth. Honey strained upward, opening her mouth wider, meeting his tongue with hers, eager to taste him just as thoroughly. The more they kissed, the more feverishly she pressed herself against him, the more she wanted. He paused for a heartbeat, and she shivered, reaching for him.

"If you're gonna back out, you better do it now." His gritty voice was rough as gravel.

Her lids were heavy as she blinked them open and focused on him. "Not…backing…out," she muttered, licking her swollen lips.

He peeled his jacket off her then, and her denim jacket underneath it. When his hands cupped her jaw, pulling her to him, she got on her tiptoes to lean toward him, balancing by clutching the crooks of his elbows.

She traced the heat of him through the soft cotton of his shirt, running restless hands upward toward the solid thump of his heart. She dissolved into the kiss, clung to him while he ravaged. There was no lying about it now. She'd fantasized this moment since the first night at the hotel when he appeared like an angry god, kicking ass, taking names, and messing with her equilibrium in a way no man ever had before.

His hands moved to cup the back of her head, long fingers feathering through her short tendrils. He murmured, "So soft," over and over as he rubbed his lips over hers, then nuzzled her neck and her throat, repeating the words like a mantra.

"Jake…" Her voice was breathless, needy.

"You like that, pixie? Tell me what else you like." His rough whisper tickled her ear.

She shook with the need to tell him every single thing she'd dreamed he would do with her and to her. Starting with how good it felt to revel in the attention of a man who considered her preferences, her desires.

"You haven't made a wrong move yet." It was an effort to form words when his lips were skimming over every bit of skin exposed by her short hair and the plunging neckline of her dress.

"Good to know I'm on the right track," he said. Cocky, teasing Jake was back.

His hands smoothed the silky fabric covering breasts, cupping their slender weight, as his thumbs circled and teased her nipples, bringing them to painful points.

He eased one finger into the neckline, sliding the sleeve down one shoulder till her breast was visible.

"God, Honey." His voice shook. "No bra?"

"Never wear them. I don't need one." She shrugged, and her small breasts bobbed with the motion, her entire body fever hot in anticipation of the next brush of his hands or his lips on her sensitized flesh.

Positioning her right in front of him, he hooked his thumbs into both sides of her neckline and pushed it down over her shoulders till her arms were trapped against her sides and her breasts propped up to his scorching gaze. He lifted his hands to the small orbs, and wet heat pooled between her thighs when she saw the slight tremor of his big, tanned hands as they rested on her pale skin.

His hands eased over her, smoothing and cupping, caressing and teasing till he lowered his head and lifted them to his mouth, suckling one then the other. Honey squirmed, sharp jolts of electricity arrowing from her nipples to her core. The buzzing was loud in her ears, her breathing harsh, her gasps turning to moans.

"Jake, please…"

He lifted his head, eyes glittering like black diamonds. "Are you ready? Don't want to rush you, but it feels like I've been waiting forever, for this, for you."

He skimmed his hand up her thigh and under her dress. Her new *Miranda's Moments* thong was soaked, and her thighs quivered as his broad hand covered her.

"I want… Are you…?" His voice halted, and he rested his forehead against hers, his breathing harsh and uneven. "I want our first time to be right."

"Right?" Feeling the way she did now, Honey knew there was no way their coming together could be anything but right.

"On a bed, I mean." His deep whisper was hesitant. She placed her lips against his jaw, rubbed her cheek against his stubbled chin. She looked up at him and waited till his hooded eyes focused on her.

"Let's go upstairs, then." She took his hand, and they left the kitchen.

His bedroom was similar in size to the one she occupied on the top floor, except his was dominated by the king bed resting near the floor on a low platform. They stood in the middle of the room. Only the shaft of moonlight through the windows pierced the absolute darkness.

"Still with me?" His heavy-lidded eyes held a question in their depths.

"All in." She leaned into him, her entire body from breast to thigh, melting against his.

"Good." His hand skated down the front of her dress, callused fingers snagging on the silk as they found her breasts again and lingered over them, gathering one in his hand and lowering his mouth to suckle the nipple through the thin silk. "I can't believe you went out without a bra."

"I don't own one."

He let out an agonized growl as his hand moved

down to smooth over her tiny belly charm, rubbing over her there then lower to the edge of her panties. With another grunt he gripped the hem and tugged the dress over her head, one hand dropping the fabric while the other came up to tease and touch. Their harsh breathing was the only sound in the room as his fingers played, his hands seeking and sketching over every inch of her from the small indent of her stomach to the curve of her rear.

She tilted her head down toward her boots. "I might need help getting these off."

"Then you might have to leave them on." His grin shone white in the moonlight.

She shrugged. "Maybe I could use the height." She stretched her hands to his shoulders, her avid mouth searching for his lips.

His hands came out to cup her bottom, drawing her up in a rough motion over the coarse black denim. She loved the scrape of it against her, couldn't get enough as she rubbed and writhed against him. He groaned and lifted her, coaxing her legs wider to clasp his waist.

"Now I've got you." Both his hands squeezed her ass.

"Now I've got *you*," she answered and slid a hand down to cup him over his jeans. At his harsh breath, she poked her tongue out to trace a scorching path along his throat.

His arms shook. "Oh, yeah, that feels so…" His voice was guttural, low.

"Tell me what *you* like," she whispered against his lips, feeling her feminine power and the need to give pleasure to this man.

"You're doing it. Everything. But I want to make

this good, make it last."

He backed toward an armchair, his hands still grasping her rear, as he spoke. "If we get into bed right away, I don't know how slow I can go. Might be over in seconds. Damn, with you it might be over in seconds anyway."

He dropped into the armchair. Honey straddled him and rubbed against his arousal. She worked the buttons on his shirt open, kissing and licking each piece of skin revealed.

He tilted her chin up with his forefinger. Took her mouth in a deep kiss. Held her head to his marauding mouth with one hand while the other teased her nipples.

She found his zipper and slowly drew it down, watching as his erection sprang out, bold and needy. His head fell back, and his eyes were glimmering slits as he tracked her every move.

"It turns me on to watch you." His voice was hoarse. "It turned me on the first time I saw you—defiant and combative when I called you out. And then to see you again later that same night? I'll never know how I let you be, how I stayed away."

Honey knew. Jake had an essential goodness in him, a sense of what was right. He'd connected the dots about her situation the first night, and he hadn't taken advantage. But she'd learned enough about him to know how much he valued his chief of security persona. He wouldn't want to be called out for being, of all things, kind.

She slanted a smile at him and raised a hand to his jaw for a moment to keep his focus on her face.

"That works for me because you know, it makes me so…when you watch me." She stuck a finger into her mouth, then stroked it along his lower lip as her other hand found its way back to its previous task, taking his arousal, hot and hard, in her hand.

He sucked in a harsh breath as his jaw clenched. "Easy, pixie, I'm like a rocket right now."

"I can switch gears." Honey kept her hand on him as she slid off his lap to kneel on the thick rug. "Now you can watch me do this." Her head lowered, and she pressed a series of open-mouthed, pouty kisses all along his length, ending with a lick at the tip of his head.

He bucked like a bull. "Ah, no. I can't, no, I can't take any more."

"But I've…barely started." She raised a brow.

Chapter 12
Sweet Dreams Are Made of This

He lifted her back up onto his lap and set his mouth on hers. Still kissing that sinfully sweet mouth, he stood, and with Honey once more secure in his arms, he swayed.

The room, as familiar to him as the back of his hand, spun around him, and he reeled like a drunk. He'd only had a couple of beers at the restaurant and a gulp of wine downstairs, so there was no reason to feel this way. Like he was out of control, overwhelmed. Like this was a moment, a night, he'd remember forever.

Honey was giving him everything, her arms were tight around his neck, and her perfect breasts crushed against his chest.

There wasn't any more time. He had to have her now.

He broke the kiss. Honey gave a startled yelp as he released her, and she slid down his body. When her booted feet hit the floor, she rounded on him.

"Jake, what?"

"Time to be in a bed. I can't wait." He shook his head. "I'm sorry if..." Gone was the smooth player he showed the world, and in his place was a guy at the end of his tether.

"I promise, next time will be a little more..."

"Don't say anything. I don't want to wait either."

Accepting that permission, he yanked back the duvet and nudged her over to sit on the bed. She perched on the edge of it, hands folded primly, incongruous given her lack of clothing and somehow a major turn on in light of everything they'd done so far and would soon do.

Then she stood up again. "Jake?"

"Yeah?"

"Yeah, so here I'm here practically naked and you, you're…"

"I hear you." He toed off his shoes, tossed his shirt onto the chair they'd just vacated, and shucked his jeans.

"Honey, get on the bed, and I'll take those boots off you. As good as they look on you, you won't need the height. No one needs vertical when they're horizontal." He winked and flashed his usual confident smile.

She crossed her arms over her bare breasts and tapped one boot on the rug beneath her foot. "I can't lie on the bed till you take them off. These boots will mess up your sheets."

"Do you really think I care about that?" He chuckled, torn between desire and a belly laugh. "Sit on the edge, then," he said.

He dropped to his knees in front of her, gripped one ankle and then the other as he slid the boots off her.

Now she was naked aside from the skimpy scrap of lace that covered her.

"I kind of like you in that position." Her eyes, so dark they looked black, danced with mischief as they ran over his body.

His sweet pixie was propositioning him. Again.

"Oh, really?" He raised a brow.

"Yeah. We're practically face to face. And I get a front row view of..." She licked her lips and reached toward his shoulders, but he lifted quick hands to stop her. Took her hands secure in one of his.

"I'm face to face with my own personal paradise here." His hand, the one that wasn't holding hers, covered her heat, and his thumb began a rhythmic stroke of her folds over the lace.

Her head tilted back, and her knees splayed open as she moaned. She watched him through slumberous eyes as he drove her. She writhed and pushed against his hand, and finally he gave in, snaking a forefinger under the lace to touch her. Satin smooth, tight, and ready. He added another finger to the first, and her legs gaped. "Jake!"

Yeah, his name sounded great on her lips. He kept up a steady pace and released her hands so she could steady herself on his shoulders.

"Damn, you're so beautiful, let go," he whispered his encouragement before he leaned forward to put his mouth at the soft center of her, first over the lace, then he scraped back the material to find her damp flesh under it. At the touch of his lips on her swollen skin, she arched her back, belly heaving with her gasps, hands at her sides squeezing the duvet. He braced a forearm behind her to keep her upright and close to his marauding mouth.

"Give me all your honey, that's it, yes." She bucked and moaned as he tongued her. When her keening cry sounded, and she shook her release, it only took the weight of one hand on her belly till she fell back on the mattress.

He licked his lips, his breathing as ragged as hers. Her eyes opened, and she rose up onto her elbows.

"Now don't you look satisfied?" she said.

"I'd say the boot is on the other foot." But he knew what she meant. He couldn't wipe the satisfied smile off his face. Seeing Honey lose herself so thoroughly and knowing he was responsible for it gave him a high he'd never felt before.

She opened her arms. "Come here."

He knelt next to her, wanting, needing to be as close as possible, but fearing he'd crush her.

"Come closer," she whispered. "I want to tell you something."

He leaned in. Her eyes were cloudy again, a grayish brown that wasn't really brown, gray, or even hazel, but more like the color of a turtle dove.

"Thank you, Jake."

"Oh, I'm not done yet." As he made the promise, he eased his finger along her bottom lip, and she snaked out her tongue to suckle it.

"You better not be. We've got all night." She ran a finger down his chest, circling his nipples before sliding her hand all the way down to the hard flesh of him jutting between them. She scooted to sitting on the mattress, and both hands circled him.

He sucked in a breath.

"Honey, I…" He gasped as he felt her hot mouth on him.

"I won't let you finish this way…unless…you want to."

Then her hands and her mouth owned him, and he shuddered, letting her have her way with him, as he knelt on the bed before her like a pagan slave. Finally, his hand covered her head, found purchase in her short hair, forcing her head back and away from him.

"Basta, enough, it's time." But still he found himself unable to cover her, sure the weight of him, never mind his ferocious need to take her, would hurt her.

She solved his problem by pushing his shoulders till he lay back, still breathing heavily, his erection pulsing like a torpedo between them.

Kneeling at his side, she tugged the damp lace off and straddled him. Took his length inside her inch by inch till she was seated hard. She bit her bottom lip as she began a slow rocking. He blinked his eyes open and closed once because this, yeah, he couldn't believe it—this was his fantasy of her come to life.

She swayed and rocked her hips, speeding up and slowing down, setting a sweaty rhythm. Her breasts bounced with each movement, and he lifted his head to suckle and fondle them till they were rosy peaks. When he saw she was close, he took over, gripping her behind to hold her steady as he ground his hips, pumping upward. A couple of hard thrusts and he was there, following her under the rushing waves.

"Hang on." He planted rough kisses on her swollen mouth, pulsing like an out of control piston.

His life force erupted, and he shuddered. She called his name in a long whimper before she fell forward onto his chest, her skin slippery and warm.

His hands smoothed over her golden skin from shoulder to thigh, and he slowly swam up from the ocean of intensity this woman evoked in him. He pushed rational thought aside because he didn't want to surface, he wanted her again, and damn, he was still hard and tightly seated inside her and…

"Oh, fuck me…"

"Right now? Well, if you insist…" Honey's giggle tickled the hair on his chest, but he sat up anyway, dislodging her to run a distracted hand through his hair.

"The joke's on us. We did it bare." He shook his head at his stupidity. "I apologize. I've never done that before. Don't worry, I have no medical issues. I'm completely clean. Damn."

Chapter 13
Rude Awakening

"I am too. And I'm on the pill. No worries, Jake. It's okay."

The pill had been her birth control of choice ever since her doctor recommended it to regulate her painful and erratic cycle. She didn't mind the slight curves it fostered on her otherwise boyish figure either.

"It's…" He shook his head in disbelief. "I've *never* been with a woman without being fully prepared. I pride myself on it. Protecting her. Protecting me." Anger and bemusement laced his deep voice.

His fingers tore through his hair again as he turned away from her to plant his feet on the floor and sat facing the darkened windows. His tight jaw and the rigid set of his shoulders impelled her to act when all she wanted to do before this moment was catch a quick nap right there till the next time they made love…had sex.

She scooted off the mattress, picked up her blouse, and pulled it over her head. She grabbed her boots, eyed her thong abandoned on the bed near Jake, and decided not to reach for it.

His beautiful back to her, massive shoulders bunched and tense, the tattoo of rushing waves that covered him from shoulder to shoulder she was too lust crazed to appreciate earlier pulsed with each deep exhalation.

"I…I'm going upstairs to get some sleep," she croaked. He didn't say a thing, and she slipped out, closing the door behind her.

****

Awkward city.

Body still throbbing, Honey fumbled her way into a quick shower when all she wanted to do was pull the covers over her face and cry. How good would it have been to sleep in each other's arms in the king bed and wake him and his seriously hot body up in an imaginative way? What just happened?

What's wrong with you, Honey? Snuggling and sleeping in the same bed was not what their relationship was about. This was only about scratching a sexual itch, and they would be going their separate ways when she started her internship. That was the plan.

It was perfectly understandable Jake freaked out thinking he'd risked getting his temporary hookup in the family way. Wasn't it?

Amazing that neither of them raised salient details like birth control and the basics of how to interact on a daily basis in non-hookup hours. She had shifts at Duffy's three nights a week and agreed to help him in his office.

Were they supposed to stay out of each other's way at all other times? Put their "meetings" on a master calendar? All of the sudden, the whole hookup idea seemed dumb and unworkable. What if Jake met someone else during the time of her lease, someone else he wanted to hook up with—or more—instead? They'd discussed *nothing.* Honey could admit, on her part at least, once they'd decided they were going to do *it,* she could hardly wait for the main event to begin.

Did that make her an unsophisticated yokel? Probably, but she'd change that going forward. This would be the way of her sex life from now on, and she had to think ahead. Career goals first and relationships solely on her terms.

Jake had admitted he'd never had a woman live with him. They'd both glossed over the finer details of what it would mean to be together even in a short-term way in their frenzy to get inside each other's pants.

Tomorrow she'd put her legendary organizational skills in play. She'd devise a plan to put herself and her career first.

But sleep didn't come easy, with the unrelenting, chaotic thoughts chasing her into her dreams. What if Jake already decided "been there, done that?" What if the flat-chested girl with the spikey hair was not worth giving up his freedom, even for a month, to meet and bed whoever else he wanted? What if they became just housemates? Simply landlord and tenant? Not even friends and without any benefits whatsoever?

That would suck. Because Jake, the lover, had everything. She could still feel him tending to her most secret flesh, and the recollection heated her body. The way his corded arms and sculpted thighs strained and shook to remain still, acquiescing to her tongue and mouth as she played with him. The intensity of his gaze fixed on her, his hands and his mouth, skillful, pleasure giving, and generous.

****

Honey belted the terry robe. It was warmer than anything else she had and more than covered her T-shirt. It was early enough Jake might not even be up.

She'd bought groceries, including breakfast food, but his coffee was to die for.

She'd grab a cup and search out whatever brand he used for future reference before turning back upstairs. Honey had the day to herself. She could help out in Jake's office for a couple of hours—unless he decided to renege on that plan too.

"Looking for something?" His deep morning voice halted her hand on its way to open the upper cabinet.

She tried to assess the voice before she turned around. It wasn't as harsh or commanding as that first night at the Pierre. But it wasn't that husky tone of last night, the one with need and laughter at its base, the one she'd replayed in her head all night long.

It was neutral. Landlord-tenant. Nothing more.

Honey tugged the robe's belt, making sure it was secure around her middle before turning around. Ridiculous given last night, but yeah, they were in the bright winter light, and her hair was askew, and she was barefoot…

Just turn around, Honey!

She turned, hands fiddling with her belt as she hitched her chin higher.

"Just trying to see what coffee you use." She shrugged like it was no big deal they'd been sweaty and naked only six hours earlier.

"I use Illy, but I add cinnamon to it."

She nodded. Wished she'd already downed a fortifying cup but sheer nerve would have to carry her through.

"Jake…"

"Honey."

They spoke at the same moment.

"You first." He nodded curtly, a polite smile curving his lips.

"It occurs to me"—*I stayed up all night wondering*—"that we need to discuss more than we have already, some ground rules, I mean if we're gonna continue…"

Everything she had to say had been so clear in her head last night, and now in the face of the hottest male she'd ever met, no, the hottest male on the planet, who right now was looking at her with a seriously furrowed brow, her brain ceased to function.

She focused on the center island and not the way his T-shirt and basketball shorts, which she now knew as his workout gear, hugged his shoulders and thighs.

"First." He bowed his head and gripped the edge of the marble countertop, then pierced her with a somber gaze. "I would never; I mean I've never before forgotten about precautions with any woman I've been with. I apologize."

She waved a hand. "Like I said, I took the precautions. I can take care of myself. And we're both healthy. But the way you reacted, I wonder if you're regretting this arrangement and whether we need to allow for the idea that it might end sooner than…"

Hi harsh voice interrupted. "Is that what you want?"

"No! I mean, no." She tamped down her voice to something less than a screech. "I went into this with my eyes open. With the knowledge that it's all temporary, but that still leaves things pretty open-ended and…"

"Is that what you want? Open-ended?"

"No." The word burst out again, and her face heated at her vehemence.

"If I was going to make excuses, I'd say I forgot to use my own contraception because last night was…" His cheekbones stained a deeper bronze. "Last night was…" He looked down again, shaking his head. "I've never… I don't want to end things prematurely. Not unless you do. I have a couple of requests though."

She raised a brow. "So do I."

He inclined his head. "You first." Still somber, still formal.

"While we are together." She swallowed at the intimacy of that word. "For this month, it's just the two of us. No one else for me. And I expect the same thing from you."

"Not a problem." A faint smile. "That's exactly what I was going to say."

Oxygen came back into the room, and Honey sucked in a big breath. She smiled. "Glad we're on the same page. Is there something else?"

"Oh, yeah." A dirty grin covered his face, and his voice dropped an octave. "Just that when you wear that robe, I get an uncontrollable urge to take it off you."

"I do have a T-shirt on underneath this, you know," she said primly.

"That can be remedied." He opened the belt in one motion, and the heavy terrycloth fell open. He pulled her toward him, pushing the robe off her shoulders at the same time. It puddled on the floor as he lifted her onto the counter stool. When he reached for the hem of her T-shirt, she raised a brow.

"Fair's fair, Jake."

His wicked smile said he expected that remark, and he yanked his own tee over his head in one motion before removing hers.

"Damn, Honey. No panties?"

"I left them in your bed."

He lifted a brow. "Oh, yeah. You'll have to come back up there if you ever want them back."

"Or I can do without them." She grinned at the severe expression on his face as he absorbed that concept. Oh, man, she loved winding him up.

He moved in on her, pulling her between his legs where she felt the rock-hard evidence of his need. An answering flood of sensation dampened her core, and she shivered.

"Come here, pixie. I'll warm you up."

His mouth found hers, and he savaged it as if they hadn't been together hours before. Her body answered his; she rubbed her still-sensitive breasts against his chest, her nipples aroused to tight points. She broke free of his mouth to press small kisses on his cheekbones and chin, her tongue poking out to flick at his earlobe.

His deep voice puffed the hair at her neck. "I want you again. Now. Is it too soon?"

Unembarrassed, she placed her hands on him, weighed his growing length and girth. "No, not too soon." She looked back at him, eyes half-mast, and the want rolled through her. "I need you now too."

"I'm all yours." He lifted her, and she circled her legs round his waist like before. She set her mouth to his, and the next thing she knew they were in his office. She helped him shuck his shorts, and he eased back on the sofa, bronzed legs splayed, his manhood rigidly at attention. Looking into his eyes, Honey lowered herself onto him, inch by delicious inch. She started a rocking motion, but he settled his hands on her waist and halted her movements.

"Condom," he said on a gasp.

"Right, of course." She released his body from hers.

He reached into the side table by the sofa, and Honey didn't want to wonder why he had condoms there or how many other women had been in this exact place doing this exact thing with him. She would not think of that now. He rolled on the protection in a practiced motion, smoothed his hands over her hips in a signal for her to continue.

She took all of him in one move, and he threw his head back with a groan.

"Ah, Honey, sweet Honey." His hands fixed on her hips as he controlled their pace, building up their pleasure in increments, slowing her down when she would go faster.

When she was near her edge about to go under, he slipped his hand between them and stroked her till the heat inside her bubbled over and bathed her in a flood of her own juices. Her scream matched his groan, and then they were spent, breathing hard. She dropped her face into his neck, inhaling his unique scent, tongue flicking the warm skin there.

After a long moment, she raised her head to look at him. His head tilted back against the sofa, his jaw slack, eyes closed.

Chapter 14
Honey, Honey Bo Bunny

He was spent. So drained it'd be a challenge to open his eyes. He hadn't felt this loose, this mindless, or this satisfied in a long time. Maybe ever. And no, breathing in and out, using those deep, measured, military breaths designed to bring him back to reality didn't work this time. Because as long as Honey's sweet, soft bottom rested on his lap and her warm exhales tickled his chest hair, the want, the gnawing need would be there too. He was getting hard again already. This woman turned him into a stick of dynamite. And yeah, she'd been messing with the rules that governed him twenty-four seven since that first night.

What time was it? *Get up, Jake.* Work out, then work. With a last secret inhale of her neck, he lifted her off him in an easy motion and dealt with the condom. But she wasn't having it. When he sat again, she snuggled back into his side, not any more ready to get up than he was.

"How is it possible to feel this good before coffee and before seven a.m.?" Honey's drowsy voice drifted into his ear.

"I don't know how I'm gonna work out with a hard on, but…"

Her eyes widened. "You're still…?"

"If I'm late to my appointments today, you know who's to blame." He lowered his brows, and his voice took on a stern edge.

"Hmm." A drowsy smile curved her lips. "I'll get coffee in a minute and be back down here by eight." She burrowed closer. "A little tired right now."

He tugged the throw off the back of the sofa and covered her. She was just closing her eyes again when he said, "Why Honeysuckle?"

Her eyes snapped open. "What the? No!" Her husky voice was vehement. "If you only knew how much I was teased." Her voice quavered with a mix of anger and pain.

Stop, Jake. Stop asking stupid questions that make her feel bad.

"Forget it. It's a beautiful name. Honey suits you." His voice dropped. "Because you taste so sweet." He let the tips of his fingers toy with her lips, still deep pink and puffy from their lovemaking.

She cuddled into him, arms curved round his waist. He tucked the throw more securely around her cooling flesh. His body was a furnace—hot as usual and especially since he'd been with her. His SEAL training meant he'd endured hours in cold water, in a pool tank, in the ocean, on his back half-submerged battling waves, towing cargo or a portable dinghy in rough seas, and just plowing through the waves doing laps.

Water was now his element. He'd conquered it. And cold was his bitch.

"Honey is Honeysuckle as you know," she murmured. Her eyes were half closed, and her chest rose on a thoughtful inhale. "My mom, like I said, was young when she had me." He felt her shoulder rise and fall against him in a shrug. "And she'd always hated her given name, Wilhelmina. So as soon as she left home, she christened herself Willow."

He nodded, his chin rubbing against the soft lavender hair on the top of her head. He was not about to question why or how her mother had left her on her own to fend for herself and two younger brothers. What would be the point? Had his mother been any better?

"So she gave me what she considered the most romantic name her nineteen-year-old self could think of."

"And Hill?"

"That's our family name, my grandpa's name. Mom took Jansen, my grandma's surname, to use professionally." She shrugged again. "Not sure why."

His mamma had been and was still obscenely proud of her ancestral name Boniface. From the House of Boniface. Although Rome was far from the Tuscan countryside of her birth, she carried the name and the aristocratic snootiness of her forebears into Roman society.

He'd been christened Giancarlo Teodoro Silvio Boniface Riccobono, surname courtesy of his father.

At first, he was tormented mercilessly at the Connecticut prep school where he landed after Francesco died, after his parents split. Though broad and tall compared to other twelve-year-olds, he was no match for the seniors who ruled the campus. He'd quickly renamed himself Jake Ricco and ditched the refined cadences of his Anglo-European English into something more All-American. Very quickly during his six years there, he became the protector. Every kid he met—even the nasty ones—was a stand-in for Cesco, and he never failed to help anyone smaller or weaker. He earned a reputation as a defender, and even the older, bigger guys respected his physical prowess and the way he, as he grew tougher and stronger, never used his size against them.

"I hear you. My full name is Giancarlo Teodoro Silvio Boniface Riccobono. Man, that name was rough. Soon after I started school here in the states, I decided I was gonna be Jake Ricco."

She drew away from his side to look into his face, her dark brows rising up till they were covered by the feathery fringe of her silver hair. "Why do parents *do* that? I mean, Giancarlo is beautiful, it's just the rest of it is sort of…" She paused, pulling in the corner of her lip with her teeth, searching for the word she wanted.

"Overkill," he supplied with a grimace.

"Yeah. I mean, unless you're a royal or a Hollywood type, why burden a kid that way? If I ever have a kid, he's gonna have a meat-and-potatoes name, a plain, good name like…" She stopped again.

"How 'bout Charlie?"

"Exactly. Perfect." She nodded at him, and when her eyes crinkled up in pleasure, he flashed on a mental picture of a tiny Charlie, with pale hair and dark eyes just like her.

"And for a girl?"

"Hmmm…" A thoughtful exhale. "I've always liked the name Cara. Or maybe Annabelle." Her eyes took on a faraway look that pulled at him.

Cara. Annabella. He said the names to himself, drawing out the syllables in the Italian way.

Whoa! What the fuck was he doing sitting naked with a woman who'd just rocked his world with outstanding sex discussing baby names? They had an agreement. They both knew what they wanted from each other, and it wasn't anything more than hookup sex.

There was every likelihood children would be in both of their futures but not *their* children with each other. There was no doubt his promise to his mother included the promise to procreate. She was crystal-disgusting-clear on it. He was the replacement heir, the spare, and one of the many demands of that role was the creation of a new generation of his bygone line. With a suitable woman from a family with a bloodline, and most important, a bank account his mamma envied.

He grabbed his shorts and stood to yank them on.

"See you back here at eight."

****

The struggle was real.

Honey wanted to focus on Jake's desktop keyboard. She tried to employ her customary attention. The ability to hyper-concentrate was what got her through years of high-level math and science classes. She pretended to check his calendar. Again.

Who would've thought a month ago she'd be happily embarking on an affair with a man who looked almost as good in black jeans and leather as he did out of them? Or that she'd have enough information to make the comparison?

She wouldn't be able to take a full breath till Jake was out the door to his appointments. If he didn't spend most of his time in the field, she'd never survive this month. As he moved around his office, picked up the pages she printed, slid them into a folder, she held her breath, demanded her gaze not to stray toward that leather sofa where only an hour ago they'd taken each other to a naked, sweaty nirvana. Her body was on a hair trigger of want. She was incapable of going slow with him, and he knew it. It was Jake who'd controlled their encounter, slowing down the pace and prolonging their pleasure. She was determined to take control next time, and she couldn't stop thinking of all the ways she was going to accomplish that.

But damn, it was only nine a.m. And double damn, he knew what he was doing to her as he circled his desk for the bajillionth time, so close the heady combination of lemon and leather on his freshly showered skin teased her aroused senses. If he leaned over near her again, she swore she'd grab him by his belt or by his fine butt and plaster herself against him and demand he...

That buzzing was the phone.

"Haven Security." Her voice was scratchy from her racy thoughts. She pushed a strangled breath out, listened.

"Yes, Mr. Ricco would be happy to see you then. Sure, I'm putting it on his schedule right now. What? No. I'm helping out for a while. Regina's on vacation. Aw, that's kind of you to say..."

He hovered even closer, and she glanced up to see Jake yanking his hand under his chin, fake-slitting his throat in the universal sign for cut it short.

"Thanks. Will do." She ended the call.

"Who the hell was that?"

"One of the interviewees."

"Cross his name off the list and cancel the interview."

"How do you know it was a he?"

"Was it a female? Then cross her name off."

"Jake, what's gotten into you? His resumé made the cut. The guy was making conversation."

"The guy was flirting."

"And I can handle myself."

"I know you can. But you shouldn't have to in a work environment. And I don't want… I don't want…" He stopped. "For this month, it's just me and you. That's what we agreed."

"The guy's fifty, Jake. Besides…I agreed to this arrangement too. For this month, it's just us. My ex cheated on me. I'm the last person who'd do that to someone else. Short term hookup or not."

He pushed his cell into his pocket and strode to the door. He opened it, then turned back to her.

"Either way, I don't want to see him. I won't be able to work with him." The skin of his sharp cheekbones darkened as he said it, but his eyes were flint hard when they met hers. "See you later." She caught her breath again at the double meaning he didn't bother to hide from his tone.

"Um." She licked her dry lips, trying for a phrase to inflect her response with something casual and flirty but couldn't make it happen. Instead she said the only thing that came to mind, the truth. "I can't wait."

His eyes smoldered to black as he nodded once and left the room.

By eleven, she'd cleared more of his backlogged paperwork and judged herself free to go. She grabbed an apple for right now and tossed a clementine into her purse for later. Jake had advanced her a week's pay as his temp assistant with the suggestion she buy herself a proper winter jacket. Jake loved to give suggestions like that.

But even though it was three weeks till Christmas, it was a mild winter for the city. Compared to the harsher temperatures upstate, the occasional dip in temperatures here among the heat-absorbing skyscrapers hadn't bothered her a bit. A winter coat was nowhere on her agenda.

She had much better uses for the money burning a hole in her account.

One was a Christmas tree. It wouldn't be Christmas without a real one, and it would take a really big one to properly fill the spacious front room in her apartment. Besides she had a trunkful of her own handmade ceramic ornaments, a mixture of her personal collection and samples of those featured in her online catalog for sale. She'd take a photo of her handiwork once the tree was up and post it on her social media. She'd dropped everything to execute her impulsive flight from Caryville, and it was time to restart her usual posts. She'd sold most of her inventory, so the next item on her list had to be securing rental space in Brooklyn with a potter's wheel and oven.

Practically outside the door on the next corner, a tree vendor set up temporary shop. Yards of curb boasted evergreens of every height and variety. The sales guy was bopping to the beat of his boom box blaring Michael Buble who proclaimed it was beginning to look a lot like Christmas.

Honey paced back and forth, examining all the bigger trees. "Listen," she said to the kid who'd introduced himself as Duane and who was patiently unfurling every tree that looked promising to her. "Just find me the tallest, fattest one you have and tell me how much. If I can afford it, it'll save you some time."

"Don't mind opening them for you, miss." Duane looked down at his boots while his ruddy cheeks colored some more. "But check this one out." He aimed his thumb at a Douglas fir leaning against a makeshift wire fence at the back of the lot.

"Ooooh." She nodded. "Oh, yeah. That's the one. I'll take it."

That tree would be spectacular in her space especially with the old school, colorful vintage bulbs the vendor had on hand. "These are going fast. Just right for yer old-fashioned Christmas, ya'know?" he said.

Old-fashioned bulbs they might be, but Honey paid upscale New York City prices for everything. She squashed down the memories of all of the years she, Donnie, and Derek had gone to a local Christmas tree farm and cut their own, first with Joss's supervision but in the last few years on their own. While the vendor was tallying up her bill, she texted them. Time to invite them to visit. She sketched over her breakup with Rick, promising them more detail when they came down.

Honey slid her paid receipt into the back pocket of her jeans. "Okay. If you can hold all of this for a while, I'll be back later this afternoon to take it back to my apartment."

"Sure thing." The guy stowed her lights under his makeshift counter and put a red sold ribbon on her tree.

The rental of space at the ceramic cooperative in Williamsburg was pricier than she wanted to pay but an expected cost of doing business in the city. Calculations flew through her mind as she wondered how much more she could charge for her creations. Maybe adding a "made in Brooklyn" etch on the back of them would make them more desirable? The issue was how she could turn a profit with the inclusion of shipping costs since she hadn't signed up for any holiday fairs in the city to sell anything that way. She could only rent the pottery workspace for a month before she was scheduled to go to Long Island to her internship, but until then she could work any day she wasn't at Duffy's or assisting Jake. Then there was the time necessary to make the ornaments and knickknacks that were her bread and butter while also finding time for the larger or more original pieces that stretched her creative muscles.

On her way back to pick up her tree, she stopped at her car and took the huge carton of ornaments out of her trunk. She'd sort through what was salable inventory and what she could put on the tree once she was back in her apartment.

Duane's dad was back from his break when she returned to the tree corner, so Duane volunteered to carry the tree and everything else back to the townhouse with her.

Honey heaved out a breath and stopped, uncurling her hand from around the tree's trunk and stretching it.

"This is it. Thanks, Duane. Good thing it was only a block, right?" She grinned at him. She might be challenged by the weight and awkward bulk of the tree, but his lanky frame, like Derek and Donnie's, was deceptive. Duane didn't break a sweat. She sank a hand into her jeans pocket for her key.

"I can help you inside with everything." He scanned the townhouse. "What floor are you on? Is there an elevator?"

Chapter 15
O Christmas Tree

"No, there isn't. I can take it from here. Duane, is it?" He pushed a ten-dollar bill into the kid's hand.

Honey hadn't heard him approach, and now her head swiveled round. Then she practically jumped out of her skin when he leaned in and caught her lips under his in a brief, hard kiss. But she didn't object. Far from it. Her hands came up to grip him on the outside of his shoulders, and when he stepped back, she clung for a moment, her breath whooshing out of her mouth in a sharp burst.

He kept the kiss quick, but the point was to deflect the bug-eyed teenager looking on. No question he'd met Honey a moment ago, and true to form like the rest of the dudes on the planet, this kid imagined himself in love. Or in lust. It didn't matter which. It wasn't happening.

Even when she was being friendly and business-like, it was obvious her bohemian pixie vibe meant every guy from puberty through senior citizen tried to work his game on her. Even the guy on the phone this morning hadn't even *seen* her, and he was purring like a tiger trying to get into her pants. It wasn't right, and yeah, she could take care of herself. She'd done it time and again since he'd met her.

But she didn't need to worry about stuff like that

while he was around to protect her. Not during their time together.

"Thanks, son. You'd best head back down the street. Looks like you have the after-work crowd starting to come by." Jake jerked his chin toward the corner where passersby were swarming the Christmas trees, weaving in and out of the maze-like space with Duane's father scooting between them in his red Carhartt jacket like a burley elf.

Jake lifted the box of ornaments onto one shoulder and grabbed the tree by its thick base with the other hand.

Honey carried the bag of lights and slid past him to open the outer and inner doors.

Jake half dragged, half carried the tree into the hallway and stopped, lifting one brow.

"You want this up in your apartment." It was a statement not a question.

"Uh, yeah, I mean, unless you'd rather… Where do you usually set up yours?"

"Mine?" His mouth flattened, then his lips parted on a harsh sound he tried to turn into a laugh. They'd never had a real tree. His father had put up a small, fake silver one a few times when he was a kid. The kind that sat in a crowded corner on the top of the TV. Gradually even that minor effort at sprucing up for the season had stopped.

He closed his eyes trying to picture what his mother did every year. He couldn't recall. His years-long pattern was to arrive on Christmas morning, and after the long overnight flight, he usually catnapped at his hotel. He would meet her later at a restaurant and treat her to Christmas dinner, a practice not at odds with the Italian upper crust. Had he ever been inside the apartment she kept in Rome these last few years? No.

He made his obligatory visit every Christmas. Every year he heard again what a disappointment he was and what his duty was to her, to Cesco's memory, and his family name. Was told he must come back to Italy and marry one of her hand-chosen, wannabe society women. The latest one had a father with a resort on the same coast where he and Cesco had taken their nightmare swim. She was an MBA and positioned, as an only child, to take the reins of the company when her father retired. There was no one else in their line, and the family assured Franca the match would take place. "Because it must," Franca said. "And because you're good-looking enough she'll want you to father children with her." He would be thirty-three next year, and last Christmas he finally agreed he'd keep his promise and comply with her plan in the new year.

As in, next month.

Franca even suggested he get his sperm tested. "For viability and volatility," she said. "George Clooney ran a big risk waiting as long as he did. He had the money though, and we don't have that luxury. You need to father at least one child with her. But preferably two." And if that little speech didn't shrink his dick, nothing had the power to.

But should he complain? As Franca reminded him time and again, he was alive. Cesco was not. It was time for him to bring back her family name and be the son Cesco would have been. So he'd marry, and damn him, he'd fuck his arranged match. Even if he had to pretend she was a silver-haired pixie with a cupid's bow mouth. Because maybe if he finally kept his promise, the nightmares would go away.

"I don't put up a tree."

"*You don't put up a tree*?" She said it in a scandalized, disbelieving tone reserved for pathetic losers. "With all the space you have in this gorgeous, traditional home?" She shook her head sadly. "Is it a time issue? It does take effort, but in the end, it's well worth it."

"Well worth it for two weeks and then pine needles everywhere?"

Her face suffused with color at his response, and he smothered a grin. He was about to get schooled on the joys of authentic Christmas trees, and he couldn't wait.

"There's no substitute for a real tree with a real scent. I've yet to find a box or a bottle that can impart the exact fragrance. Decorated with all of the ornaments you've collected over the years. *And* I have all of my own ornaments. I mean I've made them. Then when you have a fireplace, like you do?" Her face got red again, and she powered down her speech when she saw he was grinning from ear to ear.

"I guess you can tell I'm just a tiny bit obsessed with Christmas. Just help me upstairs with this." She pushed out a breath. "Please?"

"Yes, ma'am."

The four flights weren't half bad. He took the majority of the weight from her and had the pleasure of watching the subtle sway of her jeans-clad hips as she slowly climbed the steps in front of him.

He lingered to find a towel to rest the tree under while she went back up to the corner to buy the tree stand she'd forgotten she needed. He hung around while she dithered over where to put it, then set it in the place she chose.

"Okay. One last thing. I need a ladder and that's it."

He nodded, eyeing the nine-foot fir whose limbs, now unfurled, were beginning to come down and fill the space in the corner of the sitting room near the six-foot windows that fronted the building. "To hang lights. Need help with that?" he offered, not that he had the vaguest idea how to do it.

"No, I've done it a million times. I'm good here." When he hesitated, about to offer up his brawn if not his expertise, she said, "Really. When it's all done, I'll call you, and you can come up and see, and then I dare you to tell me Christmas trees aren't worth whatever it takes."

Whatever it takes. Damn, she was cute. "I can't wait," he said with a wink. And because he couldn't think of a good reason to stay that didn't involve tearing her clothes off, he left. This tree business was obviously a big deal to her, and she needed to be in her moment.

It was pushing seven o'clock. He'd rushed through his appointments today more ruthlessly efficient than usual because he was starving. But not for food. He was keyed up and needy for the woman who lived in his house, and he couldn't see why they shouldn't make the most of every second they were here together. He'd dawdled this morning, unwilling to leave her. She was in his system now, and he wondered if one month would be enough, but it would be. It had to be.

Hundreds of times today, he'd pictured her—him inside her, an angel's smile on her flushed, heart-shaped face. He crushed the fantasy now because he could wait…almost. First, dinner—no—first, a swim. Then a cold shower.

Thirty minutes later, he checked the fridge and pantry. One of the many cool things about living in Greenwich Village was access to the best Italian food markets in the city, if not the world. Twice a month, he received a delivery from a grocer three blocks away. He always ordered the fresh homemade pasta, which rivaled anything he'd ever tasted anywhere, as well as olive oils, cheeses, tomatoes, and antipasto imported from near and far—Italy and California or New Jersey and Brooklyn.

Jake took frozen meatballs out of the freezer and set them next to the jars of homemade sauce. He grabbed the cheeses and olives out of the fridge and set up a charcuterie board.

He texted Honey on her progress with the tree, and she didn't respond. No doubt she was up on the ladder. Dammit, why did he text? What if she reached for her phone and fell? Accidents happened every day. That fact haunted him most of his life. But when an accident could've been prevented, well, that had to be somebody's fault, right?

He took the stairs two at a time to the top floor.

Pushing open the door quietly so as not to startle her, Jake stepped inside the door without making a sound.

She was on the ladder, perched on the second rung from the top, reaching to place an ornament on the tree. She paused and tilted her head, then hooked the ornament to her chosen branch. Then she tilted her head again, and holding the top of the ladder, leaned back to see its effect from a different angle. She was so painstaking he marveled she'd accomplished as much as she had in an hour.

Giant, old-school lights blinked in layers of red, gold, and green, glowing from deep inside the generous arms of the Douglas fir. Small fragile ornaments, some shaped like stars, seashells, and Santas, graced the upper third of the tree.

On the cocktail table, a red felt cloth was unfurled, and covering it were all of the ornaments yet to be given a place on the tree.

"You made all of these…" he murmured.

"Yikes! Jake!" she screeched, teetering on the ladder, and he braced himself to catch her, but she didn't fall. She righted herself and shook her head at him. "You can't sneak up on me like that."

His face heated. "Yeah, sorry. These ornaments are all your work, aren't they?"

She climbed down the rungs to stand beside him.

"Yes," she said, pride plain in her voice.

"They're…gorgeous, really something."

"Thanks." She looked him in the eye. "What would you pay for one?"

"Um." He scratched his chin. "I…"

"Oh, right. You are the *no Christmas tree* guy. Yes, all of it is my work. I have my own collection, which basically is everything I've ever made or designed. Whichever ones I have duplicates of I sell. If it's popular, I make some more. As of today, I have rental space to create more inventory. I need to figure out my price point though. Cover the additional expense of the rental… I haven't had time yet to research what other people might be doing."

"Delicate. Glowing even without the lights from the tree." He wasn't looking at the ornaments though, pretty though they were.

Her face, already rosy from her exertions, colored some more. She made a face at him. "You're distracting me."

"Do you want me to leave? I came up to tell you I'm making dinner, and to see the tree of course." He placed the Santa ornament in his hand back down on the felt.

Chapter 16
Learning Curves

"No, that's fine. I'll only be a couple more minutes."

"I can help." His gaze zeroed in on hers. "If you want."

"Sure. Great. The more the merrier." Why was he so formal?

She climbed the ladder before common sense sent her back down again.

"You're so much taller I don't need the ladder, if you want to help. How about I pick the ornaments and you put them up?" She made her way back down the ladder, and as she stood next to him, the top of her head barely reached his shoulder.

"You being on solid ground is a great idea, pixie. Just give me basic instruction. You only need to say it once. I'm a quick study."

She swallowed, but the sour taste still coated her throat. His sincere smile twisted something tender in her belly. She kept her gaze down, tried to focus on the ornaments, schooling the shocked frown from her face because how sad was this? Jake just admitted he'd never hung ornaments on a Christmas tree. His parents had a shit ton to answer for in her book. Even Joss recognized the joy trimming a tree gave her and her brothers and let them have at it.

She only nodded and picked up a seahorse, a translucent green-gold that had been the very devil to get right. She placed it in Jake's broad palm and held her breath as he examined her work using a careful finger to stroke the fine tail and the green ribbon that served as a hanger.

She pointed. He hung. And they moved around the tree in record time until it was her turn to be the hanger of ornaments on the low branches.

"Which should I choose?" Jake flung an encompassing hand out to the array on the low table.

"Up to you, Jake. Like you said, you caught on quick." She grinned.

"Only because I'm hungry." He flexed his palm over the taut plane of his abs, abs she knew were beyond perfect. Which gave her an idea.

"How would you feel, I mean, would you object if I took your picture at the tree? For my social media feeds and website. People with objects sell better than objects alone. You can look it up."

"I believe you. But I…"

"I can take it so that your face is in shadow but maybe your profile shows when you're reaching up to place the ornament. Jake, the women who buy the ornaments, and yes, it's almost always women, will go nuts over you."

His mouth flattened. "Sure. Yeah. Tell me where you want me to stand. Because like I said, I'm hungry." His smile was lopsided and didn't quite reach his eyes.

She raised her cell phone to take the photo, then put it down again.

"You don't want to do this. The tree looks great. And we're just about done here. Are you inviting me to dinner? I *can* cook, you know."

"So can I. Tonight's my treat."

"Okay then, thank you." This dinner would be special even if he couldn't boil water. Because Honey couldn't recall a single time, not even a birthday, when someone cooked for her.

"Listen, it's…okay. If it'll help your business to photograph me, then go ahead." He spread his arms wide and nodded at the windows. "Now the sun's set, the way the tree's lights glow, I get why you want a photo now. It all looks…inviting."

"If you're sure? You don't have to do anything really." She snapped a few quick photos of him facing the window with the tree behind him and couple more when his gaze honed back to her. Then a few more as he slowly circled the tree using a careful forefinger to examine the variety of her designs.

The photos would be dynamite on her website and social media. But for the love of Christmas, why was a guy as drop-dead gorgeous as Jake so visibly uncomfortable when she requested a photo? No question he knew how hot he was.

It had something to do with how she asked him. What had she said? Women would go nuts when they saw him? Damn right because he had a droolworthy, buff body, the eyes and lips of a fallen saint. He was an unbelievably perfect specimen of manhood. But he wasn't reveling in that reality. Did he think she was objectifying him?

Aarrgghh. She knew nothing about men outside of the two scrawny teenagers who were her family. In her ignorance, she'd managed to screw up a compliment and marketing idea and turn it into an insult. *Way to go,*

Honey.

"Jake." She put a hand on his forearm, suppressed a shiver at the warmth of the corded tendon and sprinkling of the hair there revealed by his cuffed shirtsleeves.

"I'll show you these before I post anything. If you don't like them, I'll delete them all." *Maybe not all.* Would it be so wrong to save one of him for herself and only herself for when their time together was over?

His low voice was the darkest chocolate. "No, it's fine. I thought about it. I want you to have them. Use them however you want. Maybe you'll let me take a couple of you too?" He raised a suggestive brow, and heat suffused her face.

"Maybe." She croaked out the response as damp heat tingled between her thighs and a bowling-ball sized lump clogged her throat. "Did you say dinner? Let's go eat." Her voice was rusty, and she wobbled down the stairs ahead of him on noodle legs.

What is wrong *with you, Honey?* Yeah, sex with him was amazing, but now that she experienced it, the constant urge to be with him that way should start to fade, right?

But instead, the opposite was happening. The more she was with him; the more she wanted him. Something about the intimacy of sharing space, finding out that he'd *never* trimmed a Christmas tree. The details large and small about *him* as a person were making him into much more than a hookup. She was out of her depth, swimming frantically in dangerous waters, and all she wanted to do was let go and sink deep into him, drown in him. All she could think about was the next time they'd be together, and how much she craved knowing everything about him.

Everything. More. Again.

No. Now was not the time to worry about any of this. She still had a few weeks before her new job started, and she wouldn't waste their time together worrying about the inevitable end. She'd be in the moment. Things would be better when she started working at the cooperative tomorrow. When she could focus on her own stuff and her own career, she'd be able to put this temporary thing between her and Jake into a much smaller, much healthier space in her head.

She stalked over to his sink and pulled open the nearest drawer, finding nothing but barbeque tools. "Where do you keep your aprons?"

"I told you." His stern chief-of-security voice was back. "I'm cooking. Sit on the stool while I get things started. It's going to be simple but delicious."

"And I can't help?" She'd done ninety-nine percent of the cooking for Joss and the boys since she was fifteen and had long since mastered everything from eggs any style to Thanksgiving turkey with all the trimmings.

"This is my gig." He took an apron from a different drawer. It said "Boss Man" underneath a cartoon Dick Tracy. "From Regina, my executive assistant."

"Suits you." And of course it did. The apron only drew attention to his bronzed skin and powerful physique, and instantly Honey flashed back to where she'd been first thing this morning. Sitting on her hands trying her best not to grab him.

He filled a pasta pot from the wall faucet built into the backsplash at the stove and tossed in some salt. "If you want, you can get some wineglasses out and pour us something." He nodded toward the glasses hanging behind him.

"Aye, aye," she said and slid off the stool to comply while he took a lethal-looking knife and efficiently diced onion and garlic, setting it to simmer in a pot before pouring in the plum tomatoes from the jars on the counter.

"That smells like heaven," she said a couple of minutes later after he brushed chopped parsley and basil into the pan with the butt end of the knife and added meatballs. "So a man who can cook…and cleans as he goes. I'm impressed."

"Yeah, you learn to keep the decks clear in the navy."

He shrugged, and her gaze lingered on his massive shoulders before moving to the black chest hairs peeking out of the open collar of his white shirt.

Damn, girl, keep your focus. Converse.

"Jim said you were a SEAL? That must've been a heavy decision, you know, to join up?"

She still felt the stab of guilt over her choice to pursue a ceramics degree rather than the more financially secure engineering degree. But either way, she'd worked to pay expenses during both high school and college. Most of the kids she'd known had jobs too, but few were self-directed. Most had been content to bumble about for a good long while in search of a job or if they were lucky like Rick, slide into Daddy's business in town. Any of her classmates who'd enlisted joined at the infantry level. To pursue SEAL training on top of basic and succeed at it was only for the toughest of the tough.

He shrugged again. "I did it for the usual reasons, I

guess, something to do with wanting to be part of a team. Be a part of something bigger than me. Definitely, the desire to serve too. But to want to be a SEAL? You've got to have something to prove. I was no different. I was a kid. Excited, stupid, you name the adjective." His lips twisted into a self-deprecating smile. "And I needed to prove something, to myself and to other people."

"And?"

"And what?"

"And did you prove it?"

"Yeah, um, no, actually no. I learned. A lot. I learned the mind *can* force the body to endure pretty much anything. But...I also learned the body—no matter how strong, how skilled, or how fast—the body can't compel the mind to shut out its demons."

He looked up at her with unfathomable black eyes. "Some things you can't outrun."

He gulped his wine, shook his head. "Damn if I know how that all came up..." He ran a hand under the back collar of his shirt.

Honey forced a grin. "Me either. All I wanted to know was how you learned to cook."

He loosed a bark of laughter, and a little of the sexy glitter came back into his eyes. "Genes, baby. I'm Italian. It's all in here." He tapped his chest with the flat of his palm.

Honey shoved away the dozens of questions and comments fighting to come out of her mouth. Did she even have the right as his one-month hookup to quiz him? His past was his. Still, she'd bet he didn't open up about himself to many people. She wanted the privilege to learn more, to go beyond his achingly beautiful body, and find the man beneath the surface.

But not right now. Right now was about the present and the two of them. She ran her tongue over her lips. "Yeah, but will all that bragging stand up to a taste test? Let's see what you got there, Ricco."

He strode toward her with a wicked smile, taking off his apron and settling down onto the stool beside her in one quick move. Then he leaned in so their faces were barely an inch apart, and the gleam in his eye matched the lusty curve of his bottom lip.

"Keep it clean, Honey, unless you want to skip dinner and see right now the dessert I've got for you."

And oh, man, the struggle it was to keep her hands in her lap instead of climbing into his, once she saw the obvious evidence of his arousal.

"Hmmm, shouldn't we have sustenance to build our strength for later?" She fluttered her lashes, her rapid breathing giving lie to her teasing words.

"Coward," he said, chuckling.

Honey reveled in the unwilling laughter in his hard voice as much as she welcomed the fist of need coiling inside her belly.

His lips were almost on hers, and excitement rippled through her throat as she maintained her playful pose.

"Coward?" Her voice was breathy. "You're the distracting one, keeping me from tasting your tempting…" She licked her lips again and watched as his hands come out to grip the edge of the marble.

He pushed himself up to stand. "I forgot the cheese." His voice was gruff, strangled. Then he turned back to her, all polite host. "Do you want cheese on your pasta?"

"Jake, I want to taste it all, exactly the way you want me to." She watched as his fists clenched and unclenched at her words.

Chapter 17
I Can Resist Everything Except Temptation

Jake gripped the cheese grater tighter to disguise the faint tremor in his hand. This hookup was backfiring on him—big time. Living with Honey in the same house was turning out to be way too intense. She tempted and challenged him in a way no woman ever had. Yes, their hookup had been born because they both acknowledged and gave in to the heat between them.

But he'd never counted on wanting to be with her, just *be* with her, to hang out in the daylight hours. He didn't expect to care about how or with whom she spent her time; he never thought he'd be curious about her work, and now he'd cooked dinner for her.

Making dinner at home was no big deal, because yeah, they lived together, and why not? But the laughter and the confidences he was sharing with her after only a few days were strange and totally outside his experience.

Keeping their intimacy confined to sex was the plan.

Now that plan was shot to shit. She was a genie sprung from a bottle, and now that she was in his life and he in hers, he had no clue how he'd get back to just sex. Even though he wanted it, wanted her, all the damn time.

"That's good." She put a hand out to stop the

stream of grated cheese over her pasta. Her dancing eyes sparkled like topaz, and damned if she didn't poke the tip of her tongue out in concentration as she twirled the spaghetti onto her fork.

"Oh, man, this is really good." Her eyes closed on a sigh as she sat back after she'd demolished half her portion in moments.

He couldn't be bothered to wipe the dopey smile off his face. He liked feeding her even if all he did was boil water and dice a bunch of fresh herbs and mix it all together. He walked their plates to the sink.

"I can't take credit for any of it. I get these ingredients from the market on Thompson Street. But I do get off seeing you enjoy your food."

"Oh, do you?" Now her eyes took on a teasing glitter. They were both one hundred percent aware that now they'd finished their entrees, it was time for dessert.

He walked toward her, eying the way she lounged back on her stool. "Yeah," he said, "you were in a hurry to finish, so either dinner was very good…"

"It was…"

"Or you want to get to the dessert portion of our evening."

"You did make certain promises, Mr. Ricco. And yes, I very much enjoyed dinner. As a matter of fact, my clothes are feeling"—she arched her back and wiggled in her seat—"tight after all that food."

"Is that so?" His gaze skimmed over the T-shirt hugging her braless breasts.

She waved a hand in front of her flushed face. "Is it warm in here or is it just me?"

"Oh, it's warm, pixie."

He couldn't wait. In a quick maneuver, he whisked her from the stool onto the lower portion of the bi-level center island, ignoring her surprised intake of breath. He eased her thighs apart to stand between them before running his forefinger over the thin cotton of her T-shirt, giving the peaked nipples a flick. She jolted from the same electricity that flew up his arm.

"Ms. Hill, I trust your meal has fortified you?" His gaze tracked her heavy-lidded eyes, satisfied she was as hot for him as he was for her.

"Oh, yeah. I'm up for anything now. And I see you are too." Her sultry lids dropped to his lap, and damned if she didn't wet her lips with her tongue again.

And that was it for him. He swooped down to capture her mouth under his, straining so hard against her slight body she swayed backward. He put a forearm behind her back to keep her right there with every bit of her from breast to thigh plastered against him.

Nothing tasted as sweet as her lips, and he couldn't get enough. He drank from them again and again, breaking off only for little forays to the satin skin of her ears and neck. Every time his lips left hers, she tugged him back down, her small hand firm against his neck, whispering, "More."

Impatient with the clothing separating his skin from hers, he slipped the tee over her head, then watched as she shivered under his hands as they moved over every inch of her breasts and torso.

"Honey!" He couldn't keep the stern command out of his tone because damn, he was on a hair trigger. "Is this where we're going now? Do you want me? Here? Now?"

"Yes. Here. Now." Her lips parted on a smile as

she skimmed a hand down his stomach to tug his shirt out of his pants, then moved on to unfasten his belt. "This is exactly what I want."

He planted a kiss on her nose. "This…is why I can't get enough of you. We're always on the same page."

"Hmm." Her face sobered. "Are you saying I'm predictable?" She scraped a questing hand along his zipper while he yanked her jeans down her thighs and all the way off her legs. Catching him off guard, she reached down to find him heavy and hard in her hand.

"Ah, God, never. You're, um, edible, delectable." His hand closed over hers to stop her exploration. "I won't last if you keep that up." He retaliated by running a bold finger along the satin dampness of her thong. "It's like I've been waiting for you forever, and it's only been…" He closed his eyes on a long breath.

"Yeah, a little more than twelve hours." The surprise in her words matched the crazy timetable in his head. What was happening here? In the service, he'd always been rough and ready for leave, after training sessions designed to build and exhaust body and mind, and missions that demanded every ounce of mental and physical concentration. He'd exercised control, he abided by consent, but still when it came down to it, any woman would do. Since then, building up his business had consumed his waking hours, and eighteen-hour days didn't leave much time for women. He was up front. If she was into a one-night thing, okay. If not, no harm, no foul. And always, always was the knowledge pushed to the back of his mind that the time would come when he would keep his promise, return to Italy full time, and enter into a marriage designed to resurrect his ancestors' legacy and return both prestige and financial stability to the Boniface name.

But this was the here and now, and the sight, the scent, the sound of this one woman had him wrapped up so tight, and his fractured breathing told him he was on the edge—again—for her, just her. Damn right, they'd use every second of the month they set as their outside limit. The end would come soon enough. Too soon. But until then he was on lockdown for Honey and Honey alone. Twenty-four seven.

He forced himself to stop for a second. Stand still, breathe, and observe. Absorb this woman who had his stomach in knots and him hard and hot as a poker.

She was exquisite, splayed before him like a wet dream, her skin an even gold with light freckles on her nose and shoulders. Her tight nipples were like cherries, and her slender neck was exposed to let him suckle the sensitive skin there.

He battled an animal urge to mark her there with his teeth, fought a primitive instinct to show the world his claim on his pixie princess.

She lifted heavy lids, beckoning him with a tantalizing smile and a raised brow.

"One of us still has *way* too many clothes on." Her challenging gaze roved over him again.

"Don't care. Not this time," he muttered. "Can't wait." He didn't have the brain cells to form sentences or the patience to take off the rest of his clothing. She was here, she was his, and he needed her now. He slid his palm under the hot silk of her rear, pulled her to the edge of the marble, and positioned himself at her entrance. She urged him forward, with her legs around his waist and her feet at his back, and then he was there where he needed to be. Inside the sweet world they created. The escape they found together whenever and wherever they chose.

Her lush lips opened on a moan, then she bit down on her lower lip and sucked in a breath as he rolled on protection and surged inside, filling her tight space, forcing her muscles to stretch and contract. In spite of all his plans, he couldn't go any slower. With his arms bracketed on each side of her body, he was close enough to hear every gasping breath she took. So close his chest hairs scraped against her flushed torso. But he wouldn't allow her to bear the weight of his heavier body as he pumped in a hard, punishing rhythm. Sweat beaded her upper lip, and he leaned down to lick it off with his tongue. His fingers found her nipples again and again, and he delighted in tormenting them. His lips brushed her ear. "You got me crazy, Honey, so hot, so damn tight, I'm not gonna last…"

Her impish smile appeared, and she gripped his shoulders. "Take our time next time," she breathed, running a soothing tongue along his lower lip, as she clasped him tighter with her legs. With that permission, with the amazing realization there would be a next time and a time after that, he pushed into her with wild, painfully heavy thrusts, hands clutching her knees as he finished with a guttural stream of praise and curse words.

When he fell forward, his cheek landed against her chest, near her neck. Her hand came up, languid, to stroke his cheek, then sank into the damp hair at his nape, feathering lightly against the back of his head. Usually he couldn't take any touching after sex. Usually he needed to shake out his limbs and do something to break contact, to move on from the intimacy of the moment.

Now he was sunk in the unlikeliest of positions, bent at the waist resting his cheek against the warmth of this woman's velvet skin and supple body, with neither the energy nor the desire to move one inch. Only the knowledge that her back lay against the cold marble and she was trapped under his heavy body propelled him to gain his feet and deal with the condom.

He eased the zip of his pants half way up his still throbbing erection, laced gentle hands under her legs and shoulders and gathered her fully into his arms. Not stopping to find a blanket or her clothes, he angled down to shoulder off the light switch and headed to the stairs.

She spoke against his neck, her lips tickling skin he'd never considered an erogenous zone till now. "Jake, I can walk, you know."

"I know you can, but it seems you lost all your clothes, and even though I want to keep you naked tonight, I don't want you cold."

"Keep me naked *and* warm, huh?" Her dark brows lowered, but her frown turned into a giggle. "How're you going to do that?"

"Well." He deposited her in the middle of his bed. "Body heat, pixie." He finished unbuttoning the shirt she'd started to unbutton earlier, kicked off his boots, and stripped off his shirt, jeans, and boxers. "Fair's fair. I'll be naked too. The way I see it, we have all night to keep each other warm. My pride won't let me sleep until I show you just how good I can make it for you." He watched as she licked her lips, her intense gaze traveling over him and his rampant arousal as he stood near the mattress beside her.

"News flash, Jake. It was perfect downstairs. But…" She looked at him from underneath her lashes in the way that made him want to pin her under him, but he wouldn't do that. Not ever.

"Far be it from me to stop you from trying to improve on perfection." She angled herself up to place a hand on his straining flesh, and Jake sucked in a tortured breath and tightened his lower abs to let her play for a moment. When she would've taken him in her mouth, he backed away.

"Let me put it this way. I won't stop till you tell me you've had enough or we both fall asleep. Okay? So where were we? Right, yeah, you were just about to let me warm you up."

Seeing she was in the perfect position, he stroked his hands down her smooth legs in a slow up and down motion, widening them till she was completely exposed to him.

Then he knelt on the rug and worshipped his pixie princess.

"See how good I can make it? Tell me, how long do you think you can last; how long do you *want* to last? I could feast on this sweet honey all night. Are you all warmed up now? Guess not, you're still shivering. I better warm you up some more."

With every question and comment, he teased and tormented her sweet flesh with his fingers and tongue—playing her, playing with her till heat was pouring off both of them and the sheen of sweat on them made her legs slippery. He held on, his hands moving to grip her just tight enough to keep her just where he had to have her. He pushed her to the writhing brink of the waterfall, and when she was about to go over, he brought her back again and again, ignoring her panting pleas and disjointed moans till she groaned his name and begged him to finish her. So he did. He drank her in. Everything about her—the salty-caramel taste of her, the slippery smooth skin of her, the panting breaths bursting from her, the clutch of her hands gripping the sheets and his hair as she bucked against the unrelenting tide ripping through her.

He dropped onto the mattress at her side, satisfied by her radiant smile. Her eyes, now the clear gray of a rain-soaked pavement, searched his.

"Wow." She ran her forefinger down his chest and back up again to his jaw, lingering to trace his lips. "I'm officially speechless."

He hid the grin that split his face by nuzzling into her neck.

"And boneless as a bowl of noodles. Must be all the pasta I ate." Her eyes fluttered shut, and he pulled the sheet up to cover them.

****

He blinked his eyes open to the barest hint of dawn light filtering through the silk drapes and judged it thirty minutes before he had to get out of bed. But yeah, his body was up already. His erection saluted Honey as she slept on—her arms crushing the pillow under her chin. He couldn't remember the last time he'd slept so deeply or so well, but he had no urge to get out of bed. Not yet. Not while Honey was curled up beside him with a sexy half smile on her dreaming face. They'd exhausted each other last night. Good. He tugged the sheet over them again and carefully rested his arm over her waist.

The vivid sex dream was back. Since he'd met her, every morning he woke up horny and hard as an untried teenager. It didn't matter how the events of any day drained him. He fought it sometimes because damn, it was like he was on a Viagra diet, but his body and his mind played him and coerced him till every muscle was tight, rigid, and restless with need.

But he'd take those dreams over the vicious, detailed nightmares that still plagued him after twenty years. Before now, before his time with Honey, the true-to-life, sight-and-sound recollections had only given him rest when he was on a mission. If he was honest, what kept him in the teams was the complete numbness he experienced as he set out, single-minded to accomplish his assigned goal. The frozen feeling, the complete absence of anything else in his conscious or unconscious state, kept him going back for more. As long as he was out there, focused on completing a task, succeeding in an operation, organizing, planning, and completing a mission, the nightmares could be kept at bay.

Then his dad had taken ill, and once he decided to leave the teams, the nightmares returned full force along with the realization that day by day, he was watching the only person in the world he loved and who loved him back waste away.

When cool air hit his pulsing erection, his eyes snapped open.

This was not a dream. This was the earthy reality of his woman sharing his bed at dawn and using her mouth on him like he paid for it.

"Honey, what the?" His shoulders lifted off the mattress as he groaned.

She lifted her head, a teasing light in her eyes.

"Oh, did I wake you? I'm trying to be quiet, but it's"—she gave his erection a wink—"too hard."

He loosed a gritty chuckle. Only Honey could make him laugh when he was harder than steel. "I'm right on the edge." He lifted a hand to cover her lips just as she feathered her hand down his chest and over his belly till it settled again on his jutting flesh.

"Please. Let me do this for you." She pushed his shoulders till he fell back on the pillows. He lay on the cool sheets, his harsh breaths the only sound in the morning stillness. The air was thick with the scent of her, of them, their sweat, their arousal, the night before. She played with him much as he did with her, and her perfect mouth was heaven. Through half-closed lids, he memorized her, inhaling agonized breaths. And then savoring the sight of her pale hair against his much darker skin—the sight of her tasting him—and that was it. Game over. Against his will, he rocketed into a shuddering release.

Honey sat back on her heels, a satisfied smile on her lush lips. "Why should you have all the fun?"

Chapter 18
Private Paradise

Fun was the last thing on his mind as he stood military straight in his tux, a big, "fake Jake" smile plastered on his face as he glad-handed a splashy group of Long Island's elite at Connor's "Keep Montauk Wild" Fundraiser. Honey ruled his thoughts, and since she wasn't here tonight, all the fun was already sucked out of the evening.

The irony of it was of course Connor would've welcomed Honey at his event. The mansion by the sea was chock full of glitz and glamour. But not a silver-haired pixie in sight.

So why hadn't he asked her to come with him?

He had his reasons. For one thing, how irritating would it be to put up with Connor's ribbing and speculation about why he invited a specific woman, because showing up at these things stag was his usual MO? Added to that, he accepted these invitations not only to support his buddy and the cause, but also to mix with the movers and the shakers who were the bread and butter of his business. His date deserved the bulk of his attention and not to feel like an accessory while he schmoozed. He called BS. Honey was nobody's accessory. With her agile mind and sense of humor, she would've challenged and charmed anyone she met, whether he was with her or not.

Dig deeper, Jake.

It was also a fact that these events on the east end of Long Island were, even in the depths of winter, a mecca for an amazing array of gold-coast women, and tonight was no exception. In the past, if he'd been lucky, and yeah, cocky Jake would say luck had nothing to do with it, he'd count on meeting a like-minded woman for a night of mind-numbing, anonymous sex with no regrets and no repeats.

But that wasn't it either. He wasn't looking for a night's entertainment. He was simply *not* interested. All he could see in his mind's eye was a mouth so sassy and sinful he sported wood any time he flashed back on one of their encounters or even one of their conversations.

So why hadn't he asked Honey to Connor's event?

Tonight Connor had arrived with a gorgeous woman, the kind of statuesque brunette Jake always used to go for. But when he introduced himself to her, he did a double take at the sight of the enormous ring on Lacey's engagement finger and was forced to hide his astonishment that none other than Connor had put it there.

He concealed his shock by going with his fall back, party-Jake attitude, flirting with Lacey, and hell, yeah, the sole highlight of this lonely evening without Honey was seeing Connor stone-faced and possessive, rapidly putting distance between Jake and his woman. Lucky they were in a public place, at Connor's own event, when Jake yanked his chain because Connor's navy reputation as a brawler was well earned. Of course, Connor had nothing to worry about. Lacey was looking at Connor like he hung the moon for her.

Besides, Jake had perfection at home. At home. *When was the last time he'd thought about the townhouse as home?*

It pained him to acknowledge Honey would've loved coming to tonight's event. In the Uber on his way there, he'd remembered how she told him just yesterday she was torn between doing some of the sightseeing she always wanted to do in the city and making the most of her hours at the artists' cooperative. Unspoken was their agreement, that unless she was on her shift at Duffy's, every night was theirs—alone, together. He was so needy he'd considered asking her how much she made a night at Duffy's so he could pay her whatever it was to stay home. But the idea had died a quick death at the thought of Honey's ballistic reaction to a suggestion like that. It sounded way too much like he'd be paying for her time because their nights always ended one way—in his bed.

In fact, tonight was his first night away from her since the first night. He'd managed with her help to arrange most of his schedule to coincide with her nights at Duffy's so when they were both working, all he had to do was arrive at the pub in time to walk her home.

He should've invited her. She would have reveled in the festive holiday lights, appreciated the ornaments dripping and shimmering from the towering Christmas trees in every corner in this glittering room in the mansion by the ocean. She would've been eager to discuss and support Connor's Foundation's goals to protect the east end beach environment.

But here was the ugly truth—Jake was selfish. He couldn't make himself forget their time together was limited. Plain and simple, he didn't want to share.

Besides, these functions were not only filled with glamorous, successful, well-heeled women, they attracted their fair share of rolling-in-it masters of the universe.

Why should he expose her to those guys? Dogs who'd pant after her, lapping up her unique charm and vying for her attention when he craved her entire focus on him?

Guys like him.

No. Calling himself a dog was an insult to dogs. He was an asshole. He was a jealous asshole.

He worked the room like he usually did, slipped into the skin of the laughing, carefree Jake. A few people asked for his card, and he provided it. But when he'd circled the ballroom once, he got out of there as soon as he decently could. Connor probably didn't notice anyway, wrapped as he was in Lacey's arms on the dance floor, gazing at her with a single-minded focus Jake had never seen on his face before and would've ridiculed if the look didn't remind Jake uncomfortably of the way he couldn't help trying to memorize a certain heart-shaped face.

So now what? It looked like two of his closest buddies were settling down with the women of their dreams. Where the hell did that leave him?

Dreading the inevitable day he finalized his pre-arranged match in Italy and Honey moved out and on to her internship.

Don't feel sorry for yourself, asshole. It was only ever going to be a hookup. Remember. You're alive. Cesco isn't. And maybe when you finally make good on your promise, the nightmares will stop.

****

The Uber was just turning the corner onto Jane Street when she called.

"Jake? Are you home yet?"

"Just about."

"Good."

"What's up?" He checked his watch. "And where are you at one in the morning, if you don't know that I'm not home yet?" He hated the sound of panicked jealousy in his voice.

Her voice cooled but stayed matter-of-fact. "I'm on Bleecker Street in a bar. Um, it's called Roll with It. Do you know it?"

"Honey, what the hell, yeah, I know it. It's a dive, underage age drinking, fighting, what the hell," he repeated, then forced his voice into an even tone. "What're *you* doing there?"

"My brothers are in town, and they've gotten themselves in a bit of trouble. Can you come?"

"Yeah. Stay right there. I'll be there in a minute."

He directed the driver to turn east toward Bleecker Street. Honey's words played over and over as his mind conjured up all manner of sick scenarios young kids fall prey to in the city. Her voice had sounded calm though. As a matter of fact, it'd acquired a steely quality when he questioned her whereabouts at this hour. She wasn't pleased, and damn, he'd usually been able to keep his need to know everything about her under control. She *could* take care of herself. Honey didn't need him to protect her. She could decide to go out with her brothers at any hour, and it was literally *not* his business. But they were in some kind of trouble, so she'd called him. He couldn't get there fast enough.

When they got to Bleecker, he left the driver and

his car to fight the vehicle and foot traffic. The usual late-night Greenwich Village horde flowed all over the streets, tonight supplemented by the visiting holiday crowds. He sprinted up the last block, dodging the strings of half-drunk, strolling tourists.

Honey's hair was a beacon in the low-lit interior as he pushed through the front of the room, past the small crowd head nodding and singing along as a Queen cover artist proclaimed—they were the champions—to reach her in the corner by the pool table. She was flanked by two, tall, scraggly-haired teenagers, who themselves were positioned in between two beefy and broad NYPD officers.

He approached and nodded to the officers. Good thing he knew them because who knew what Honey's brothers had been up to?

"Alonzo. Dennis. What's up?"

"Hey, Jake. Yo, Jake," they answered before Alonzo stepped forward.

"So here's the deal. I get a call, and I'm about to bust these two identical baby bozos for the fakest ID I've yet to see this whole year when their sister"—he looked disbelievingly from petite, fair-haired Honey to the tall, dark-haired young men at her side—"says she knows you, and they're friends of yours, and can she please call you?"

"Right." Jake looped his wrists casually in front of him, nodded. "Okay, so yeah. She *is* their sister, and they're all friends of mine."

Jake rubbed a hand along the back of his neck as he took a good look at the twins, then decided, confident.

"This is Derek." He pointed to the one who was slightly behind Honey. "That one's Donnie," he said, jerking his chin at the identical one who had his jaw set at a pugnacious angle. "They're all friends of mine and all staying with me. I was out at an event"—he waved a hand at his tuxedo—"or I would've short circuited this plan before they got here."

"Well, as long as you can vouch for them…" Dennis, the older officer, shook his head and lifted a disgusted brow until it disappeared inside the bill of his hat.

"I can." Jake clasped his hands behind his back, the picture of relaxation.

The younger cop stepped forward again and got up in Derek and Donnie's faces. "Listen up. You were lucky this time. If I see you two again tryin' to buy drinks with this crappy ID, which, by the way, is a personal insult to me that yer walking around with, there's nothing you'll be able to do about it. I'll haul your asses down to the precinct just to make an example of you. Understood?"

Derek and Donnie nodded quickly and kept on nodding till Jake interjected.

"Officer Dolan didn't hear you."

"Yessir," they said in unison.

"And next time, you better bring your ID too." Dolan looked down at Honey with a half-smile, and Jake stepped between them.

"Back off, Lonny." Jake knew his smile had a savage edge. "She's of age."

Jake couldn't stop himself from resting a proprietary hand on Honey's shoulder as they all headed out of the bar. The walk back to the townhouse was accomplished in silence.

Once inside, Jake loosened his bow tie and took off

his jacket, as he ushered them all into the kitchen.

He poured himself a scotch, and with a lift of his brow, asked Honey what she wanted. "White," she answered.

He took a quick gulp of his scotch and offered each of the brothers his hand.

"Pleasure to meet you, Donnie. Pleased to meet you too, Derek."

They mumbled their embarrassed hellos, and Jake waved a hand toward the stools at the center island. "Sit down, guys."

Derek slouched on the seat as if trying to make his five-foot-ten body disappear while Donnie only circled behind his.

Donnie leveled a direct look at Jake. "How did you do that? How did you know which one of us is which? You've never met us before."

"Observation. You're the drummer, a little more of a talker. Derek over there has calluses on his fingers and hands from the guitar. Your sister talks about you two non-stop." He glanced over at Honey who was sipping her wine. She raised a brow, which almost turned into an eye-roll. She was uncharacteristically quiet and obviously pissed. At her brothers for obvious reasons and him for his jealous quizzing earlier.

"That's cool." It was Donnie again. "Rick got our names wrong probably eighty percent of the time." He shook his head. "And he's known us since we were in first grade."

Derek snuck an uneasy glance at Honey at the mention of Rick's name. She mouthed back at him, "No worries."

Jake's lips twisted. "Yeah, I met, er, Dick. He

didn't strike me as a guy who had superior observational skills." The boys guffawed, and this time Honey did roll her eyes, then held her palms in front of her.

"Enough. I'm in the room, okay? No more deflecting. You two let me know at the last minute you were arriving for a visit. That means I didn't mention it to Jake who's my landlord. Then before you even come over here, you decide to go out to get hammered using phony ID. You guys aren't even sixteen yet… When you texted me to come over to that bar, that's the first I heard you were in town. C'mon guys. Really?"

Donnie shrugged. "Carl, you remember him, Honey? He told us about a few places on Bleecker Street with live music. As long as we were down here and your place being so close, we thought, you know…we don't *look* underage, and well, we figured…we're only here for the weekend so…"

"It was dumb, Honey," Derek apologized. "Thanks for getting us out of the situation, um, Mister…"

"It's Jake. And your sister is right. What if I hadn't been around? What if those cops decided to make an example of you? They like to do that especially during the holidays." He let that sink in before he threw them a bone.

"I was planning to ask Honey to the Met tomorrow. There's an Asian ceramic exhibit there." Her gaze shot to him then, and his face heated because he hadn't asked her yet. Who knew if she thought it was a worthwhile exhibit or maybe she'd already gone?

Sitting in the Uber, feeling like crap because he hadn't asked her to Connor's event, he'd googled a list of art galleries and ceramics exhibitions in the city and came up with the biggest, showiest one he could find. "You guys can come with or you can do something else and meet up with us. Sunday night there are clubs with live music all over the city especially now in the holiday season. I don't know what you want to hear, but we can all go check some out before you have to head back."

"That would be awesome, Jake. We have a really late bus back Sunday night because we're on break so, yeah, that's awesome." Derek was nodding and beaming.

"Final question, then I'll show you where you're going to sleep. You guys hungry?"

Honey burst out laughing. "Fatal error, Jake. These guys might be rail thin, but…"

"Yeah, I know, I remember being their age, and I was a swimmer, so I was always hungry. I used to scarf up Devil Dogs by the box."

He remembered the piss poor selection of food at boarding school and forcing himself to eat whatever he could stomach, including whatever junk food he could grab in the cafeteria. Everyone training on the swim team had to consume mega calories. And his homesickness for his dad was always wrapped up in his craving for authentic Italian. Sometimes Dad had cooked, and sometimes they just went out in Little Italy and celebrated. Having an Italian dinner with Honey the other night had been the first time he made a dinner like that without memories of his father turning the food to acid in his stomach.

He and Honey worked in tandem to prep a quick meal for the boys who downed two glasses of milk each, plus sandwiches piled high with Italian ham, turkey, and mozzarella.

Jake handed Honey the key to the third-floor apartment. "Sorry, guys, I didn't know you were coming, or I would've stocked up on ice cream, cookies, and cake. Honey and I finished all the dessert." It was an innocent enough comment, but Honey flushed, no doubt recalling their midnight feast the other night, as he wanted her to. She turned her back on him and headed to the door.

"I'll grab some extra towels and meet you upstairs," Jake said.

Chapter 19
Reality Check

"I can't believe you found such an amazing apartment in the city, Honey." Derek stood in the center of the bedroom. He was clearly hit with the same kind of awe she'd felt when she first moved into Jake's townhouse. In his case it looked like there was a large dose hero worship of Jake mixed in.

"Yeah, it's sweet, and I only have it for a month, so that's how I can afford it. If I had to pay rent here any longer, I'd be out of money in a couple of months. Next month I start my internship, and the hours are weird and long. On top of that, it's a long commute, so I've started looking for another place near there. Probably a share house or a studio apartment. So I have to enjoy...everything here...while it lasts."

Honey had already forced herself to check the online listings a couple of times. No surprise, Jake and her apartment here were fantasies on every level. There would be no duplicating either of them. She'd entered into this arrangement with her eyes open though. She knew both the dream man and the dream apartment were temporary. If Rick and her ill-fated apartment deal with Trey were the dregs of experience, Jake proved to be the apex.

Her first hookup was flawless. Score one for Honey and the hookup gods. How had she found a guy attentive enough to her conversation to be able to tell identical twins apart on his first try?

But yeah. With every detail she discovered about Jake and after every blissful night, she was ever more conscious of the temporary nature of their relationship and the knowledge that for her, Jake wasn't just a hookup anymore. Maybe he never had been. He was the real deal. Somebody who paid attention to her in bed and out, somebody whose secrets she wanted the right to know and whose future she wanted to be a part of.

Every day she woke up sure this would be the day she'd tell him. The day she'd admit her feelings for him went beyond the physical. But he hadn't given her the slightest indication he wanted something more. He had a life that didn't include her as evidenced by his black-tie event tonight. But man, if he did, she'd sign on in a heartbeat.

She owed it to herself to be honest. But working up the courage was tough. Because part of her knew telling him how she felt might end it all that much quicker. Who could blame her for wanting to live inside their happy bubble as long as she could?

The first step in Honey's career, her internship, was a few weeks away. But the knowledge that moving toward her goals meant saying goodbye to Jake left her trying to figure out how she could crowd a little bit more of Jake and every perfect moment into their short-term affair than the day before. Left her memorizing those moments so she could pack them up and take them with her when their time was up.

Logic told her to forget about the end game and focus on today. Forget about all the ways she thought she and Jake meshed so completely because she had zero experience hooking up, and Rick had proven long term wasn't her strength either. Logic demanded she check the box that read short-term sex—no, amazing short-term sex—and move on.

The co-op was her happy place. Every hour back working in a studio was productive; she was creating at a fast pace. And her massive daily output came with the reward of more time in the evenings with Jake.

"Oh. I thought…never mind." Derek's flustered voice trailed off. He flushed to the roots of his flopping dark hair, and his brother snickered.

"What he wants to say is…we thought, we think, you and Jake are hooking up." Donnie put it out there, turning from the window and looking Honey straight in the eye.

"This isn't our business, Don." Derek elbowed his brother.

Honey ignored the heat of her flaming face and managed to keep her big-sister bravado in place. "No, it isn't your business. All I'll say is this time next month I'll be living in a different place, and I'll have a new job so when you come see me, we'll have someplace new to explore."

Upbeat as she always was with them, she hooked her hands through their elbows. She'd been their surrogate mom for so long, their champion big sister, it was tough to be anything but positive and strong. Would she ever open up to them about something so private, something that's ending soon anyway and she wanted to keep all to herself? Especially on the heels of her embarrassing breakup with Rick? No. *Never*.

Who would ever want to admit the silly deluded dreams, now abandoned, that'd kept her tied to

Caryville these last three years since her graduation, the hankering for some pipedream about family she'd made up instead of pursuing her career? At least Donnie and Derek benefitted. It would've been tough to leave them with just Joss when they were twelve. Now at fifteen plus, they were pushing six feet tall. They weren't the cuddly babies she'd fussed over as a ten-year-old.

Her personal life was a mess, but they could understand her desire to work at her career.

Their mother and Joss were prime examples of the power of pursuing one's profession. As much as Honey was proud to finally embark on her chosen career, it hit her hard now how solitary the life could be. She'd swear Joss had never had another woman after her mother. And grateful as she was there hadn't been a parade of women in and out of their lives in the years since her mother left, he must've been lonely. He was definitely bitter. And what about Willow? Had her mother found a replacement for Joss or maybe multiple replacements? No one she'd ever mentioned, even in passing. No one she wanted her kids to know about anyway. Or had there been no one since Joss for her too? Had Joss been the one? Did she still care for him even though her career took first place?

"Too bad, he's a cool contact to have in the city." In the way of teenagers, Derek let the subject go and turned to face Honey.

"Yeah," Donnie chimed in, "really too bad. He knows all the cops *and* all the best places for music…"

Honey refocused on her brothers and forced a chuckle. "Let's make the most of tomorrow, then."

Jake appeared at the door as she opened it to leave. He handed the towels to her, and she stacked them on the dresser near the door.

"Goodnight, guys. Oh, I almost forgot. Tomorrow I'll show you the Christmas tree in my apartment. You're gonna love it. It's epic."

Jake was still on the other side of the door, and he lifted a brow as Honey put her finger to her lips and took his hand. They went back downstairs to his bedroom.

Jake stopped just inside the door. Clasped her shoulders with heavy hands, then waited till she raised her gaze to his. "I wasn't sure if you'd want to…be here, be with me tonight. What about Derek and Donnie?"

"They already asked. And I told them the truth."

"Really?" His straight black brows shot up in disbelief.

"Well, not exactly truth but not an outright lie. I told them I'm a short-term tenant, and I intend to make the most of my time here. And that *is* the honest truth."

He started to unbutton his tux shirt. Honey flopped into the chair by the bed, her legs flung over the arm, her gaze riveted to Jake.

The moonless night turned them to shadows in the room. Honey reached over to turn on the lamp.

"What are you doing?" He stopped midstream, the shirt half off his shoulders.

"I'm watching you undress." She'd never get tired of him—or his body, in clothes or out of it. It didn't matter if he was in a T-shirt, a tuxedo, or a leather jacket. She wanted to commit every single thing about him to memory. The grace and strength of his large, tanned hands, the faint sheen of sweat at his temples, there since he'd raced into the bar during tonight's encounter with the NYPD, the dusting of coal-black hair that trailed from his chest down to the waist of his pants. He kicked off his shoes and tossed his shirt. She couldn't suppress her sharp intake of breath when his hand reached the buckle of his belt.

She couldn't tell because even with the lamp on the room was still mostly in two a.m. shadow, but his expression looked like it clouded, and his movements turned awkward. Just like when they trimmed the Christmas tree. Damn.

"Am I making this weird? You have a beautiful body. I can say that because I'm an artist." She wanted to waggle her brows, but something in his uncomfortable stance made her settle for a solemn smile.

His gaze was as intent on her as hers was on him. "I'm no artist, but…" The weighted moment passed and he shook it off, lifting a leering, suggestive brow.

"But small-breasted blondes turn you on?"

"Guess they do. Guess one does," he amended huskily. He was naked now, and the proof of his attraction was staring her right in the eye. "Come over here," he said.

Her body awakened as much to the gravelly whisper as to his seriously sexy body. "You'll have to be quiet," he said. "No matter what. We don't want to answer any nosy questions tomorrow." Heat poured off her skin at his words.

When Honey stood on shaking legs, he opened his arms, and she ran into the warmth of his chest as he lifted her against him. "Time for you to lose these clothes too," he muttered in her ear. Obliging, she lifted the T-shirt over her head. His hands and his lips immediately latched onto her breasts, and when she would've given a little squeal of delight, he placed a hand over her mouth. "Shhh."

He eased her down till she was in the middle of the bed and then helped her shimmy out of her jeans. Honey grabbed his shoulders to pull him down to cover her. Jake vaulted onto his forearms.

"We've never done it like this," she whispered. "And I want to."

He shook his head. "It's the most basic way of all. And you know, pixie, I like to think I have more finesse." He lowered his dark brows.

"You do. But I want to feel you. On me as well as in me." Amazing, considering everything, the self-conscious heat that suffused her skin as she said it.

And she was still whispering, because this felt like a revelation that was too personal, and even though they were talking about a plain vanilla sex act, somehow the thought of Jake on her and over her and in her was the most erotic and romantic coupling her imagination could conjure. *Because it was with him.*

"Truth? I think I'm going to hurt you if I'm on top."

"No, no, you won't. I'll tell you if you do."

She reached for him.

"No. Not the first time," he said. "I can't, not the first time."

They could never go slow the first time no matter what they did.

"I promise it'll be all right. I'll tell you if it isn't."

"Okay." He lowered himself slowly, his forearms straining, rubbed his body up and down against hers. Teased her lips apart with his tongue. "You know I always end up giving you want you want."

Her face lit with a pouty smirk. "I count on that."

He showed her he knew—based on instinct and their experience—everything she wanted. Confident hands scraped over her hips and thighs till she was panting and breathless. Her hands climbed up his back to his shoulders, pulling him down, down to her, not satisfied till his sweat-slicked body was plastered on top of hers and he was totally inside of her aching, needy body. And all in complete silence.

****

They were side by side now. Jake arranged the sheet over their cooling skin like he always did and reached over to brush the sweat-dampened hair from her forehead. She sighed and burrowed into his chest.

"Thanks," she said. "For getting Derek and Donnie out of that situation. I owe you one."

His low chuckle rumbled under her cheek. "However much I like the idea of you owing me one anything, it's no big deal. I still remember being an overgrown fifteen-year-old."

"But twins egg each other on. Which makes it worse because Donnie usually has a brilliantly dumb idea, and Derek doesn't want to say no and seem like a wimp, and then, well, you saw what happened."

"Yeah, I saw. I had a brother. It was like that with us too. We weren't twins, but we were a year apart. Very close."

"You *had* a brother?" Oh, no. The pain he tried to glide over with his flat words was there, throbbing under the surface.

"Yeah, he died. I was twelve, and he was thirteen."

She sat up. "Oh, my God. Jake. You were a boy.

How horrible. I'm so sorry." She placed a hand on his shoulder, and his flinch rejected the contact for a moment before he relaxed under the warmth in her eyes.

"You don't have to tell me about it, but if you want to talk, I'll listen."

Seconds passed. His eyes blanked till he focused on nothing at all. "It was all a long time ago. And I wasn't a boy. I was old enough. Old enough I should've known better. He drowned." His voice was as dark as she'd ever heard it. Not stern, just weary and so sad.

Her mind raced. *Not a boy?* Who put that ridiculous idea in his head? Having a front row seat on boys, from babies to toddlers and now immature teenagers, Honey was an expert. Twelve-year-old males were boys.

She settled back down again, her head on his chest, her arm stretched across him to comfort his much bigger body with her own.

Would he tell her about it? He would if they were friends. They were friends, weren't they? They'd gone way beyond hookup in her eyes, but that didn't mean he saw it the same way.

"It's okay," she reassured. "If you ever want to talk, I'm here. As a friend."

"Friend with benefits." A low rumble of laugher colored his voice.

"Those are the best kind."

Chapter 20
Elf on the Shelf

"Have a minute? I'm in the neighborhood. I need a favor."

What could Vlad want at seven a.m. on a Monday?

"Sure. Come on over."

Jake knotted the towel around his hips as he walked to the front door and unlocked it. His laps were done, and he'd head to his weight room to lift after breakfast. Honey was probably in her apartment on her yoga mat, stretched into one of those complicated back bends that was as erotic as it was athletic. They'd agreed the only way to accomplish their morning fitness routines was to go their separate ways before breakfast. Otherwise, more often than not, they couldn't resist sweating together—the old-fashioned way.

Yesterday, all day, they'd gone full-on tourist. Derek and Donnie tagged along on their trip to the Met. Not the Honey-focused outing he planned. But one thing was obvious. Honey's brothers were proud of her, and their back and forth with her about the differences between Asian and Italian ceramic impressed him. His only intent was to make Honey happy by taking her to the exhibition. He didn't expect to enjoy it. Now, he'd ask her to let him go to the co-op with her so he could see her in action, observe her creative process in person.

They oohed and aahed along with the rest of the tourists as they stared up at the gigantic Rockefeller Center tree. Then they talked him into ice-skating. Not pretty. But what was gorgeous was Honey's laughter as she raced ahead, cutting a fast and graceful path through the holiday crowd lumbering around the rink, leaving Jake and her brothers clumsily following in her wake. Afterward they gorged on supper in Little Italy before they hit a couple of music venues. When he and Honey dropped the boys at the Port Authority for their bus, extracting promises to text when they got back home, they were all exhausted.

Honey put a hand on Jake's forearm as soon as they went through the front door of the townhouse. "It seems I'm always saying thank you." He started to shrug off her thanks, but she gripped him by his biceps, pulling on them till he was looking back into her eyes, which were right then a warm chocolate. "No. Really. We covered a lot of ground for their first trip to New York City. Feeding me is one thing, but you treated *all* of us. You really didn't have to. It's so generous, Jake. You spent your whole day with us. You've got some fans there in those boys."

He pulled away to touch a forefinger to the tip of her nose. "Stop thanking me. I had fun. Did you?" She nodded. "That was the goal. I only wanted to make it memorable for them. For all of us."

After he left her to keep his promise, he wanted to have this memory to pile on to the others he'd already locked away. It was a week till Christmas. Only seven days to create enough memories to last him through the rest of his life.

****

He opened the door at Vlad's discreet knock.

As always, Vlad was the guy who was immaculately turned out no matter what the hour. Today he was decked out in a bespoke business suit, perfectly knotted tie, and hand-tooled shoes as he checked out Jake's framed poster art on the walls of the front hall.

"I like these." Vlad nodded at blown-up, black-and-white photographs and colorful advertising posters for various Italian sports cars. "Did you take these photos? Sabrina has a great eye…"

"Nah, I bought them. A photo is as close as I've gotten to buying a car in the city."

Vlad laughed, and Jake realized he could count on one hand the times he'd ever seen his friend crack a smile.

"Looks like married life agrees with you, man." Jake pulled him in for a bro-hug before they shook hands.

Could be his imagination. But no, Vlad's cheekbones darkened before he met Jake's gaze full on.

"I didn't expect to be…so…happy," he admitted. "Or want to…actually need to make someone else happy. And I shouldn't have shown up like this. I, ah, hope I'm not interrupting."

"Interrupting? What do you mean?" Yeah, duh, he was in a towel, but Vlad knew he swam every morning.

"I mean, because, ah, your elf, she's off the shelf."

Jake took a second to process the phrase. On rare occasions, just like him, if he was emotional or caught off guard, Vlad's English deserted him. He rolled back the sentence to figure out the meaning, then ran a hand across his chin. "My elf?" Had Vlad completely lost it on his honeymoon?

"He's talking about me, Jake."

Honey's husky, before-coffee, morning voice came from the top of the landing. She was gorgeous as always—barefoot, hair darkened with sweat, in skin-tight yoga pants and a red tee.

"I *thought* I heard the door open." She cocked her head as she descended the stairs.

Then she walked right up to Vlad. Held out her hand in her straightforward way. "I'm Honey Hill."

Damn, but if he had to knock Vlad's teeth down his throat, he would. If Vlad dared to utter one crack about her name, the color tips in her hair, or her presence in his home at seven in the morning when Vlad knew he never invited women to his place overnight, Jake would do him serious damage. And no regrets. Even if Vlad blackballed him to every single one of his business contacts.

Vlad gripped her hand. "Vladimir Grigory. Pleasure."

Honey's heart-shaped face crinkled into a grin.

"Ohh, so you *are* real. It's been weeks since you've shown up at Duffy's, right? I was beginning to think Jake was only *pretending* he had friends."

Vlad's half smile turned into a full flash of white teeth. "I haven't made it to Duffy's lately. I'm a newlywed." He shrugged as if it was all the explanation needed.

"Congratulations. I wish you and your wife a long and happy life together."

Just like that Honey defused his tension while simultaneously infusing the moment with her trademark humor.

"Vlad, come into the kitchen, have some breakfast, tell me what's going on."

"No. Thank you. I can't stay. I have to ask you if you can do something on a professional matter. It's time-sensitive. That's why I'm here so early. It involves…" His deep voice trailed off.

He glanced over at Honey where she stood inside the loose circle of Jake's arm.

"It's okay, Vlad. I trust Honey. She's been helping me in the office."

Vlad lifted a speculative eyebrow. Jake had no trouble reading that look. Vlad knew better than anyone how seriously Jake took his business. If Honey had his trust, she had to be more than…more than what? More than a woman in his home at seven a.m. in yoga pants? More than a hookup?

He shut down that line of thought and focused on what Vlad was saying.

"It involves a friend of my wife, name of Lacey Reed. She's being blackmailed."

Lacey? Connor's fiancée?

As Vlad began to divulge the details of his request in his precise English, Jake sensed the moment Honey hung back to give them privacy. Vlad was aware of it too, and Jake watched as his shoulders relaxed. Jake was caught between wanting Honey to stay and wondering how she knew leaving the room was the exact right thing to do.

After Vlad left, he found Honey in the kitchen. Over the course of time she'd been here, Honey took most of her meals with him in the main kitchen. "I like your coffee better than mine," she'd said with a flutter of her lashes, which led to him asking if that was the *only* thing about him she liked…

Focus Jake. He didn't allude to Vlad or his request but instead asked her about a subject that continued to bug him.

"You never told me the details about the dirtbag who tossed your stuff when you first moved to the city. I could try to track him down. Possibly get your stuff back."

"Wow." She pushed out a breath that told him she didn't expect what he said and didn't want to dredge all this crap up again. He didn't want to either. But he wanted to help her out, protect her if need be.

"Sure. Why not? I guess your connections would help. So his name is Trey Sanders, and all I have are his cell phone number and the address where we shared the apartment. He never responded to any of my calls or texts after he did it, which is no surprise, so who knows if the number's even good anymore?"

She tucked one of the short wisps of her hair behind her ear and fiddled with it, the way she did. "I don't know anything else about him…and all because I was so determined to find a place…fast. The price was right and I was impatient."

"No judgment here, Honey. I just…it bugs me. I could try to find him, and I want to."

"Trey was angry. I have a feeling he tossed everything. There was nothing of real value for him to sell. It was just my stuff. You know, clothes, some books, and photos." She made a face. "And a couple of ceramic pieces."

"He took your *work*?"

Honey chuckled at his outrage. "Well it's not like I was toting around a Rembrandt. And I should've found out more about him. It was an impulse move. I decided everything too fast. And the ceramics, I only kept them because they have sentimental value. They were the first pieces I made. Very amateurish but you know…" She brought up a couple of photos on her phone, one a yellow bowl, the other a small ornament of a house. "I'll send these to your phone."

"And give me his cell too." Jake swallowed the thick bile in his throat. What if the scumbag hadn't tossed her stuff? What if he still had Honey's clothing, pictures of herself and her family? He schooled his features.

"Okay. Good. I'll see what I can do. I can't make any promises."

"Right. No promises."

"Honey?"

"Yeah?"

"Why ceramic art?"

She smiled. "I was little, just before we moved to Caryville. Willow had work in the area, and as part of it, we visited a museum attached to Alfred U. We always rambled around checking out a new town in those days. It was fun. For some reason I was fascinated by this exhibit of ceramic ornaments. I thought it was cool; they were all original and so tiny. Mom let me join in a kid class, I got my hands dirty, and that was it. I was hooked. And you know I kept that first creation; that's that little house ornament you see in that picture. They were easy to transport, which was a big deal because we were always on the move back then."

He examined her face for long moments after her rambling explanation, so long color climbed up her throat.

"Thinking about that loser Trey and the major asshole that's blackmailing Lacey, if you want, I mean, do you want more info about me? I don't want you to feel unsafe."

Chapter 21
Tell Me No Secrets

Did she want to know more about him?
Um, yeah. Only everything.

She had the benefits part, and oh, man, they were sweet, but what she craved was his friendship. She wanted to know everything. From the moment he'd been born till the seconds before they clashed in the corridor at the Pierre. She wanted to know why he planned to sell the beautiful home he'd renovated with his dad. Why even joining the SEALs hadn't helped him in the battle against his demons. The right to know the details of the death of his brother and the privilege to comfort him.

But they'd agreed upfront. They were a short-term hookup. No future and no promises. When she thought about it, their kind of honesty was rare in a world filled with cheaters like Rick and the serial ghosters who ruled the dating world. She and Jake gave in to their attraction like adults do. When it was over, they would walk away. Like adults do.

But what if they decided they wanted more? Could they move on to something more open-ended, a continuation of their affair with no end date? No. Honey discarded the idea before it took full possession of her thought. That road would be way too messy.

Honey couldn't afford to live in this townhouse

longer than a month, and she didn't want to. She wanted Jake, but she needed her independence. She'd come to New York to establish her career. But what about when she moved to a place of her own? Could she and Jake keep whatever it was they had going then? To see where it went?

There was no doubt in her mind what she wanted. She'd say yes to more of Jake in a heartbeat. But Jake?

Maybe Jake was ready to move on. Behind the deliberate, expansive charm of his smile, she recognized a loner. Did he regret opening his home to her, benefits or not? After the—let's be real—convenience of a live-in hookup, was he ready to mix it up again, go back to business as usual—single-guy style?

What if what she called their "connection" was simple novelty for him? She was the girl who strayed down to the city from the wrong side of the tracks. Bet he hadn't had too many girls with purple tips in their hair and a bejeweled belly button. Or, oh, man, of course he had. Jake was…Jake. Magnetic, stern, gorgeous, and considerate—in bed and out. Was there a woman he couldn't have if he wanted her? Yeah…no.

What was it Jim Duffy had said about Jake's dating habits? "*A revolving door of sophisticated arm candy.*" Jim had warned her, and now the thought of Jake with another woman hit her like a shower of flaming arrows to her chest. Her heart actually burned, and she rubbed a hand over her chest as she squeezed her eyes shut against the pain.

Stop it, Honey.

This line of thinking was doing nothing for her. She had to enjoy her time with Jake for what it was.

Time would tell her the truth of it—whether Jake was the best thing that had ever happened to her or the biggest mistake of her life. Or both.

"I hope you think we're friends." She looked into his eyes, willing him to see *her. Honey.*

"We are." His gaze traveled over her face so thoroughly heat bloomed in her cheeks, and she pressed her palms up to cool them before continuing.

"From where I stand, I see a good guy. I can tell from the way you treated my brothers, by the attention you give your clients, to me." She tilted her head, looked him in the eyes. "I don't have to ask you anything else."

He nodded.

"But…if you decide, if you want to tell me anything about yourself, I'll listen." She gave him a small smile, willing him to share something, anything, he willingly wanted her to know.

"Have I ever told you how many times a night I can make you…?" He waggled his dark brows.

And that was it, folks. Just like that they were back on the playing field they both excelled on. Honey looked away to hide the frisson of pain his words caused even as she told herself not to waste any more time on what ifs and maybes. This was what they had. And it would be enough as long as it lasted.

"Gosh." She pushed out her lips in a fake-disappointment pout. "*Just at night?* Gee, how old did you say you *are* anyway?"

"Oh, you're going to pay for that, Ms. Honeysuckle Hill."

She giggled. "I certainly hope so."

He swooped down to lift her into his arms, going-over-the-threshold style, and her heart wedged in her throat. *Stop. It. Honey.* No promises. No future.

"You're in the field today," she reminded him.

"Not till ten o'clock, which gives me a good, two, *daylight* hours to show...you..." He punctuated each word with a teasing stroke of his tongue along her lower lip.

Oh, man, she loved winding him up. Within moments, they were both on a hair trigger, and she loved it. Loved him. Loved him for playing along, that was. For stoking both her desire and her funny bone with his words.

Jake proved age was just a number once in the comfort of his king-size bed and then again under the waterfall nozzle in the shower.

"What do you have to say for yourself now, Ms. Hill?" He was wrapping her up in his terry robe after knotting a towel around his hips.

"I'd say it's a shame you have a ten o'clock. I'd like to put you to a formal, twenty-four-hour test. You know, under ideal conditions. With no interruptions."

His gravelly chuckle slid down her backbone like warm honey. "To be continued then, pixie. Maybe my ace assistant can clear my calendar?"

With an absentminded focus, he parted the robe he'd just closed around her, revealing her small breasts again. He ran his warm hands over them again and again, palming the nipples into painful peaks, cupping her sensitive breasts into fullness once more as if he hadn't had his hands on them and on her for the better part of two hours. From there, a rough but gentle forefinger circled the lavender stone piercing in her navel till goosebumps prickled her skin. His nonchalant possessiveness pushed her senses into overdrive, and her body softened and yielded, readying itself for him all over again. She squeezed her thighs together. "Ah, Jake. You've gotta stop now." Her arms grappled the air to hold onto him. He was her weakness, as well as her strength, and she needed him like she needed her next breath.

"Stop? You know I can't. I don't know how I'll settle my mind on anything but you today. I close my eyes, and I see you. I open them, and here you are. I want, I need my hands on you all the time, Honey, and that's the truth."

This could be enough. She would say it to him. She had to. They could claim each other, and keep each other for however long it took. Till they saw where it went. Hadn't he said at the very beginning *if it's what we both want, where's the problem?*

She swallowed a gagging gulp of air, trying to get the invitation out. To tell him to clear his calendar, his entire calendar, right now and spend the rest of the days they had together—together.

But she wouldn't do that. They both had responsibilities.

Somewhere she dug up a smile. Pressed her swollen lips to his once before she stepped away and re-tied the robe. "Text me," she said over her shoulder as she ascended the stairs to her own place. Clearly, their twenty-four-hour marathon was destined to take place only in her imagination.

****

But Jake surprised her.

——*Don't eat dinner. There's a cool place I want to take you. You have to be ready by 6. You in?*——

—Sure what's the place?—

—It's a surprise—

—You hate surprises—

*—Yeah, (*she could almost see him grinning*) but you love them—*

—True. Is there a dress code?—

—I want to say clothing optional, but we'll be outside. Buy the coat you keep telling me you're going to get. See you at 6—

Honey still hadn't gotten around to replacing her winter jacket, but she had a cozy sweater she could wear. The weather was practically balmy compared to what she was used to upstate.

At six o'clock she was ready, wearing bargain black jeans, metallic T-shirt, and boots. Her chunky turtleneck was at the ready slung over the stool in the kitchen.

At six thirty she was hungry, wondering where he was and waiting for a call or at least a text.

When seven o'clock came and went, she told herself not to worry. Jake had to be dealing with a work emergency. She knew this because he was annoyingly punctual in every area of his life. Which was why she kept trying to push back on his morning appointments and create enough daylight for them to make the most of their remaining time together. If he wasn't back, there was a good reason. But why hadn't he called or texted?

At seven fifteen she texted him. Nothing. At seven twenty she called him. No answer. She marched back and forth along the hall, her boots clunking in time to the out-of-control beat of her heart.

Something was wrong. The certainty was bone

deep. She was as sure of it as she was of her stupid porn star name. She had to look for him. No. Not until—she ran into his office. Checked his calendar. His last meeting had been at four p.m. with a client who needed a bodyguard/driver and a state-of-the-art home security system for her family. He'd met with this family before. Today's meeting would've been a short one to review the equipment installation and finalize placement of personnel.

She ran her perspiring hands along the fabric of her jeans, her hand shaking as she tapped in the digits for the client's phone. But before she could hit send, her phone rang. She jumped. Put the phone to her ear.

"Ms. Hill?"

"Yes? Yes!"

"This is PCA Reynolds at Mercy Hospital. We have a Jake Ricco here. He was in an accident. Unconscious for a time. He just gave us your name. Can you come down to the hospital?"

"Of course, yeah."

"Follow the signs to the emergency department. 17th Street and First Avenue."

She bolted from the townhouse, and in one moment, every single piece of her fledgling knowledge of the city and how to get around it flew out of her head.

Subway? Uber? She stopped, heaved in a gulping breath, scanned her surroundings to get her bearings. Even downtown, the streets were jammed with people making the most of the holidays in an unseasonably warm Manhattan December.

Oh, man, which of the impossibly tedious methods of city transportation would get her clear across town fastest?

Finally, a yellow cab pulled up. She tried to swallow, but her heart was a cannonball in her throat. She stared out the window onto the street thick with pedestrians and vehicles, blind to everything but two facts. Jake asked for her, and he was well enough to do so.

Fifteen long minutes later, she wove her way past the doctors, nurses, and staff at the end of their shift, streaming down the long emergency department ramp. She headed straight to the ED's circular nurse's station.

"Hi, someone called me… You have someone here, patient Jake Ricco?" Honey spit out the entire question on one long exhale.

Without lifting her gaze from the computer screen, the staffer asked, "Name?"

"Honey. Honey Hill." With a conscious effort, she lowered her voice to medium volume and tried to excise the panicked tone.

After hearing her name, of course the staffer took a second to look away from her screen. She flicked a glance over her that said she was mildly surprised Honey wasn't sporting hooker heels and double D boobs before she resumed tapping her keyboard.

Honey refused to react. She gave the woman a smile so sweet it should've rotted the woman's teeth. *See?* her smile said. *I can be patient.* She could stay calm. No. She couldn't. She *had* to see Jake. She pushed out a hyperventilating breath, raised her fingers to her temples, and pressed hard, but nothing eased the pounding, squeezing throb that hammered from the inside out.

"Pod B, number seven. He's the one with all the

ruckus round him."

She jerked her chin toward the gurney with multiple white coats and pastel uniforms moving and hovering around it. After a bored eyebrow-raise at Honey's hair, she turned away to pick up her ringing phone.

And yeah, damned if Jake wasn't surrounded by a slew of hot female medical personnel pulled straight from the set of *Grey's Anatomy*. Her gaze honed in on him, and he wasn't moving. He was as motionless as a Michelangelo statue and just as pale.

She brushed past them, pushed her way to the edge of the gurney. He looked… Was he breathing? She raised her hands to her mouth to cover the scream pushing its way out, then forced her eyes to observe. Yes. Yes, he was breathing.

She expelled a nauseous breath, released her death grip on the gurney's rail. Faced the collection of colorful scrubs. "I'm Honey Hill." Her low voice cracked on the words. "What happened to him?"

Pastel peach had a clipboard and read from it. "He was run over by one of those electric bikes, a delivery guy going the wrong way. Hit his head on the pavement. Lost consciousness briefly. Passersby called 911. Apparently, his phone flew out of his hand, and the screen shattered. It was locked anyhow. He's fallen asleep again."

"Where's his shirt?" Heads swiveled in her direction. After the recitation of events causing his injury, clearly the staff hadn't been expecting such a basic question. And Honey wasn't sure why it was the first thing she had to ask.

"There was a lot of blood." Turquoise scrubs raised

a disbelieving eyebrow after stating the obvious, no doubt rethinking the advisability of releasing Jake into Honey's care.

Honey winced at the sight of the deep violety-blue bruise mottling the skin of his right shoulder.

"Blood? Where?"

"From his head wound. But thankfully no broken bones." The doctor slowed her speech like she was speaking to a fifth grader. Probably a fifth grader would've known better than to ask. "The bleeding is stopped now, but you know, there's a lot of blood when an injury involves the head. That's why we called you. We couldn't release him after he lost consciousness unless it was to next of kin or someone who lives with him." She directed a pointed look to Honey's ringless left hand. "Do you?"

"Do I what?"

"Do you live with him? Are you next of kin?"

"Yes, I live with him. I can take him home. Would you... Where's his shirt? I don't think... He wouldn't want to be...exposed like this. Where's his shirt?" He was lying on a gurney in the middle of the frenetic emergency department in a room that was more like a closet with an open curtain around it.

Why hadn't she thought to grab a sweatshirt for him before she left the house?

"There's blood on it. Here it is. But you might want to take a blanket instead."

Navy blue uniform handed Honey a plastic bag with Jake's bloodied, wadded-up white shirt in it along with his cell phone, wallet, and watch.

"He's asleep again. If you can't get him to wake up now, we'll have to keep him at least overnight for observation."

Honey leaned in toward Jake, only to be elbowed back by the doctor with a determined pageboy and lethally high Louboutins.

"It's probably best if he stays overnight. If he goes home, someone will have to watch him all night. We weren't able to get a complete history from him…"

"I can watch him. I've stayed up all night to watch sick twins with strep. I can do this." Honey leaned over Jake again, put her lips to the side of his ear. "Jake? It's Honey. I've come to take you home. But the doctors think it might be better for you to stay overnight. Do you want me to bring you home?"

"Hell, yeah. Going home." His gravelly response brought a wave of relieved laughter from everyone in his open room and drew brief looks of amusement from the friends and families hovering around their loved ones in the rabbit warren of curtained rooms.

"Okay, then," Honey said.

A collective swooning sigh was released from everyone who watched as Jake lowered his broad-shouldered, hard-muscled, swimmer's body from the gurney to ease into the wheelchair, looking like an injured action hero with a bruise coloring a large swath of his right shoulder, a bandage on the back of his head, and five o'clock shadow darkening his jaw.

The female population at Mercy Hospital and probably a good portion of the males could be forgiven for thinking a god had stepped down from Mt. Olympus to walk in their midst. Jake gave a disjointed smile and a half wave and whispered, "Get me out of here."

When the Uber pulled up, Honey fussed over him, supporting his elbow as he slowly gained his footing from the wheelchair and took halting steps to the car.

If she was any judge, his bruises were making themselves felt, and his head was throbbing.

She held the discharge instructions in front of her like a bible. "It says here you can have more painkiller in two hours."

"Okay." He nodded and winced. "Fine. I'll be fine as soon as we get home."

Honey hovered behind him as he climbed the stairs to his bedroom—the one she'd shared with him every night since the first night.

"I'll get into bed and rest."

She stood guard outside the door as he used the bathroom, then watched him ease down onto the bed. He slowly slid off his boots, and Honey reached down to help.

"Honey, I'm okay. This is nothing. I can take my own boots off. I may or may not have a concussion, but they gave me a CAT scan, and it came out negative. So the odds are I don't have one. This hard head is good to go. I've been worse. Much worse."

"I guess. But I'm gonna stay. Just in case you need anything. I promised the doctor."

"Sure." He smiled his fallen angel's smile and patted the bed beside him. "Come here."

She ignored him and tucked an extra pillow behind his back. "You should try to sleep propped up, not flat on your back."

"I will. And I'll rest easier if you're next to me. C'mere," he said again.

"Hang on." Honey went to the sink and filled the canister he always kept by the bed with cold water.

No doubt she'd be able to stay awake. She'd done

it countless times over the years when her brothers were sick. But Jake should stay awake too. Or at least she needed to check his pupils every half hour or so.

"Can I get you something?" She gripped her hands together, tried to think of anything he'd need so she could put it to hand before she turned the lamp off.

"You can come over here and stop worrying. Can't believe I was mowed down by an electric bike." He loosed a raspy chuckle. He reached up to touch the wound on the back of his head. Shook his head in disbelief and grunted.

"I can heat up some soup for you." But maybe not, she thought. Would food make him nauseous?

"I'm *fine*. Not hungry."

"Ok." She couldn't think of anything else he might need. She toed off her boots and edged toward him on top of the duvet.

"I'm sorry about our date." He lifted his palms in an I-can't-believe-what-happened way.

Her eyes crinkled up with her first smile since his text this morning. "Well, as surprises go, this one was right up there."

He chuckled. "You must be starving. You should go down and get something, some soup."

"No, not right now. But I will get something later on if I am."

"Put you head on my chest. Try to rest."

"No, I... You're the one who has to take it easy."

"I rest better with you here next to me."

Her stomach flip-flopped at his casually spoken assurance. She looked away to hide the pleasurable warmth that shot straight down to her toes at his admission. Resting her head against the muscled warmth of his chest, Honey felt the reassuringly solid, steady beat of his heart under her cheek. She sucked in a deep breath, inhaling lemon and leather, antiseptic, sweat, and Jake.

She closed her eyes, and when she opened them again, his bedside clock said ten minutes had passed. She could do this. She'd sleep in spurts and check on him for signs of concussion. She set her cell to a twenty-minute vibration alarm and snuggled in on his uninjured shoulder.

He shivered, and she raised her head.

"Are you cold? Where do you keep your shirts? I'll get you one to put on."

His eyes stayed closed. "Shhh. C'mere. It's okay. Not cold."

Chapter 22
Drowned in Your Sorrow

"I'm cold, Cesco. I told you this was too far."
"Yeah, well, you're shivering too. Let's turn back."
"Zia Marina said…"
"Yeah, I know she's not our real Zia, but…"
"Basta. No more. I'm not *a baby. We have to turn back. The waves are big here, and the water's freezing. Let's go."*
"It's okay, Cesco. Hold on to me. Yeah. Hang on. Hang on. I'm trying. It's the current."
"Don't let go, okay? Whatever you do, don't *let go of me. It'll be okay, don't let go. I won't let go of you either. I'm trying to swim. Hang on, Cesco. I have you. Hang on. Cesco? Cesco?"*

Honey sprang upright after the first couple of strained words in the one-sided conversation. Jake, still asleep, was in the grip of an epic nightmare. His breaths burst out in harsh, labored gasps, his voice morphing from the serious, stern tone she was used to, to something frightened, on the desperate edge of panic. Frozen, her hand covering her mouth, her breath clogging her throat, she couldn't listen to another agonized word. She had to wake him.

But even as she debated the advisability of shaking him awake, his eyes opened wide, stared at nothing, bloodshot. He shivered violently, and she groped for the blanket at the foot of the bed. Tugged it over him. The room was dark except for the dim light of her phone, and as she promised the doctor, she'd roused herself every twenty minutes or so to check on him. But this last time before her phone vibrated, his words, the argument he was having in his dream, was loud enough to waken both of them.

This was about his brother.

Water, shivering, current, waves, swim. Jake had been with his brother when he drowned. Jake had tried to save his brother. "*Hang on Cesco. Don't let go.*"

Jake had watched his brother drown.

How old did he say he'd been? Twelve?

She reached across him for the water on the nightstand. He pulled himself up onto his elbows and took the flask. Without a word, he drank and kept drinking till he drained it. She watched his throat work as he swallowed, his eyes wide, unfocused, and shocked.

"Cesco is your brother."

He blinked once, then turned his head slightly toward her. "Yeah."

"Jake, I'm so sorry."

"No. I'm sorry you had to hear... I usually don't speak during it."

"Usually?"

"During the nightmare. I don't usually speak. At least I don't believe I do." He rubbed a hand over his eyes for a moment before letting it drop back onto the duvet. "You didn't need to hear all that."

"*I* didn't need? What about you? The burden of that memory..."

Slowly he slid up to sitting and propped himself

against the pillows.

"It's what happened. My brother drowned. Because of me. I couldn't save him. I wasn't able to save him." He said the words with a practiced, emotionless assurance that made it sound like he was reporting the weather.

She rounded on him to stare into his face, knew her own face held shock and disbelief. "Because of *you*? You can't possibly believe that. You don't, do you?" Her voice was an urgent whisper.

"Of course I do. I was there. I was responsible. That's what happened." Still spoken in that flat monotone.

"You were a kid, Jake. It was an accident."

"You weren't there, were you?" His rough voice was charged with aggression and some emotion she couldn't decipher. "*I* was the stronger swimmer. *I* was bigger. Younger but bigger."

"You were twelve. You were both boys. It's a miracle *you* survived."

"Not a miracle. A curse. I couldn't explain how I survived. To anyone. How do two boys go out to swim on a warm day and only one comes back?"

"You said it yourself. There was a current. Besides, do you even remember what happened? How could they ask a child to explain something like that?"

"Oh, yeah, they asked. And I remembered. If only I could forget. Some nights I go to sleep begging to forget for just one night."

"Jake." She pulled the blanket up over both of them and deliberately lay her head down against his uninjured shoulder, like she was about to sleep. "If you want to talk more about this, I'm here. I won't bug you with endless questions. Especially not tonight. You need rest. You're probably concussed."

Long moments passed as his chest rose on his inhales. Then he circled his uninjured arm under her shoulders and gathered her into his side.

"Like I said, I was twelve, and Cesco, my older brother Francesco, was thirteen. It was Easter break, and we were on the west coast in Tuscany. My mother's family was from the area. Boy, we loved it there. We ran wild." She heard the fleeting smile in his voice. "Explored the entire countryside on our bikes or wandering around on foot. We ran circles 'round our nanny, Zia Marina. Cesco especially. He, Cesco, was a beautiful kid, blond, blue-eyed like our mother. Zia Marina could never say no to him whether it was an extra snack after lunch or staying up later to read or watch television. Telling our parents we deserved to get the latest video game.

"Anyway, that day in April was unseasonably hot. The temperature was pushing ninety degrees. Cesco and I both wanted to swim. Zia Marina told us to cool off in the shallow end because early in the year the water was bound to be cold.

"And yeah, the water was freezing, but there was no way we were staying in the shallow end. We went out too far, and I think…I think Cesco got a cramp because one minute he was swimming, like really powering well beyond our boundary, and the next minute he called to me. I swam out to him, and we started to go back. But the waves were fierce, and it was taking forever to make any kind of progress. I kept telling Cesco to hang on to me, I felt strong, no cramps.

"But the waves kept coming at us, and there was an

undertow. After one really strong one battered us, I don't know. He let go. I lost him. I looked, I really tried to find him, but I couldn't. I didn't know what to do. Finally, I swam back and ran for help. We searched. Our family. The local police. My parents hired a helicopter to aid in the search, but a storm came in that night, which was why the waves were so churned up. That was the last time I saw Cesco. I mean, until they recovered him a couple of days later."

"Oh, my God." Honey swiped a hand at the tears that streamed down her face before they could drip onto his chest.

He didn't look at her. He just kept his face forward as he continued. "It broke our family apart. My mother was never the same. I mean, how could she be?"

"But thank goodness *you* survived."

"Yeah, but…"

"But what?"

"But somehow I always knew that if someone had to die, she would've preferred it was me."

"*Oh, no, Jake*. I'm sure that's not right. Your mother?" She got up on her elbow and peered into his face.

His lips wobbled, then pressed together. "Cesco was the oldest. She called, still calls him, her golden boy. He was named after her. He resembled her aristocratic ancestors, and I take after my dad. So when they split up, I went with my dad."

"They split up after Cesco died?"

"Yeah, within a year. Not an actual divorce though. My mother just stayed in Italy fulltime, and I was enrolled, you know, in that prep school in Connecticut. She didn't want me with her." His mouth flattened.

242

"But she didn't want me raised with my dad in the city where he was working eighteen-hour days building his business. I needed to be groomed as a gentleman so I could have a gentleman's career." He issued a harsh laugh. "She was *not* happy when I dropped out of college to join the navy and forget about her thoughts on me running a security business."

Honey was speechless at Jake's revelations, and she wanted to challenge every single one of them. Instead she changed the subject. "My mom is supportive of my career. But from a distance. She couldn't understand why I wanted to stay in Caryville."

"Where you grew up?" The sigh Jake released told her he was relieved at the subject change.

"Mostly, yeah. My mom is a road warrior. When we settled in Caryville, I was nine. That was after she met Joss, the twins' dad. We'd already bounced around a lot before she got settled in her career and started making a better salary. By the time we got to Caryville, I was ready to stay in one place. So I did. Even after she left Joss. I wanted to stay there because I wanted a home. Not that she asked me to go with her. She wanted me to stay there, get my education. And it would've been a bummer for her and lonely for me if she took me on the road. She had no interest in homeschooling me, and truthfully, I wanted to meet kids my own age. But by the time I did, the damage was already done."

"Damage?"

"Meeting new kids never went well. I was already awkward. I spent my early years around adults listening to talk about science and the environment and work. Dorky McDorkster. I was clueless when the girls or boys in my school talked about anything else. My social skills were nil." She shook her head and closed her eyes at the memory. "I was small for my age, with long, sloppy braids. I wore overalls."

"You sound adorable." He ran a forefinger along the side of her cheek, and she edged closer to his warmth.

"It was a long time ago. I've grown up." She squeezed her eyes shut. "But yeah, trust me, that wasn't a good look for me."

"No, you trust *me*. I wouldn't change a thing about you. Then or now."

Honey resisted the urge to fling her arms around his neck for that. She wished she could hug the young boy who'd endured so much, but she forced a laugh instead. "Now I know you're concussed. Time for the painkiller if you want it."

"Nah, but maybe I'll close my eyes for an hour. Till seven."

****

Jake awakened a little less than sixty minutes later, relieved that his body clock was still in working order and able to awaken him when he wanted it to. He put a tentative hand to the back of his head. Some soreness but the mild headache was almost gone. He could take something over the counter for the remnants of it, but his guess was after a decent breakfast he'd be good to go.

Honey was curled up on top of the duvet next to him, her hand clutching the pillow under her head. Should he waken her? No.

She had to be exhausted after awakening every twenty minutes or so all night to check on him. Her golden skin was pale, her sprinkling of freckles standing out in sharp relief across her nose and cheekbones. As he watched, her hand flexed on the pillow, and she pulled it deeper under her chest. Oh, hell, yeah. If he could be that pillow.

He'd gone to sleep that last time listening to her as she told him to—just zoning out as she talked about her brothers and their music, her ceramics, all of it in a low and soothing singsong voice he had no doubt she'd used before on her brothers.

That in itself was exceptional. He usually awakened from the nightmare in a cold sweat, certain no matter what time it was, he was done sleeping for the night. That was how it'd been for twenty years unless he was on a mission.

This time after her gentle nudge, he managed to tell her what happened all those years ago or at least the basics of it. It was the first time he'd spoken to anyone about it since the endless repetitions of that day he recounted immediately after it happened.

And then somehow she'd eased him back to sleep.

Back in the SEALs, right before he decided not to re-up, the teams' psychologist had sat him down after his last assignment. Told him that while he excelled at making sure his teammates adhered to proper procedure and rules, he was putting himself in more and more danger with every mission. That doing so could be bravery in certain situations, but that his over-the-top actions had reached a point where he was unnecessarily risking his life as well as the safety of his teammates. Para-suicidal the doc called it, and did he want to talk about it?

Yeah, right. No. He declined to discuss it but the

knowledge he might harm his teammates because he couldn't turn off the shit show in his head decided him. He chose not to sign on for another tour and went home to spend time with his dad.

He missed the purpose in his life and his teammates, but he was crystal clear on one thing. There would be no more death on his conscience. After his dad passed, he redoubled his efforts building his security company. He'd found his ultimate calling and it was good to be an agent of protection and safety instead of the source of loss and misery.

The calling he would put into the hands of Connor and his handpicked manager when he left for Italy on Christmas.

He and Honey only had a few days left. He had to reschedule the surprise she'd missed last night. He slid out of bed and headed to the shower.

Chapter 23
Christmastime in the City

Jake actually laughed when she suggested he take the day off after the accident and his trip to the emergency department.

"Not possible. I'm too busy, and besides, I feel fine."

He hadn't said another word about his recent accident or the horrific one that claimed his brother's life, but the fact she knew what happened lay between them. If Honey was reading it right, Jake was relieved she knew, but he never would've willingly told her. The shock of the concussion and her presence in his room precipitated his revelations. Otherwise, she'd have no idea the burden he'd carried around all these years. The one he still carried.

But what to do now? Bringing up the subject would be tantamount to shoving a knife in his chest…and hers. Because she'd never seen such open suffering on a face as she saw in his—both during the nightmare and when he recounted the tragedy later. It'd be cruel to bring it up again. Unless he wanted to talk about it, which obviously he didn't.

Weird, what he wanted to talk about was Christmas. He peppered her with a ton of questions about what she, Joss, and her brothers did to celebrate the season, about all of their favorite songs and foods and decorations. She played along because yeah, she'd be missing all of it this year as she claimed her new life in the city. Reminiscing and laughing with Jake brought her brothers closer.

Today was December 23rd. Jake had rescheduled the surprise, and Honey had to admit she was giddy wondering what he had up his sleeve. They'd exchanged another series of texts yesterday.

—*Ok. Tomorrow. Honey's surprise Take 2. Be ready at 6*—

—*Try not to get run over this time, ok?*—

—*It would almost be worth it to hear you go toe to toe with the staff at Mercy again*—

—*Hmm. So you* were *listening? I guess you enjoyed them checking you out in your weakened state*—

—*The only one I want checking me out is you*—

—*Well wear a black shirt. Just in case. You know. Blood*—

—*I* will *get you for that, Ms. Hill*—

At the appointed hour, she was ready, and Jake came through the door at six p.m. as planned.

They got into the Uber, and Jake raised his brows at Honey's chunky sweater.

"No coat?"

She shrugged. "It's fifty degrees."

"And getting colder," he said.

"I have scarf," she responded, fluffing it up around her face. "I'll be fine. So where are we going?"

"Still a secret."

"Well, I can see we're heading uptown…"

"Do I have to blindfold you, pixie?"

"Um…" Fifty shades of erotic images popped into

her mind, and her face burned like hellfire. Bottom line: yeah, she'd try pretty much anything—but only with Jake.

"I'm still tourist enough to want to see everything. I've barely been in the city a month. So no. No blindfold"—she raised one eyebrow—"this time."

Jake's chuckle was dark. He took her hand, threaded her fingers through his, pulled her hand to rest it on his hard thigh, and covered it with both of his.

Honey's curiosity spiked when the car left Manhattan and entered the Bronx. There hadn't been time yet to see much of Manhattan, and the only other part of the city she knew a little about was the part of Brooklyn where the ceramic co-op was.

Then she saw the lights and the sign: *Bronx Botanical Garden Holiday Train Show*. The driver pulled up to the curb. "We're here," Jake said, and then, "Surprised?"

"Yes, and intrigued." Eyes wide, Honey scrambled from the car.

His smile was just as wide and almost boyish. "Good. Let's go in." He took her hand as they followed the sign toward the Enid Haupt Conservatory.

"Are we joining a tour?" Honey scanned the swathes of people milling about the entrance to the gardens.

"Nah, I have our tickets, and I know my way around. When I was talking to you about what you do around the holidays, it came to me that the only thing I did with any consistency was come up here with my dad to see the trains."

Her heart—it stopped, then jumpstarted in a painful rhythm. Jake was sharing a personal memory with her, a tradition.

"We came here most of the years I was in prep school. Dad was fascinated by the work of the artist, a guy named Paul Busse who builds these. The track is about a half mile long. The whole train and all the surrounding New York City landmarks are made up of stuff you might find in a garden—twigs, leaves, acorns."

"Wow. This is so cool. Look! A mini Statue of Liberty. This is really stunning, and then when you add the lights everywhere…" She spun in a circle, sighed. "I love it."

"I know. I can't believe the detail. I thought you'd appreciate what went into creating something like this."

"This miniature version of iconic New York landmarks. It's amazing."

"And then there's the train. I loved it here, so I wanted you to see. Whenever I would come up here with my dad, it was just the two of us. I could forget…everything else."

Honey pictured the younger Jake, lanky like her brothers, wide-eyed, caught up in the coolness of what the artist built, but in the end happy to be with his dad doing something just with the two of them. Thankfully it was clear the elder Mr. Ricco, er, Riccobono, had had a positive relationship with his remaining son.

"They have a fire pit and a place to buy drinks. There's also a shop. Do you want to check out the ornaments?"

Couldn't he *tell*? Her heart was in her eyes. *Oh, Jake.*

"Sure, all of the above," she said.

He wrapped his arm around her side as they

meandered around the grounds of the gardens, under the holiday lights, weaving between families and carolers.

They wandered around for an hour before Jake called a halt.

"Part two of the evening is dinner on Arthur Avenue, which is the Bronx's Little Italy. But they don't take reservations at most of the restaurants, so…"

"Say no more. I'm ready. You had me at Little Italy."

In the end, they got into Jake's first choice, Zero, Otto, Nove, with no wait time. It didn't hurt that Jake smiled his show-stopping Jake smile, and the woman behind the reception desk practically drooled.

It was late when they got back to the townhouse. Honey, powered by espresso, cannoli, and holiday vibes, floated up the stairs to Jake's suite.

****

He shrugged out of his jacket, and nerves made him roll the collar of it up and back a couple of times before he draped it on the back of the sofa.

"I have a gift for you. For Christmas."

Her cupid's bow mouth turned up at the corners at the same time as her eyes crinkled. "And I have one for you too. But Christmas Eve is tomorrow." She tilted her head in question.

"Yeah, but technically it's tomorrow now." He made a show of checking his watch. "It's one in the morning." He worked to keep his voice light. He needed to start the process of saying goodbye. Time was running out.

"Okay, sure…let me go get mine." She left the room, oblivious to the dark mood settling over him.

He sat on the sofa, dropped his head into his hands, closed his eyes, and listened to the tap-tap of Honey's light tread up the stairs to her apartment. *Shake it off, Jake. Make this last night together as perfect as the past weeks.* But there was no help for it. Once he said what he had to say, it would be over. The only question was whether he'd come clean with every detail or simply rip off the Band-Aid and go.

"Jake?" Her voice sounded at the top of the stairs. "Why don't you come up, and we can open our gifts here…"

"Sure." He tucked the boxes under one arm and met her at the top of the stairs. She turned on the wireless sound system, and Frank Sinatra poured out, promising to be home for Christmas—if only in his dreams.

Her eyes gleamed with something that looked like anticipation or maybe it was just the amount of wine they'd had at dinner as she backed into the living room. The Christmas tree winked and glowed in the far corner, and as Honey predicted, emitting the faint trace of pine, the exact scent of which was likely impossible to replicate. The room was like a card depicting the warm romance of the season. He had to memorize it all.

Especially Honey. With her sparkly top and radiant eyes, she could be the angel on the top of the tree, if the angel wore Gucci boots and had spikes of "I did it for Christmas" red on the tips of her pale hair. In contrast, to tease her after her remarks about his accident, he'd worn a black shirt and black jeans and yeah, his mood matched. *Shake it off, Jake.*

"You first," he said, presenting her with two large boxes wrapped in solid red paper and shiny gold ribbon.

"Wow, this is a mystery and"—she lifted the top one, held to her ear, and gave it a shake—"almost too pretty to open."

"Well"—he shrugged—"you know *I* didn't wrap them. The salesgirl was very helpful."

"Oh, I bet she was." Honey smirked, and he cracked a smile at her patented eye roll.

"C'mon, open them." He sat on the sofa beside her, entertained by her unfettered enthusiasm as she plopped both boxes on her lap.

Like a kid, she ripped off the paper in seconds, flipped the top box open, and lifted out the fuzzy golden jacket. She stood, slipped her arms through the sleeves, twirled, and posed in front of him. "It's so cozy and warm. I love it."

He used his stern voice. "You need a coat. The city gets raw in the winter, and the wind is a bitch. I don't want to think of you being cold. The saleswoman helped me with your size. It's very warm. She said it's called, ah…"

"Yeah, I've seen these, a teddy bear coat. It's adorable. I love it."

"Didn't know if you would prefer real fur…"

"What? No, it's perfect, Jake. Thank you. I can't believe there's something else?"

"This one's more boring, but I wanted you to have it." He shrugged again as she lifted the lid from the second big box.

She shook out more fake fur, this time a blanket, one side fuzzy, the other side water resistant.

"It's to keep in your car just in case you ever need it. It's thermal. The manufacturer guarantees it will keep your body temp up to 98.6 degrees."

She grinned. "Got it. They're both really thoughtful. Mine's going to seem frivolous by comparison. I couldn't, I didn't…"

"No worries. You don't need to say anything."

She took a small velvet pouch from underneath the tree and placed it in his open palm. He fumbled opening the tight drawstring, the package awkwardly small in his broad hands. He struggled to inch his long fingers inside. Finally, he unwrapped the tissue paper to reveal a small ornament attached to a silver ribbon.

He grasped the ribbon and held up the silvery blue bauble. Iridescent splinters of light danced inside the glazed and painted ceramic, the luminous sphere shimmering as it captured the light from the tree and the lamp.

Honey twisted her hands in front of her. "It's meant to be Polaris. The North Star. I thought as a sailor you might appreciate it and…of course you don't need to put it on a Christmas tree. It can hang in a window. I couldn't figure out what you might want…"

You. I want you.

"Or need…"

You.

"Thank you. It's original and it's you. Someday when you're famous, I'll be able to say I have one of your authentic works."

"Ha ha, it *is* one of a kind…"

"I will treasure it." *Say it, Jake.*

He stood up, paced toward the tree, then turned and came back to her. "Ah, the reason I wanted to exchange gifts tonight is tomorrow I'll be heading to Italy to spend Christmas with my mother. I've gone every Christmas since…Cesco and…"

"Oh." She stopped swaying to the Christmas music in her new coat and stared at him.

He registered the confused stillness of her expression.

"When do you get back?"

Tear off the Band-Aid, Jake.

He squared his shoulders. "I'll be there indefinitely."

Her eyes rounded, and she gaped at him.

Chapter 24
When It's Over, It's Over

Indefinitely?
Wait. What? What was happening here?
What in hell was going on?
Her vision went black for a second as his words repeated in her head, each one hitting her with the strength of a hammer smashing against her chest. Jake. Leaving. Italy.

Staying indefinitely, a.k.a. you, Honey, will never see him again. What the fuck, what the fuck, what the fuck, why?

She snapped her lips shut, schooled her expression into something other than the gut-wrenching shock chilling her flesh. She swallowed past the broken glass in her throat to speak, but it didn't matter because there wasn't one word, profound or profane, that could express her emotions in the face of his bombshell.

It took her several long beats, but she lifted her chin in a futile attempt to keep the tears filling her eyes from pouring out.

There was no way she could produce a smile, but she forced the rusty words. "You've gotten really good at this surprise thing."

Faced with her distress, he looked away from her, his lips tightened, and his eyes shadowed. He rubbed the back of his neck before he returned his gaze to hers.

"I always go back at Christmas. But usually it's a round trip of two or three days, tops. But this time is…different. And I figured, the thing is, if I'm not coming back… I don't know how I would say goodbye to you twice. Don't know if I could."

He took a step toward her, reached out like he'd run a thumb under her eyes to wipe away the tears streaming down her face, but Honey put her hand out, palm facing outward to stop him, and fell back another step.

Not coming back…not coming back…

In and out. In and out. She forced her breaths to slow, tried to relax her shoulders and spine, reflexively pushed the stray wisps of her hair behind her ear. But slowing down the action didn't mean it wasn't happening. This wasn't a lucid dream or whatever they called those surreal experiences she'd read about on Buzzfeed. This was real.

She was living a nightmare.

She cleared her throat, swallowed the tears. "You don't owe me an explanation, Jake." *But WTF?* "Like I said it's…a surprise. We agreed…" She flashed back to that handshake in the Japanese restaurant. "To a month long, um…"

Man, she'd only known him a few weeks, their month was not up, but suddenly boom, their time was up. Her time was up.

He was nodding. Quick jerks of his head that told her he wanted this conversation finished.

"I want you to know—you can stay in the apartment for as long as you need to. As long as you want to. My buddy Connor will be placing a manager to work here with my PA, you know Regina, to manage

Haven until I can make some final decisions. He's also gonna oversee the sale of the townhouse eventually. Makes it easier having someone on the ground here rather than trying to do it all long distance."

The information was coming at her too fast to process. "Easier. Yeah. So you really aren't coming back… I thought you were just, you know…dumping me."

"Damn, Honey." He took another step toward her, but she wasn't having it. She backed away till she couldn't smell the lemon and leather of him, far enough so she wasn't tempted to launch herself into his arms and do something crazy like beg him to stay.

She pressed her lips together. But their trembling wouldn't stop—the harder she pressed them, the more they shook. Processing his words was nearly impossible when all she could hear inside her pounding head was the drumbeat of *not coming back…not coming back.*

"So you're leaving your home, your business…" *Me.*

"Yes." He reached for her, but she held her hand up.

"Why?" *Why now? Why are you leaving now? Why are you leaving me? Now?*

"I made a promise. I put it off for as long as I could, but…"

"A promise to go to Italy? To give up everything you've built here?" She didn't try to conceal the confusion or the hurt in her eyes. "I don't understand."

"I promised my mother, a long time ago, I'd go back and be… I promised I'd live the life my, Cesco, would have lived…"

"You…*what*? But you're not Cesco. You're Jake.

258

And besides, who knows what Cesco would've done?" Her voice was getting strident, and she took a breath. What difference did it make why? He was going.

He closed his eyes for a moment, and when he opened them, they were stark, with pain etched in the deep line between his eyebrows.

"Franca doesn't see it that way. Her ancestors were Italian nobility. She's obsessed with her heritage as a royal. She had plans for Cesco. When he died, she put it on me, hounding me to do what he would've done. I fought it and ignored her…for years. But then I started to think *maybe…*" His beautiful lips twisted before he dropped his head, color invading his cheekbones.

"Jake? There's no Italian monarchy anymore, is there? And what do you mean by maybe?"

"Maybe when I go back, if I do as she says, the nightmares will stop."

The hope in his voice mixed with the pain she always heard when he spoke of his brother stopped her. He was looking for something. Something to ease him. And all she knew was—she wasn't it. Whatever it was, it was something she couldn't give him.

"What must you do?"

"There's a woman, only daughter of a society family with some money and some noble ancestry. They're trying to expand their tourism business. They want to do it internally…through marriage. I would be…a name, a face, a heritage." He lifted a shoulder.

"You mean marriage as in you—getting married, having kids…"

"Yes." He averted his gaze and nodded.

And as his words sank in, shock piled onto shock until her mouth flooded with saliva, and she was seconds away from heaving up her dinner. She fisted her shaking hands over her mouth and breathed through her nose. But the churning, nasty tide of sick wouldn't go away. She pointed one hand to door, the other clutched at her stomach.

"Leave. *Now*." It was guttural command.

She didn't wait to see him go; she stumbled to the bathroom and slammed the door. Turned on the cold faucet and sat on the toilet seat with her hands extended under the tap up to the wrist. But her pulses still pounded, and her stomach grated and churned fit to overflow with every heartbeat. So she turned off the faucet, then stuck her head between her knees and pressed a fist to her belly.

Of all the ways he could've ended them, Honey had never seen this particular scenario coming. How could she? Jake was leaving everything behind to live in Italy and start a new life there. With a wife. Getting married. The pounding at her temples doubled, then tripled, and it was no use. She turned the water on again to muffle the sounds of her retching.

She slumped on the corner edge of the bathtub, leaned against the wall at the back of it for who knew how long, gaining her feet every few minutes to empty her stomach. Over and over till her insides were hollow and aching. Finally, she wobbled to the sink to rub a cold washcloth over her face and swish out her mouth.

She poked her head out before she left the bathroom, and her apartment was silent, empty, and dark. Except for the Christmas tree, plump and cheery in the corner, mocking her with its happy twinkling. She walked over to it and pulled the plug out of the wall.

****

The blackout drapes kept out the early morning sunshine, but eventually the hiss, howl, and snarl of traffic and rushing pedestrians intruded and pulled Honey from her restless sleep. She checked her phone—six a.m. She'd managed to sleep for an hour. She waited till seven, but then needing the contact, she texted Derek and Donnie.

—Hey, guys, guess what? I'll be home for Christmas. Not sure if I can get there in time to help with Christmas dinner or anything but can't wait to see you—

Derek replied. *—Hey, Honey. Cool. Will Jake be coming up too?—*

—No. He's going away. And I'll be in a new place by New Year, I hope—

Tossing her clothing into her pack took only minutes. She left jeans and a top out on the bed for after her shower. She unhooked every ornament and wrapped each of them in felt. The one-time soothing activity held no joy. No music this time, no plans, no dinner cooking downstairs. The silence was deafening. Damn Jake for ruining her favorite holiday. She listened for the car that would take him to the airport as she unstrung and rewound all of her cool, new vintage lights and placed them carefully in the top of her storage box. Because there was no way she'd leave the building until he was already gone.

Jake's hard tread on the stairs shook her into checking the time. Three p.m.

Don't!

Don't come up here.

Don't you dare. Don't do it!

How did he have the balls to come up here? It would kill her to talk to him again.

He rapped on the door, two, hard, no-nonsense knocks.

She could shove a chair under the doorknob. Or maybe ignore him and sink to the floor, weeping like she'd done last night, all night—till her head throbbed and she crawled under the duvet to shield her eyes against the assault of dawn light.

But no way did she want to be *that* girl. The one who couldn't say goodbye. She straightened her back. Swallowed a hysterical giggle as she glanced in the mirror near the door. Her hair was on end, nothing new there, and yeah, no makeup on the tear-mottled skin of her face. And at three in the afternoon, she was still wearing the terry robe Jake loved seeing on her and even more, loved taking off her... *Stop. It. Honey.*

She hated him. Somehow she'd given him her heart, and he smashed it, and she had no fucking clue, not a tiny inkling what would happen. She'd promised herself this Christmas with him, this New Year, would be enough. That she'd walk away with no regrets and gorgeous memories because that was how they planned it. And yet somehow in her treacherous, secret heart, their relationship went from hookup to something deeper. But damn him, all along, all along...he'd planned a brutally fast end to their short-term liaison.

She agonized during the wee hours, questioning everything she believed about herself and him, wondering how she could've built their temporary hookup into something it wasn't. Because it wasn't like they hadn't been clear with each other from day one. Their thing was temporary, and now they were over.

If she had a conscious thought about the end of them, she would've said her thought was their parting would be mutual. Both of them leaving, maybe agreeing to meet up at some vague future moment and that promise to meet would take away the awkward.

Instead he was strolling away, and her heart was in shreds at his feet. He was moving on, really moving on. She had to do the same.

No reason to speak to him. No reason to open the door. Only a masochist would open the door.

She pulled it open.

"Hey." He stood in the threshold, a stranger in black jeans and bomber leather.

She owned her disheveled appearance, put a fist to her hip, and lifted her wobbling chin. "Did you want to give me some last-minute instructions? Why don't you text me whatever I need to do when I leave?"

His lids dropped low over eyes black with turmoil. "I wanted to see you. One last time. To say goodbye."

Her chin went higher, her jaw tightened with the need to protect herself from feeling anything. "Is that how this is done? I'm new to this. Didn't we say everything we had to say last night?" She didn't bother to take the bitch out of her voice. She forced a shrug. "This space will be hard to say goodbye to, but I'll be okay. I can…"

"You can take care of yourself. I know."

He put a hand out, raised it like he'd cup her jaw, but she jerked her head back and gripped the side of the door. Then she stood straighter, planted her feet to fill the threshold with her body because there was no way she'd let him in.

"You have a plane to catch, and I've got to get

going too."

"Get going? I was serious when I said I'd be happy for you to stay on here. However long you want. I'd like to think of you here."

She closed her eyes for a beat, then shook her head. Here without him? With memories bombarding her twenty-four seven? That was not happening. She felt her lips twist and didn't bother to reply.

She searched for the words she'd struggled so hard to come up with in the small hours before dawn. Something about wishing him well and not having regrets. She swallowed, anxious to make her voice cool and even as she said her piece.

They'd agreed to this. Their time together burned so bright. But just like fireworks, once lit, once the bright colors hit the heights, there was nothing for them to do but stream down. But now she knew it hadn't been just her body moving up—it had been her heart soaring as well. Up to spark for moments before fluttering, descending, floating, crumbling, and lost, down, down, down, helpless to stop its own disintegration. Helpless to control where she'd land.

No. She would control where she'd land.

He turned away from her, then back again. Examined his booted feet for long seconds, then met her eyes. She wasn't ashamed to admit she relished the discomfort she saw there, the disquiet. Why should she make it easy for him to say goodbye? Yeah, this goodbye was crushing her, and she wanted it to crush him too.

She had a sudden harrowing look into the future. At herself, decorating, playing music to celebrate the season. She was emotionless, a robot, going through the motions for her visiting brothers. Formerly her favorite time of the year, now destined to be the reminder of a heartbreak she knew no number of lifetimes would cure.

She forced her gaze to his face, and though it was painful to look at him, she took some satisfaction in noting the pallor of his skin under its olive tones and the deep line running between his brows, one that hadn't appeared there till last night. There was no blinding Jake smile for her. He looked as sick as she felt.

She folded her arms across her chest, waiting, and finally he spoke.

"I have to tell you, first off, I always planned to come back after Christmas, stay here, with you, till mid-January. Like we talked about. But then…" His voice was so low and gritty she had to lean in to hear. "When I… Then I decided it was better this way. One goodbye, not two because Honey…I couldn't say goodbye to you twice. I almost wish…" He lifted one hand toward her face again, and she reared back. He dropped it. "I almost wish…I hadn't met you…because saying goodbye is damn near killing me."

Wished he hadn't met her?

"You wish you'd never…" she sputtered, "met me? You had to come back to tell me that you wish we'd never met? I'm… I thought…I had feelings for you. Damn it, Jake! Damn you for saying that. Go. Get out." Her vision blurred with furious tears. Her voice rose, and in a second, she'd be shrieking if he didn't get out of her sight. She brought the palms of her hands up to cover her eyes. Pressed them hard to her aching, streaming sockets.

When she opened them, he was gone.

She sent the door crashing on its hinges, and the sound reverberated into the echoing silence. Childish? Yes. And ultimately, unsatisfying.

She shuffled to the window, hid behind the curtain in case he looked up, watching and waiting till he appeared on the sidewalk below. She bit down hard on the knuckles of her left hand as he tossed his duffel into the trunk of the waiting Uber. He paused to reach into his jacket, slid dark sunglasses on. Then he glanced up to her window for just a moment before he got into the car and left her life forever.

****

Thirty minutes later, she was on her way back to Caryville. Craven coward that she was, she was grateful to visit during Christmas. No one would guess the reason she wasn't in New York City was another Honey relationship disaster. How they'd laugh if her neighbors found out she'd managed to fall for a guy, and not because the guy represented stability or security but just because of who he was and who she was or thought she was when she was with him. Someone she thought matched her on every level. *How dumb can you be, Honey?*

The six-hour drive gave her a ton of time to wallow and wonder. When she wasn't crying. The biggest what if being, if she'd known everything she knew now, would she still have gotten involved with Jake? She wouldn't admit this to anyone else, but yeah. Yeah, she would have. The pain of his leaving left her sleepless, aching, and angry. Ten lifetimes wouldn't be enough to forget him, wouldn't be enough for her to close her eyes and not see him behind her closed lids every time.

But she'd never regret her time with him.

But not Jake. He wished he'd never met her. Those words, his last words to her, were a sledgehammer to her exposed heart. God. She needed to focus on those words and just let them pulverize her heart till she didn't feel anything at all.

When she pulled onto the dirt driveway, the windows were lit from within with a foggy green and red glow that meant the tree was up and the oven was on. More lights, the clear kind, were suspended from the porch rafters.

Derek and Donnie came running out, and Joss ambled out at a slower pace to greet her. Honey's eyes filled again because, somehow, ridiculously, she hadn't cried enough. The twins had put aside some dinner for her, and she ate the mangled but somehow tasty meatloaf because she hadn't had a thing to eat since last night except the stale Mentos she'd found in the glove compartment on the ride up.

Going back home was the right thing to do. Because the comfort and familiarity of her brothers and even Joss, giving gifts, handmade ceramic musical ornaments for Derek and Donnie and a flannel shirt for Joss, pushed out at least for short moments, thoughts of Jake.

Still, naturally because this was her sucky life, while Honey sat at dinner with her brothers, their first question was about him. They backed off quick when her monosyllabic answer did nothing to hide the quaver in her voice. Even Joss simply nodded as if he totally expected she'd say she'd stay home for only one more day before heading back to the city to get ready for her internship.

She read the thought bubble over Joss's head, which said she was just like Willow. Stopped by sometimes on holidays, then went off again. Which was horribly unfair, but she wasn't ready to do battle with him or confide in him or her brothers. Not ready to say, "Hey, Joss, you and I have more in common than you think."

She was raw.

She was out of plans and running on autopilot. She had till January 20th before she had to start, but the larger issue was where she'd stay. She had to secure a rental on Long Island or Queens, and the only thing she'd learned over these painful weeks was not to commit to a place without meeting her potential roommates and signing a lease.

But back in her old room, sleepless on the well-worn chaise that replaced her bed, the questions rushed to fill the space in her head, and every question and all the space was Jake. Did his future wife meet him when he landed in Italy? When would they marry? Where would they live? What about his mother?

Why didn't he call out his mom on her bullshit? Yeah, and why didn't she call her mom out on hers? Willow had blithely transferred the responsibilities of motherhood onto her fourteen-year-old daughter, knowing Honey loved her brothers and obligation if nothing else would force her to do everything she could to care for her them. Willow had taken advantage of the situation to suit her own life, and Honey never had it in her to complain because she adored Derek and Donnie, had loved them since infancy.

But still. Joss had helped in his way, but Honey was a fulltime unpaid caregiver at a time when she could've used a mother to help her be a little less awkward, a little less dorky. At best, Willow was her friend, the kind who came around periodically to party with you and tell you how much better her life was than yours.

That was Willow. She always sent money at the beginning of the school term, so there was that.

What would Willow say about Jake? Probably caution Honey not to get in too deep, to take care of herself, her career. Too late. Honey had dived into a new relationship, and she'd sunk like a stone.

Anxious to avoid the sympathetic stares of her brothers who had never seen her as anything less than focused and capable, and had no idea how to comfort her, she got up before dawn to start the drive back. Though she had wanted and needed contact with her family, she wasn't the same person who moved to the city a month ago. Rick's cheating had scuffed her pride. Jake's defection crushed her heart.

Halfway back to the city, her cell rang, and a New York City number popped up on the screen. She'd been puttering in the slow lane, so she easily pulled over on Route 80 to take the call rather than let it go to voicemail. It wasn't Jake's number, but her unreliable stomach dropped anyhow when an official sounding female asked to speak to her. It took a few seconds for the substance of what she was saying to sink in.

"So basically what you're telling me…?"

"What I'm saying is, we now have a position open in our back office. I saved your resumé. Your math and science background is impressive. You didn't apply for this position, but we'd like to meet you."

"I, sure, I'd love to meet with you too."

"The period between Christmas and New Year is always slow. Are you available today?"

After she finished the call, she rolled down the windows in the Ford, but she still couldn't catch her breath. She stepped out of the car on wobbly legs and leaned against the hood. Life was so freakin' weird. Looked like the universe saw what a basket case she was over Jake and decided to throw her a bone. If she got this job, it would be a financial game changer.

She was offered the position later the same day. Start date right after the New Year. More math than art but she wanted to be okay with it. She would be okay with it because the financial incentive was too great to ignore. The HR person at the museum on Long Island said she wasn't surprised Honey would back out of their low-wage internship for a bona fide position with Sotheby's. "You have a great resumé, and frankly we would've offered you the same thing if we had a similar opening. Good luck to you."

Back outside, she shivered in the feeble December sun. She wanted to call Jake to share her good news. Was she really this pathetic? She called Lizzie.

"Sooo, I'm not looking for a place on Long Island anymore. Life is coming at me fast right now, Lizzie. I can't wait to talk to you."

"Same. You can come straight here if you want, 'cause Kurt and I are done. I told him he had to go, and he moved out on Christmas Eve. I'll give you all the gory details when you get here."

Chapter 25
Wallow

The flight attendant shook him awake as the plane began its descent into Fiumicino Airport.

He downed Jameson after Jameson, Connor's *FML* alcohol of choice, until his vision blurred and Honey's face receded from his mind's eye. He fell into a stupor, missing both the on-board dinner and breakfast.

He stretched his spine in the cramped seat, then swayed to his feet to use the head. He splashed cold water on his face, examined his bloodshot eyes. He looked almost as bad as he felt.

But yeah, mission accomplished, right? He was in Italy, and he'd been unconscious for ninety-nine percent of the trip here. The cab ride to his hotel was too brief and bumpy for him to sleep again, so he looked out the window.

As the taxi wound its way into Rome, he noticed enormous Christmas trees in every piazza, decked out with ornaments bigger than his fists. Honey would love them because the Italians went all out. He closed his eyes on the image of her enchanted face, eyes sparkling brighter than the lights surrounding them as they strolled through the Botanical Garden Train Show. The Jameson sloshed around in his stomach as the taxi jolted to a stop in front of the Hotel Russie.

He decided to arrange to see his mother now before

he gave in to the urge and opened the minibar whiskey.

"I'll come over to pick you up at your apartment," he told her over the phone. "In two hours."

His change of plan from their usual dinner meeting didn't sit well with her, but he hung up before she could say anything else. What he wanted to say shouldn't have an audience.

After a shower, he was tempted to rifle through the minibar, but with no desire to eat, a shot would likely knock him on his ass before he got to his mom's apartment.

And he needed to be awake enough to tell her what he thought of her before he finally acquiesced. This wasn't an operation he would train for, accomplish, then move on. This was the rest of his life—without Honey.

He couldn't regret what he'd said. He *did* wish he'd never met her. Because painful though it would be to give up his life in New York, his friends, his work, his home—everything—he'd never seen himself sharing any of it. Every woman had been like every other woman.

Until Honey, marriage was a business arrangement plain and simple. Before Honey, the thought of tying himself to a woman to fulfill his promise was, if not okay, then a means to a desired end. And the end was relief from the weight of his guilt. Most marriages he'd observed were unhappy one way or another. So what was the big deal? Because when he fulfilled his pledge, maybe, just maybe he would sleep at night.

He'd evaded his future, this future, for years to enjoy everything that would be denied him. So sure that when the time came, one woman would be like any other for the purpose of fulfilling his promise and easing his guilt. And yeah, it was asinine, but the irony couldn't be ignored. How fucked up was it when he finally accepted he couldn't put off the future any longer, he'd met the one woman he wanted everything with? The one woman he wanted forever with?

He couldn't stop thinking about her tears. First how she'd tried to hide them, and then how she was like "Fuck you, Jake, I'm gonna let you see them. I'm gonna make you hurt even worse. I'm gonna make you remember how you walked away from me. From everything we could be, everything bright and hopeful. You're never gonna forget how you threw us away."

And you know what, dickhead, she's hurt now, but she is funny, brilliant, and sexy, and it could be she's already met the guy who'll take my place and give her everything I couldn't.

Hell, when he met her, it was because a dude had been working his game on her. Then there was the ex. The grabby roommate. Then she decided to be with him and only with him, and what had he done? He'd cut the whole thing short to make good on his fucked-up promise.

He opened the minibar and pulled out the whiskey. The shot hit the back of his throat, and his vision finally cleared. Suddenly the path was obvious. He'd attempt to make Franca understand, but he didn't care what she said anymore because all bets were off. He was going back to New York. If it was between being with Honey and the damn nightmares, bring on the nightmares. He'd face anything with Honey at his side.

****

His mother's building was old and decrepit in a

way that had nothing to do with historical Roman landmarks. There was a garbage-strewn alley next door, and the faint stench of urine was all around even on a brisk December night. This was where she'd been living? Was there something more to her need to match him to a socialite than her obsession over heritage and Cesco? Before she buzzed him up, her usually commanding voice sounded weak and breathless through the tinny intercom.

He entered the inner courtyard as a bunch of teenagers came down the stairwell, lighting cigarettes and laughing into their phones.

The staircase to the fourth floor was worn *carrara*. At his knock, she opened the door a crack, and he saw the lock was on a chain.

"It's me, Mamma," he said, reverting to Italian for her benefit. "Merry Christmas."

She swung the door wide and grabbed his arm, pulled him inside before securing the bolt.

Air kisses exchanged, he looked over her shoulder at the chaos beyond. It was a two-room apartment with a kitchen alcove. Franca was dressed to the nines in the red boucle suit she'd worn last year. And maybe the year before that…

She motioned him to the settee, where he pushed aside books, notebooks, and fabric swatches to sit carefully on the fragile seat, eying the rolls of fabric and filled ashtrays on the dusty, Venetian, mirrored cocktail table. His mother still hadn't kicked her smoking habit.

He stood again and paced to the window but resisted the urge to open it because it was cool outside. He remembered Honey's question about Christmas celebrations and Christmas trees. There was no evidence inside the apartment that it was December 25th as opposed to June 25th. Anything like that had stopped after Cesco. From the looks of this apartment, his mother's life had ground to a halt after Cesco.

Her thin bejeweled fingers pleated the wool of her skirt. She was uncomfortable he was seeing her at home where it was obvious money was tight and her legacy long gone.

"How do you support yourself, Mamma?"

She stopped fidgeting, clasped her hands together on her knees, and pursed her lips. "It isn't easy. I'm a bookkeeper for a few of the smaller design firms in the area. Furniture and clothing."

He nodded and forced a smile. "Using your MBA."

"Yes, but I've had to take on more than I've wanted to lately, and these startups, they should have an accounting department, but instead they have one staff member handling everything financial…"

"Why don't you work for one of the bigger firms? With the benefit of a large staff and higher salary?"

"Giancarlo, please, as if they'd hire me. I'm not getting any younger." She lifted a hand to her still-thick hair with its enhanced blonde streaks. "Besides, if any of my friends found out I work…"

"I get it, okay? You're proud of your heritage. You should be. But the Italian aristocracy is gone. It's been gone a long time. You have to accept that. I read the grandson of our last king is hawking pasta from a truck in LA."

She raised a dismissive brow. "Who would believe such a thing? This is what I have. This is what I know. I will not have you disparage it like your father did."

"Here." She pulled a photograph up on her phone, and as he paced back to sit on the settee again, she pushed the cell into his line of vision. "This is Emilia Castelnova, she has her MBA, and her parents are eager to make the match."

"And is Emilia on board with it?" The brunette in the photo could be anywhere from twenty to thirty, generically attractive in her sophisticated, silk dress. Not at all like a quirky blonde with the row of earrings in her right ear and a cupid's bow mouth that could go from conversational to dirty in seconds.

"Dio, Gianni. Of course she said yes. I showed her your photo too. You're a strapping man. They have money but little pedigree. You have the pedigree…"

And you're pimping me out.

"*You* have the pedigree, Mamma. I'm my father's son, remember? Why don't you look for a gentleman of your own?"

"Your father was, is… I was in love with him. I would never…marry another."

What? What in the actual? The strain of conversing in Italian so infrequently had to mean he'd misunderstood her. He switched back to English. "But you would sacrifice me and this woman so easily?"

She switched to English too and sat straighter in her chair opposite the settee.

"Don't judge me. I went against my parents' wishes to marry your father. They cut me off completely. I was left with nothing—nothing!—except for the small legacy from my aunt, which I lived on for years. I came to regret challenging them. I loved your father, but we were from two different worlds. My parents warned me. And so I wanted you and Cesco"—

her voice choked—"to have what I didn't have. Respect in society for your noble heritage. Financial security. You *owe* me."

He shook his head, started to reach out to her to grasp her hands, but she stiffened, jerking them back to her sides, and he opened his hands on his lap instead. "I do okay in my profession. I can give you security, Mamma. I can support you. My business does well in New York. You can come back with me."

"No! I will not. Have you forgotten…?"

"Dio, never. Are you joking? I forget nothing. But Cesco is gone. He's been gone for so long."

His voice thickened. He stopped, expelling a harsh breath. He wanted to hug her. He wanted her arms around him. They're both grieving, still, for Cesco and his father. But she'd never done that. Not for him anyway. She was frozen in place, hands clasped over her elbows on her lap.

And all at once, it was time. Time for him to stop wanting what would never happen because he would never make things right for his mother. Regardless of who he married, where he lived, or who he tried to be for her. No matter what hoops he jumped through, he couldn't give her what she wanted most. Cesco.

What he wanted most used to be to atone for the sin of somehow surviving when his brother had not. Nothing had ever been more important than that. For twenty years, all he'd desired was a way to be at peace. Without guilt. Without nightmares. But now something was more important than all of it.

The possibility of a life with Honey. If he hadn't fucked it up beyond repair.

"You live in the past. I know you'd rather it was

me who died that day, but I did not. I am here."

She didn't react to that statement at all; she didn't dispute that he was always a distant second to her golden boy. He shrugged, suddenly restless, and ready to be done with this conversation. He stood.

"And I've realized I'm too alive to accept this bloodless match. Even if I don't sleep another night of my life. And *you* shouldn't ask it of me. We are here. Alive. We have each other…or not…"

She was staring at him like he was crazy. She was not listening. "That is why you must do this…you must honor your brother's memory. *You live*. He…"

He cleared his throat. Spotted the drinks cart she had tucked in a corner near the entrance to the kitchen and strode over to it while she watched him, unmoving. Poured whiskey neat and gulped a numbing shot before returning to pace in front of her.

"Mamma, listen. And think about this. Here's what I can do. I will pay for this apartment for you. But I would request six months of the year you come to the states. You can stay at the vineyard on Long Island. Tell your friends you're checking on your family holdings in the states. You know that'll impress them. Then I can see you and make sure you're okay. But I will not marry this woman Emilia. What I *can* do, if she and her family are interested, is put them in touch with a friend of mine in New York. He knows investment advisors and moneymen. He is a moneyman. If he sees value in their business, he will help them; he'll invest in their expansion."

"But what about what you did, your ancestors, you changed your name… Dio, the shame…"

"I am Jake Ricco now. And I'm proud to be Jake

Ricco. I'm American, a veteran. The past…"

"You do dishonor to your family name, your brother…"

"Basta. No more. It's your choice, Mamma. You can keep his memory alive in other ways. But not through me. I'm done here."

He suggested a quiet side street near the Vatican for dinner but ended up taking her to a restaurant near the Spanish steps as usual. It was an indication of her situation that she even agreed to dine with him given their conversation, but she did. She wouldn't miss the opportunity to dine well, see and be seen. There was no more talk of his refusal to follow her plans for him. She made small talk about people he'd never met whose reputations were burnished on social media.

Dinner, which Italians like to drag out especially on holidays, was a quick hour. Franca's figure had not rounded with the years like some women her age. She was society all the way, not a traditional Italian mamma. In deference to the day, it was Christmas after all, she drank one glass of prosecco and ate a modest fish dinner and refused dessert. Jake looked over the dessert offerings, knowing Honey would've had a tough time deciding between the tiramisu and the gelato and he would've ordered both so she wouldn't have to choose. He ordered the salted caramel gelato with his espresso.

He stayed on to organize the automated payment of her rent with his bank. He hired a cleaning service to come once a week complete with an organizing assistant to help her cull through her treasures and sell or get rid of some of it to make the place look less like a mausoleum. He extracted a tentative promise she'd consider coming to New York in June to stay for six months.

"I haven't been to America in twenty years. So…" She shrugged.

"So that's why you should. You should come to see me. I'm the only family you've got." And no, she had no interest.

"If you would consider, just think about this Emilia."

"No!" He slashed his hand through the air. "It's not happening. And if you call me about it, I will hang up on you. I want to hear how you're doing and maybe tell you about me. That's it."

Clearly, she was struggling financially and desperate to keep up appearances with her well-heeled friends. Her desire to marry him off to preserve her heritage had more to do with her dire financial state than Cesco or his dad at this point. If he provided for her—and he could—she could keep up the façade that was so vital to her. She'd have to be satisfied with that.

His hurt was as fresh and sharp as the wound opened the day Cesco died. There was no comfort seeing her. There never was. Because for his mother, nothing changed. She expressed no interest in a relationship with him. Cesco was dead. It was his fault, and he owed her. The only difference was his decision, his unwillingness to feed her narrative. But the torment of his memories and nightmares was nothing compared to the thought of never seeing Honey again.

He couldn't wait to get back to her. She soothed him; in her arms, in her body she bore some of the burden he'd been carrying for two decades. She absorbed some of his pain. And what had he done? In return he'd hurt her.

His flight was overbooked and delayed. Waiting in the lounge at Fiumicino airport, he started to text her, but the words wouldn't come. What he had to say had to be done face to face. Words coming from his heart and soul should be spoken to her in person. In contrast to the trip out, he decided to avoid alcohol. But whether he was wide awake or in an alcohol-induced stupor, his mind's eye saw one thing—the look on her face when he told her he wished he'd never met her. *Fuck it, Jake.*

His cell rang. His mother's number flashed on the screen.

Chapter 26
Say Goodbye to the Old

Honey wiped her eyes, her tears part laughter, part the overwhelming sadness consuming her since Jake left. How would she have survived these last days without Lizzie? Lizzie'd known her since middle school, and there wasn't a milestone or a crisis they hadn't shared together. Lizzie went easy on her with the Jake quizzing because Honey lost her composure every time she tried to tell her the whole story. But when Honey divulged the bare bones of her heartbreaking hookup, Lizzie declared celebrations were in order.

Lizzie topped off Honey's glass and held her own out, closed her eyes to propose another toast.

"What are we up to? Oh, yeah. Third thing to be celebrating this new year. Career success."

Honey raised her glass. "Baby steps into giant steps. I'm saying it. I'm proud of us. We rock. Cheers."

They clinked glasses, and Honey took a healthy pull on her champagne. They'd splurged on the good stuff because they both could look forward to a sweet pay increase in the new year.

"Amazing to think I'll make more with this two-week shoot of a commercial series than I did last year, all in." Alcohol gave Lizzie a goofy grin but didn't erase the delighted shock on her face.

"Girl, you worked hard enough for it. You've been

at it for years. Glad you're seeing the reward." Honey took another effervescent gulp.

"Yeah, hate to say it, but that's another reason Kurt had to go. He was draining me, not just financially because man, he couldn't keep a job, not even as a barista. But he was more downer than support system. I had to keep the faith for both of us."

Honey was silent. She could count on one hand, with a couple of digits left over, the times, in all the years she'd known him, Rick ever asked her anything about her art. Jake on the other hand engaged her, teased her, quizzed her, asked her a ton of questions about her process, organized the excursion to the exhibit he somehow figured out she'd wanted to see, and brought her brothers along. The push pull of professional calling versus family obligations was a major issue in his life too.

Wasn't that why he dropped everything? Dropped her…to go back to Italy and make good on a promise wrapped up in a family obligation?

Don't go there, Honey.

Somewhere along the way, their "it's just sex, let's give in to this thing between us" hookup had turned into the real deal for her. Happily ever after wasn't in her DNA, but her emotions were involved moments after meeting him. No point in denying it. When he offered to let her stay in his hotel room that first night, he'd revealed the gooey center inside his hard exterior, and game over—she was a goner. She would never forget him. There wasn't enough champagne in the world to make that happen.

"Okay, get your coat on." Lizzie put her glass down with a clunk.

"What?" Honey squinted and blinked, but Lizzie's mane of red-gold hair was still a fuzzy nimbus around her angular face.

"We've toasted everything from finding our new place, our jobs, to our breakups. And you're still tearing up on me. Time for drastic measures. We're going dancing."

"Arrgg, I don't know if I can walk a straight line, Lizzie. Forget about trying to dance."

"Who cares? We're going out, and we're gonna let it all out, the rage, the hurt, and the bull. No sad crying on New Year's Eve, Honey. I won't have it."

The music was deafening, the club's cover charge double the expensive bubbly they'd knocked back at the apartment, but it was worth it because dancing squashed out everything else for a time. In the crush of bodies, she let it all go. With every pulse of the strobe light, her spirit wasn't exactly lifted but more like emptied of all that weighed her down till all she felt was the booming music, her staccato breaths, and her pounding heartbeat.

They finally got an Uber, Lizzie's treat, after they both swore up and down to the driver they weren't drunk enough to get sick in his car. They weren't and they didn't because they'd sweated out most of the alcohol, and with New Year's Eve twenty-dollar Cosmos, they cashed out pretty quick.

Sticky with sweat, exhausted, Honey slipped on a sleep shirt and had her first dreamless sleep in days. She may have been too drunk to dream, but as soon as she woke up, she automatically reached for her phone. She needed her Jake fix, the photos she'd taken of him at the Christmas tree. Every morning before she could force herself out of bed and every night before she could even pretend to fall asleep, she scrolled through them, telling herself no, she wouldn't print them because, hello, she wasn't a stalker. Was she? She'd get over him. He was living his life, in another country. It was a new year, they had new lives, and if she's in *his* past, she had to put him in hers.

But sometimes just for a little while, alone in bed, she let herself remember. She searched the pictures for clues in his beautiful face about what he felt for her. And yeah, she forced herself to acknowledge it. He felt nothing. It had been a hookup, his pre-wedding, get his rocks off last tango before he tied the knot.

He'd walked away. There'd been no contact. And maybe that was for the best. She didn't want to think about what she'd do if he reached out to her, if he wanted to continue their hookup even though he was engaged or even married.

Because she didn't want to admit a tiny part of her wanted him to come back, engaged, married, or head sheik of a harem. If she gave those thoughts oxygen, they'd kill her. Because she wasn't so sure she could say no to the prospect of even an occasional meeting with him. Her self-respect demanded she say no. But she craved him like chocolate, and she didn't trust herself. She'd cave as fast as she had the first time, faster, because she knew now what it meant to be with him, because she'd committed every moment to memory and no one, no one, would ever compare to him.

She almost took comfort in the knowledge that her fantasy would never happen. She would never be tempted because he wouldn't cheat. He'd made that god-awful promise to his unhinged mother, and he'd see it through. Once he married his socialite, he'd be faithful. That was how he was made, and she had no doubt about it. That was why even though she wanted to hate him, she couldn't.

The most she could hope for was the pain would lessen. In time every thought of him would cease to be a rusty knife to her guts. She was also certain she'd never find anybody else. But she had her career, and between her studio art and her position at Sotheby's, her hours would be overfull. She was so much more like her mother than she'd ever known.

But for now, just one look, she promised herself. One quick scroll to get her through today. Maybe she wouldn't need to look again tonight. She w*ould* wean herself. But not right now.

She stretched her hand out, ran it along the edge of the end table, but her fingers didn't touch her phone. She sprang upright, pried her eyes open to search the small space. Grabbed her purse from the floor beside her, but it wasn't inside. Panic set in, and she closed her eyes again. The effort it took to recall the details of where they'd gone and what she'd worn last night was a testament to a long, drunken evening.

Okay, she hadn't brought her purse; she'd tucked her phone into the back pocket of her black pants. She checked. Not there. Her eyes jumped around the studio, taking in the detritus of a night's drinking. There nothing to see but the colorful, plastic champagne flutes, candy wrappers, empty popcorn bowl, unwashed cheeseboard.

She darted into Lizzie's area, shook her awake. "Please tell me I was smart enough to give you my phone last night for safekeeping."

"Jeez, Honey, please tell me it's later than seven a.m. and you didn't lose it after you've lost every single other thing you own..."

"Um, oh, crap." Honey flopped onto the sofa, then popped up and took Lizzie's phone. "I'm gonna call the club and the Uber."

Her final call was to the police where she was not so politely informed that she was one of a shit ton of Manhattan New Year's Eve revelers who had a phone lost or stolen the previous evening. "I don't wanna tell you you're outta luck, but..." the cop said.

Then she had to email her future boss at Sotheby's to let her know she'd "misplaced" her phone, giving Lizzie's contact info in the meantime. Then as Lizzie grumbled her way into the shower, she sat cross-legged on the sofa and snuck a peek at her Instagram from Lizzie's phone. The only photo of Jake she'd posted, now the only one that wasn't lost in her phone and unreachable on the cloud, was the one where his noble profile was in shadow, which didn't really matter because Honey had his face memorized. His broad back, the corded muscles of his arms, and long legs outlined in the fading winter evening, and the glow of the Christmas tree lights.

Staring at his picture, her skin flushed and breathing went shallow just like the first day she'd met him. She couldn't look away from him, not even a picture of him. He'd been so uncomfortable with her request to take a photo. But he'd given in when he saw it meant something to her for her business. That was when she'd started to think he might feel something for her.

How could he consider his own physical beauty a burden?

No question, he knew how to use it. But did he believe his only value, the only thing he had to offer was his body? And sure, during the time they spent together, she'd gorged on him, devoured him like he was cake and every day was her birthday. But his appeal from the beginning had everything to do with *all* of him. His personality—domineering, charming, sexy, generous, demanding, stern, thoughtful, and *so* weighted down by guilt.

Would he ever truly take joy in his physical self, or had he completely absorbed the message his only worth now that his brother was gone was as his physical stand-in? As a body who must fulfill a promise because somehow, he'd been lucky enough to survive the tragedy that killed his brother?

If she ever came face to face with her, she'd force his mother to see how messed up it was that a mother could cast aside her surviving son when fate had taken the other.

Aren't you forgetting his future wife, Honey? For all you know, they're already married. She was in the picture with him now. She'd see more than the charming surface Jake showed the world. She'd see Jake. Damn, they'd have children together. Jake's babies.

Oh, God. She pressed her hands to her temples to relieve the pressure of the vise squeezing the skin covering her skull, compressing everything inside her head. *Jake's babies.* She stared at his picture, her vision blurring with tears. *Jake's babies.*

The alcohol rolling around in her stomach since

last night wanted to find its way out. She sat on the sofa, legs folded underneath her, rocking back and forth. She couldn't make herself look away from the photo. *Jake's babies.*

Lizzie appeared in front of her, her long hair swathed in a towel turban.

"Oh, sweetie, no. No, you can't... Give me the phone, Honey."

When she didn't respond, Lizzie pulled the phone from her hand and shooed her into the shower.

****

Jake picked up the call. It was not his mother. The woman speaking urgently in a staccato burst of Italian told him his mother collapsed in the town square near her apartment. Strangely she'd listed him as her emergency contact. He returned to the city, went to the urgent clinic near the Vatican.

His mom had COPD. No surprise to him in hindsight as he'd witnessed her labored breathing the entire time they spoke at her apartment and later at the restaurant. She brushed off her diagnosis.

"Please Giancarlo, of course. I know." She waved a hand, dismissing the subject.

"Yeah, but you collapsed in Piazza San..."

"I know what happened. As you say in America, it is what it is. I like the cigarettes." She lifted a brow, laying in her hospital bed like a queen and challenging him to dispute it.

"No," he declared. "This is a game changer. You're coming to New York. To your vineyard on the island. The air is good there. It will help you. I'm making the arrangements. This isn't your choice anymore."

While she was treated, he undid all the

arrangements he'd made previously for her apartment. After a few days, he saw her settled back in the now cleaner, better organized space with a caregiver. He bought her a ticket to JFK and told her he'd meet her when she arrived, when the doctors deemed her stable enough to travel. He contacted Connor and told him he was returning to the states. He wouldn't be selling his townhouse or his business. He contacted the vineyard and instructed the manager to ready the guesthouse adjacent to the main house for his mother's arrival.

At long last, he was on a plane to New York. He called Honey as soon as he landed, but the call rang straight to message. The long cab ride was punctuated by another handful of futile calls. Inside his house, he dropped the phone as he took the stairs at a run to the fourth floor. Nothing. Her door was locked. He didn't want to check, but he went back to the kitchen and saw her key was on the hook. No note.

Of course she hadn't stayed, asshole.

He texted her.

—I'm back in New York. To stay. I need to see you. I love you—

He thought about her face when he'd said he wished he never met her.

He spent the next hour alternately texting her and calling her. Where could she be when her internship didn't start till late January?

This is New York, bozo. It's January 6. She had more than two weeks to go somewhere, anywhere you're not. Because you told her you wished you'd never met her. Remember that? And wherever she was, dickhead, she was on the other side of the phone ignoring you.

He raised his fist to the kitchen door and took a swing. The pain jarred him from shoulder to wrist. He examined his bleeding knuckles like they were someone else's, watched his blood drip to the floor.

You said goodbye, Jake. He thought of the tears that had seeped out of her eyes when he said he was going away. Until that moment, in spite of the connection that was as hot as a live wire between them, he hadn't known for sure whether he wasn't just a hookup to her. He'd blocked out the way lust was turning into a mix of passion and tenderness, fascinated interest turning to admiration and total fucking absorption in everything Honey. And it was obvious now she'd been shattered when he made his little speech, ripping the heart out of the great thing they had. She'd cried. *And you said you were never coming back.*

****

Jim Duffy was opening up for the evening when he got there.

"Jake. Happy New Year, man. Whoa, wadja do to yer hand?" He chuckled. "Hope the other guy looks worse."

Jake glanced at his fist, at the dried blood and shredded skin over purple bruised knuckles, then shrugged at Jim.

"You need something on that." Jim reached under the bar for hydrogen peroxide and splashed some on, then handed him a wadded-up bar towel with ice at its center.

"What's going on Jake? I haven't seen that look in your eyes since your old man passed, God rest his soul."

Jakes raked his uninjured hand through his hair.

"Have you seen Honey?"

"No." Jim raised a speculative brow. "The other day she dropped off a Christmas card and said goodbye. She's done working here, because, you know, her internship on the Island."

"Yeah, right, but…where did she…?"

"She finally see the light?" Jim's teasing smile morphed into a frown at Jake's expression. "You're kidding me, right? You two not together? What happened?"

"It was never supposed to be…we had an understanding. I broke it off, but…"

"But now you know that girl's the real deal? I've never seen two people happier than you together. Except maybe me and my Jeannie. Walked around like a fool, wondering how I got so lucky. What the fuck is wrong with you?"

"It wasn't supposed to turn into anything…permanent."

"But it did."

Yeah, it did. But I have…" Jake straightened up to his full height. "I had…obligations in Italy. I never expected to…" He shook his head. "I hurt her."

"You did what?" Jim's pasty skin reddened as he took another look at Jake's bloody fist. He slapped a beefy hand on the bar.

"No…no, I mean she cried when I broke it off a couple of weeks ago. And it took me doing that, making her cry, to realize I can't face never seeing her again to…"

"Get yer head out of your ass?"

"Yeah, and now she's gone. I have to tell her how I feel."

"To apologize and tell her you love her."

"Yeah."

"Well, you know what you have to do. Go find her."

Chapter 27
Operation Honey

If he treated this like a mission, if he made the lists he was so accustomed to and proceeded in his usual methodical, stubborn way, maybe he'd survive till he saw her again. Till he apologized and begged for one more chance, swore he'd never hurt her again, never make her cry. He didn't deserve her, but he'd spend the rest of his life showing he was her man. Her only man.

Restless to do something, not sleeping anyway, he drove to Long Island at six the next morning even though her internship there hadn't started yet. At a standstill in his rented sports car on the merciless Long Island Expressway, he had hours to rehash every moment they were together and how he refused to think about the time he would leave her, how he told himself their short time together would be enough. Until he did it, and it ripped the heart out of his chest.

"Sir, I'd like to help you. I really would." The young woman at the museum's reception desk allowed her gaze to linger on the growth of scruff on his jaw as she rested a hand at her throat. "But we have no one by that name here."

After he scrawled Honey's name on the back of it, he pushed his card across the desk. "She's a new hire. When she starts, can you see that she gets this card? And ask her to call me?" He looked into her eyes till she nodded rapidly. "Please."

"Sure, Mr. er, Ricco." She examined the card, then eyed him again. "Is she…a relative?"

"She's, she's my…everything." He heard himself say the words and knew the tips of his ears were reddening as he turned away. "You can tell her that too."

Six the next morning and he was on his way to Caryville. Seven hours of driving with a raging hangover later, his GPS failed to locate the old Victorian her brothers and their father lived in. He stopped for coffee and directions at the local inn, the Crown.

"You lookin' for Willow Jansen, you won't find her at that house there."

"Ah, no. I'm looking for her daughter, Honey, or her brothers."

"Her *half*-brothers you mean?" The bartender looked down his nose. "Well those boys are likely in school at the moment. Yesterday started the new semester at the high school. And you know Honey's gone. Moved away. Same as her ma. She's a smart one." He snickered. "Book smart I guess you call it. Seems our little town wasn't good enough for her."

"Or maybe your town wasn't good enough *to* her. Appreciate the directions." Jake dropped cash on the bar and left.

He found the house, a rambling Victorian with dark green shutters and a deep porch. Christmas lights were strung through the upper cornices, and the wicker porch furniture in the corner was half covered by a tarp. He rang the bell, and the booming ringer echoed back at him.

He returned to the Ferrari and leaned against the hood, zipping his leather jacket against the wind. He stared at the house, picturing a small girl in overalls, her long, unruly braids waving like ribbons of silver behind her as she skipped up the six steps to the front porch.

An hour later, he was still there when Derek and Donnie came ambling up the road at a snail's pace, their loud, octave-sliding teenage voices clashing like cymbals. Derek had his guitar slung across his back. They did a double take when they saw him, their faces going from surprised pleasure to suspicious disdain in an instant.

"Hi, guys." Jake straightened up from his slouch against the car.

"Jake. What're you doing here?" That was Donnie. His shocked voice was edging toward hostile.

"I'm looking for Honey."

They glanced at each other for a second, then focused back on him. Jake figured they just had a full-blown conversation without saying a word out loud. Twin thing. He and Cesco had had that too.

Finally, Derek said, "Sweet ride," shrugging at the Ferrari gleaming in the fading afternoon light.

"Thanks." He forced a smile, slid his clenched hands into his jacket pockets. "I'd like to speak to Honey. I…do you know where she is?"

They looked at each other again, and then Derek spoke.

"You hurt her, Jake. We liked you. But you hurt her. If you don't know where she is, that's probably because she doesn't want you to know."

His gaze searched each of their faces, not wanting sympathy but looking for something, any small morsel of hope. They stared back at him like men, not the raucous teenagers who'd snuck into a bar a few weeks ago.

"I fucked up. I want, I have to, make it right, tell her I'm sorry."

"No," they said in unison. Donnie crossed his wiry drummer's arms across his chest.

"Can you tell her I'm back in New York for good? To stay. Can you tell her, I…please tell her I love her?"

They looked at him goggle-eyed, and then Donnie spoke. "Okay."

There was nothing to do then but ask after their father who was still at work. After that, the boys waited, grim-faced, as he got into the car and drove away.

Did he have any faith they'd tell her? He had to believe they would. The boys liked him. Or they used to. But they loved their sister. They'd tell her—if only for the chance to see him grovel. The question was whether Honey cared enough to do anything about it.

****

Five more days and every idea for where Honey could be was crossed off his list. It's easy to get lost in a city like New York. Easier with cash. But he didn't flatter himself. Even though Honey didn't have cash to spare, there was no way she'd abandon her job and her career dreams to go under his radar. She was here. He could feel her.

He didn't want to believe it, but the reality was staring him in the face. She hadn't called or texted. *You lost your fucking chance with her, Jake.*

No, he wouldn't give up. Not until she looked him in the eye and told him to get lost.

His mother arrived on Long Island. He met her at the airport and accompanied her to the vineyard where she was greeted like a visiting royal and basked in the attention of the staff and the companion he'd hired to assist her. The ensuing updates from the manager, Diego, on the drama surrounding her settling in left him in no doubt the man deserved a hefty pay increase as soon as he could discuss it with his mother's relatives.

His business was booming. Thank everything that was holy, Regina was back and helping with the backlog. But there was a gleam in Regina's eye when she spoke about her granddaughter, and there was no way Haven Security could compete with the little angel whose pictures she drooled over in her cellphone. Dollars to donuts he'd be looking for a new assistant in the near future.

He avoided even walking past Duffy's. He couldn't stand to think of Honey behind the bar and him lusting after her and teasing her, all the while falling in love with her. And him with his head too far up his ass to know what was happening, to declare himself hers forever and do whatever it took to make her happy.

But mid-month, he went back to Duffy's one night after Vlad sent an SOS text saying he was with Connor and Connor was drinking himself into a stupor over his girl, Lacey. Vlad had never seen Connor so hammered, but Jake had—plenty of times when they had first enlisted, and Jake volunteered to get him home. And all the while Jake listened to Connor ramble, he thought— at least Connor knew where his woman was. He can fucking go see her and fix whatever he did wrong.

You let her go. When you had the chance to man up, you blew it. You walked away.

Every off-hour, he walked Avenue C where her actress friend lived, the one with the futon and the boyfriend. It was a long shot because Honey said she would move closer to her internship and he had no pedigree info on the friend. But he'd run down every lead that might point to where Honey was. He wasn't sleeping anyway, and when he did, the old nightmare was gone. Whether his eyes were opened or closed, all he saw was Honey.

He observed any number of people, with hair dyed every color of the rainbow, sporting tattoos and piercings of every description. No pale-haired pixies though. He walked the neighborhood till he was exhausted, then went home to dream of her again. In his nightmares, tears streamed down her face as she walked farther and farther away from him.

The next afternoon, he was in the same East Village neighborhood. It was his only lead now. Tomorrow he'd loop back to Caryville and talk to Derek and Donnie. Convince them to call her. Beg them if he had to. Then he'd check back at the museum on Long Island.

He passed St. Vincent's Church opposite the deli and went in to light a candle. It was January 22nd, Cesco's birthday. He would've been thirty-three today. What would Cesco think of him right now? He'd probably be laughing his ass off. Cesco had been the rule breaker and Jake the list-making rule follower.

C'mon, help me, brother.

Back outside, he crossed the avenue to the deli and ordered a large black coffee. Last night was another half-drunk, sleepless night. He'd crisscrossed the city, borough to borough, then come back yet again to any place that had some connection to Honey. Coffee cup in hand, he reached into his pocket for a dollar to give the guy, a fair-haired dude with a grime-streaked face, a guy he'd seen teetering against the brick wall near the side door of the deli on 14th Street with his ever-ready paper cup held out every time he'd walked past these last few days.

The guy leaned toward him. "Help me, brother," he said.

When he pulled cash out of his pocket to drop in the cup, he also grabbed hold of the small talisman he was never without. The luminous ornament, the Christmas gift Honey gave him, Polaris. He turned it over, worrying it in his hand, rubbing the glazed ceramic, his fingers sliding over the etching, *Made in Brooklyn.*

Made in Brooklyn.

No question Honey still went to the co-op in Brooklyn, no matter where she was living. She loved working there. When they were together, she'd gone there every day she wasn't working at Duffy's.

He downed the coffee in a couple of gulps, then sprinted home to boot up his computer. There were a shit ton of edgy galleries, artistic hangouts, and workspaces in New York City. Brooklyn had five ceramic workspace co-ops.

****

She'd put an apron over her work clothes in a minute. After she lugged the boxes with finished pieces to her car, she'd probably go in and work. She could go home. She needed sleep. But one or two hours at the co-op was better than sleepless hours alone or worse, debating Lizzie's righteous summing up of Jake's character.

She craved the escape the potter's wheel provided. The need to concentrate on that one thing, her work, commanded her complete attention. If she was focusing on the piece, she was not sinking down the dark hole of obsessing on everything Jake was surely doing. So she dragged ass to the co-op every evening after work and both days of the weekend.

The new position at Sotheby's was challenging but in a good way, the "learning every nuance of my job gives me no chance to focus on anything else" way. There was a ton of organizing in her role, and the focus on minutia kept her hair-trigger emotions in check. Her superiors were layering on more substantive tasks daily as she mastered the day-to-day aspects of the finance department.

Mental exhaustion met physical exhaustion, and sleep was the thing she pretended to do after she put on a T-shirt, brushed her teeth, and got into the sofa bed she'd scored online.

Most nights, she hopped the subway straight from work to the co-op, but tonight she drove because there was no storage space left here for everything she'd produced these past weeks. The studio was jammed with her output, and yeah, she'd have plenty of inventory to sell online this year. But between this side hustle, her new job, and Lizzie's TV commercial contract, when Lizzie's lease was up next month, they'd be able to afford a bigger place to rent. Something with a giant closet or basement storage or open space shelving.

Her largest, most unwieldy piece was an abstract of a giant wave with the figures of several humans struggling in its watery depths. Gerard, the artistic director here, called it all consuming and terrifying, and he'd encouraged her to enter it into some contests and exhibitions. Honey was good with that. She'd created it over a long stretch of hours right after Jake left. She couldn't wait to get the thing out of her sight. All consuming and terrifying just about summed up her emotions most days.

One more box to load. She closed the trunk, crossed the street, and headed back up the block toward the studio to get the last one.

"Stop right there."

The gravelly voice was behind her on the sidewalk. She hesitated, her step faltering for a moment. Lizzie was right. This was what happened when you were awake twenty out of twenty-four hours and hyped up on caffeine the whole time. Lizzie told her she'd start hallucinating, and now it was happening. She kept walking albeit at a slower pace, wondering if Jake the hallucination was any easier to take than Jake the actual human.

"I know you can hear me."

Definitely a hallucination. His deep voice was hollow.

Part of never seeing Jake again was hoping and praying all the details of him, his smile, his voice, his swagger would fade into blurry half recollection. It was the only way she'd survive the constant, gnawing pain of his absence.

But she was so not there. She was dug in deep, down in the fresh pain, in the clarity-of-detail stage. She wallowed, jealously guarding every moment they'd spent together in her mind, holding them tight in a box.

All the little moments, every single, stupid thing was imprinted on her mind. Maybe someday when she could stand it, way in the future she'd be strong enough to take out the memories and swim inside them, pretend the weeks they'd spent together meant something to him.

And her damned artist's mind was a freakin' cornucopia of detail about him. She forgot nothing. Just because she wanted to torture herself, she'd started on a bust of him, the first and probably the only one she'd ever create. Maybe when it was all done, she'd be able to let go. Yeah, no. Who was she kidding?

"Please, Honey."

The abject agony in his dark voice stopped her. Hallucination Jake was sad. Which made sense because this was her hallucination. It wouldn't be her hallucination if he showed up all cheery to tell her how happy he was that he'd left.

In her hallucination, Jake was sorry, so damn sorry, he let her go.

No harm in confronting a hallucination, was there? But for some reason she still had to run her perspiring palms down the sides of her gray tweed skirt before she turned around.

Wow, he looked like crap. As much as Jake ever could, anyway. His hair was longer, shaggy, not ruthlessly combed back but more like he pulled his hands through it every five seconds. The longer length made his cheekbones stand out over his stubble-lined jaw. His arms hung at his sides, his hands doing an unconscious flex.

"What did you do to your hair?"

She raised a hand to the top of her head where first

spiky purple then the red tips used to reside. But...why was he commenting on her appearance? This was not in her hallucination script.

"Jake?"

She croaked out his name and glanced around her, checking to see if people passing by were looking at her funny. Even in Brooklyn, pedestrians gave wide berth to anyone who stood on the sidewalk conversing with no one. But she didn't see anyone giving thumbs up or down on her sanity.

She narrowed her eyes. "Why did you just ask me what I did with my hair?"

"Hell if I know. Surprised me is all."

He raked a hand through his own unruly mane again.

"But you're my subconscious mind talking to me in a hallucination, so you already know I had to take the color out for my job. I minored in Psych. That's how hallucinations work..."

He took a step toward her. "You feel okay?"

"No, I'm not okay," she shouted. "Of course, I'm not okay. I'm not talking to a fucking apparition for the hell of it. I'm doing it because my subconscious wants so badly for you to be here."

She pointed at a guy across the street.

"See! That guy's staring at me because I'm seeing things that aren't there. I'm arguing with someone who's across the ocean married to someone else."

The guy across the street shouted back. "Lady, I'm watching you cause I'm waiting for your parking space. You told me you'd be done in a minute. Are gonna go, or are you gonna yell at him all night?"

Her head swiveled back to Jake, and she took in his

rumpled, untucked shirt, the scruffy half beard. This bleary-eyed guy, whose clothes were hanging off him was a shadow of the Jake she knew…had known.

"Go ahead. Yell all you want. I deserve it. But I'm so damn glad I finally found you."

"Found me? I wasn't lost. You said you weren't coming back. You wished you'd never met me."

"Sheesh. Really?" This from the guy across the street.

Jake's eyes were dark coals, and they were burning into hers. He took a step toward her, then stopped when she took a defensive step back.

"I was an ass. When you cried, all of a sudden I thought maybe this wasn't just a hookup for you either, that you felt something for me. But I made myself walk away…" His eyes burned into her again. "God, I never want to see you cry, never want to be the cause of your tears, again. Give me one chance, Honey. I swear, I won't fuck it up. There's no life for me if you're not in it."

"You look…kind of grungy."

His laugh was rough, and he gave her a long once-over, from the top of her long-sleeved white blouse past her knee-length skirt to her cute, new, black ankle boots.

"You look…corporate."

She shrugged. "Long story. I took a different job."

"I've been looking everywhere for you. I visited your brothers…"

"Really?"

His half smile was sheepish. "It didn't go well."

The guy piped up again. "People, are you getting in this car and leaving or what?"

"Honey, please. Tell me I haven't fucked us up beyond repair. I want a life with you. Only with you. These last weeks, I've been out of my mind. I can't sleep, I'm not good for anything till just now when I found you."

She took a step toward him, and they were toe to toe. "And now?" she whispered. "Now what? What are you good for now?"

"You. Only for you. I love you." His knees hit the cold pavement, his arms gathered round her waist to pull her tight into him as he pressed his cheek against her.

"I want to take you home," he groaned into her chest. "I want to sleep next to you, make love to you. I'll never leave you again."

"If this is a dream, I don't want to wake up." She pressed his head against her, combed shaking fingers through his black curls, then shivered as a tremor passed through him to her.

"It's your dream," the guy across the street said. "It's my freakin' nightmare."

Epilogue
June

Honey stretched like a well-loved, spoiled cat, her right hand drifting down Jake's broad back over the rippling mashup of green, blue, and gray waves that comprised his tattoo, traveling over his shoulders to his hip then up again to settle at his waist. She curved into him from behind, her naked flesh heating as she pressed her breasts to his bare back and tucked her feet into his calf muscles.

Just five more minutes.

Then she'd get up. Last night had been a satisfying end to a long week. Barely six months into her job at Sotheby's and her boss extended a flattering offer to underwrite her MBA, encouraging her to apply to NYU and Columbia for next semester.

That came on the heels of the news from Gerard Wentz at the co-op. The work she called Turbulence took first prize in a prestigious art show upstate.

They'd celebrated with a pasta dinner and far too much wine.

The bright sun peeking around the edges of the gray silk drapes meant it had to be close to seven. Lizzie was merciless with her yoga schedule. They'd signed up for a trendy and costly set of classes in Tribeca one of Lizzie's actor friends pulled strings to get them into. Any minute now, her phone would ping with Lizzie's text, reminding her of the time.

She curled back into Jake. There was no way Lizzie would actually come down from her apartment on the fourth floor, the one that used to be hers, and knock on their door. Lizzie had moved in shortly after the night she and Jake got together again.

Jake called Lizzie that night, thanking her for being the loyal friend she was. He listened without interrupting while Lizzie ripped into him for causing her best friend so much pain.

When she took a breath in her diatribe, Jake insisted she consider moving into the townhouse and taking over the fourth-floor rental. Lizzie had checked out the space the next day, and now Honey had her two best friends in the same place and couldn't be happier.

"If you keep rubbing your feet on me like that, you'll never get to yoga on time." Jake's rumbly morning voice settled over her like an invisible caress.

"We could always…" Eyes sliding shut again, Honey's teasing voice let Jake supply the rest of the suggestion.

He shifted to face her, his dark gaze running her length as he held her shoulders. Her body flushed, and it wasn't the perfect June weather that was the cause.

"Damn, we can't, we stayed out too late, and now we've slept in. Derek and Donnie and your, and Joss, are coming today, and then we have Vlad and Sabrina's thing…"

Punctual, list-making Jake was stressed. Honey rubbed a finger slowly along the sculpted curve of his bottom lip till he groaned.

It took Jake multiple trips to Caryville with her to inveigle his way back into her brothers' good graces.

Honey's worst moments brought out their protective side, and the tables of their dynamic were turned. She was less of a mother hen to them now and more of what she should be—a sister and a friend. School was out, and they were coming for the weekend. Jake promised them a night out tonight, chasing whatever kind of music they were into right now.

They ought to arrive at noon, which gave her some time to work in her new workspace after yoga. She and Jake had just finished the process of converting the living room on the third floor into a ceramic studio after plowing through layers of red tape for approval and variances from the city.

****

Every item was checked off his list. Everyone they cared about would be there.

Their people.

All but Franca. And Jake was fine with her absence. He accepted she still lived in her delusions, and nothing he said or did would change her outlook. With his last words, his father had asked him to be kind to his mother, so he was. But he wouldn't feed the fantasy. Not anymore.

All he wanted was to make Honey happy. She'd wanted to meet Franca, and amazingly the encounter had been relatively pain free.

Honey blasted through his mamma's icy reserve, quizzing her about Franca's MBA, refusing by literally talking over Franca, to hear a word that wasn't positive about him. She called herself his girlfriend, told her all about her job at Sotheby's, and Jake witnessed the grudging respect dawning in his mother's eyes.

Then all it took was Diego's observation noting

how much in profile Honey's face resembled the lost princess on the label of the vineyard's wine to make Franca take a second, more intrigued look at the love of his life. Diego had already gotten his raise. Now he was in line for a hefty bonus.

He had to tell Donnie and Derek his plan in order to try to get Joss to come down to the city with them, and now he'd sent them all off to explore so they didn't blab anything at the last minute. The boys told him not to count on Willow showing up, even though she was in the country. She wasn't sure she could get a flight to New York then back to her current assignment in Michigan.

Honey was standing in front of the closet with the door flung wide, freshly showered, and wearing her terry cloth robe. "This is my first baby shower. What's the dress code?"

He shrugged. "Not that robe, pixie. I'm the only one who gets to see you in that robe."

She looked over her shoulder at him, and a blush stole up her throat. He loved that he still had the ability to make the champagne color of her skin darken to a deep rose.

"Sabrina said it was more of a party than a shower, that Russians don't do baby showers, but she wanted to see her friends. I'm not even gonna give her the mobile I made until little baby Lilianna is born." She pulled a sleeveless, lavender sundress off a hanger.

"I wouldn't worry about it." He was tucking a white button down into black pants.

"You're such a guy." She swaggered up to him and let the robe slip off one shoulder. "And that's why I love you."

Emotion clogged his throat. In spite of his epic failure to recognize he was falling in love with Honey and the pain it caused them, once they were back together, they'd picked up where they left off. Honey wore so many hats, her badass corporate hat, her artistic one. But yeah, his favorite was her *I'm Jake's girl* badge.

They declared their love to each other frequently and conversationally. He never tired of saying it, and every time she said it to him, he knew he was the luckiest dude on the planet. Only last week, he'd earned her happy tears when one of his contacts, a desk cop who had a cousin in a Brooklyn precinct, located Honey's long-lost belongings. They'd been stuffed in an alcove in the boiler room of the building of her first ill-fated city apartment. He might have been giving her gold bullion by the way she leapt into his arms when he handed her the little ceramic bowl and ornament.

He pulled her into him by the shoulders and planted a hard kiss on her cupid's bow lips. "Save all that teasing, pixie. We're gonna be late."

****

The window next to the battered green door had a small, block-lettered sign: *CLOSED FOR A PRIVATE PARTY at 4 PM.*

Jake's arm came up from behind Honey to push the door open.

Her eyes needed to adjust to the dim interior after the bright June sunshine, and the jangle of voices in conversation stopped.

Then the voices yelled, "Surprise!"

Sabrina and Vlad were in one corner of the long trestle table sitting next to Connor and Lacey. But next to them were Lizzie and her brothers. And for crying out loud, was that Joss and Willow's heads close together, chatting at the opposite end of the table as if no one else were in the room? *What was going on?*

"What's going on?" Honey turned to ask Jake.

He was on one knee with a small jeweler's box open in his palm.

"I love you, Honey. Let's spend the rest of our lives together. Marry me."

She swooped down to him, threw her arms around his neck. "I love you, Jake," she choked out through a tear-filled throat. "How long have you been planning this surprise?"

The *snap, snap, snap* of a camera went off around them as Jake shrugged, sheepish. "A while."

"A long while," Connor's baritone boomed from his corner of the table. "Two of us had to get back from Bermuda for this surprise."

"It had to be the right weekend," explained Lizzie. "After Connor and Lacey were back from their honeymoon, but before Sabrina and Vlad's baby…after Donnie, Derek, and Joss were finished for the semester…"

"Excuse me for a second everybody." That was Jim Duffy. "But Honey can you say something to put this guy out of his misery?"

"Yes, yes. Yes, I will marry you. I love you, Jake." She held out her hand for the sparkling amber topaz he placed on her ring finger, then tugged him to his feet.

A cheer went up, but before she and Jake could sit down, Sabrina zipped her camera back into its case and rose carefully from her chair, pushing a tendril of hair back from where it escaped the long braid at the back of her neck.

"This could be a memorable day all around. Looks like Lilianna is ready to make her entrance." All heads swiveled toward Sabrina as she breathed through a contraction, her hand massaging the small of her back. "I thought it was Braxton Hicks this morning," she told the room at large, "but they haven't stopped, so I think this is the real deal."

Vlad gained his feet more unsteadily than his wife, took her hand in his, his eyes gleaming with emotion.

"Raise a glass for us. I'll call from Mercy as soon as we have news," Vlad said.

Willow stood, raised her pilsner high, and with her hand over Joss's, said, "To new beginnings."

Thank you for purchasing
this publication of The Wild Rose Press, Inc.

For questions or more information
contact us at
info@thewildrosepress.com.

The Wild Rose Press, Inc.
www.thewildrosepress.com

To visit with authors of
The Wild Rose Press, Inc.
join our yahoo loop at
http://groups.yahoo.com/group/thewildrosepress/